IS THIS THE NOVEL THAT REVEALS THE TRUE STORY BEHIND THE YOM KIPPUR WAR?

The Arab states are poised to destroy Israel in the Yom Kippur War. Russia is about to seize control of all Mideast oil. The plan is perfect, the agents are in place, doom is already descending on the Western world . . .

. . . unless a legendary master of Intelligence, a fearless field operative, and a beautiful, danger-hungry woman can join forces in a search to the ends of the earth for the mysterious document that alone can head off unspeakable global catastrophe. . . .

THE SECRET LIST OF HEINRICH ROEHM

"A DIABOLICAL PLOT . . . A SUPER SUSPENSE THRILLER THAT WILL KEEP YOU DANGLING!"—*Gerold Frank*

"A clever counterespionage chess game with Odessa-like verisimilitude."
—KIRKUS REVIEWS

"A scheme that could materialize in tomorrow's headlines."—PUBLISHERS WEEKLY

Big Bestseller from SIGNET

THE SECRET
LIST OF
HEINRICH ROEHM

MICHAEL BARAK

A SIGNET BOOK

NEW AMERICAN LIBRARY

TIMES MIRROR

"On the sixth of October, at dawn,
we got a definite warning from a very reliable
source that later during the day the Arab
countries were going to attack Israel."

(Speech of Mrs. Golda Meir,
Prime Minister of Israel,
after the Yom Kippur War)

The Spark

January 1, 1972

Like giant, evil-looking dragonflies the six super Frelon SA-321 helicopters hovered over the dark waters of the Suez gulf. It was a pitch-black moonless night. The aircraft cast no shadows while they crossed the low range of white sand dunes rising on the African coast of the strait. They were over enemy territory now, flying deep into central Egypt. Halfway to Cairo the choppers made a half circle, turned south and east again, returning to the Suez coast. "We'll reach the target from the direction of Cairo," the pilot of the first Super Frelon said to Joe Gonen, a lieutenant colonel in Israeli Air Force Intelligence. "Nobody will suspect anything."

Nobody did. When the helicopters landed in a cloud of dust and barely five hundred yards from the Egyptian air base at Marsa, no shot was fired at them. The detachment of Company 4, 57th Infantry Battalion, First Egyptian Army, assigned to mount watch around the secret base, were used to the round-the-clock aircraft traffic that brought mysterious visitors and heavy crates of equipment. Only after the light 82-mm. mortars and the heavy 0.5 machine guns simultaneously opened fire did the alert sirens start howling. Bewildered men rushed to their positions. But it was too late. The Israeli commandos charged with lightning speed, breaking their way through with a hail of bullets and hand grenades. In minutes they overcame the disorganized resistance in the security belt surrounding the Marsa base. They had only one casualty, a young lieutenant who was shot while igniting an explosive charge near the electrically operated steel gate at the base entrance. The Egyptian sentry on the nearby watchtower who pumped a burst of Gurionov 7.94 bullets into the Israeli sapper didn't live to see him fall. An exploding hand grenade shattered his firing platform as well as the powerful projector mounted over his machine gun. This was the last action of the battle. Scores of Israeli paratroops, dressed in olive green fatigues and reddish boots, crashed past the twisted debris of the steel gate that had once guarded the base. From the low barracks and the strangely shaped hangars human figures emerged, some of them in their underwear, holding their hands above their heads. No one tried to resist. Small detachments of paratroops swiftly set roadblocks and machine gun ambushes on the two highways leading to the camp, one from Ismailia and the other from Aswan. Fifteen minutes after H hour the secret Marsa Air Force Base was in the hands of the Israelis.

"Phase one completed; proceed with phase two. Over," said Lieutenant Colonel Gonen into his wireless transmitter. Around him paratroops were systematically scanning the buildings and piling crates of documents and equipment along the tarmac road. "Hurry up, Joe." The voice from the other side of the Suez gulf came clear and calm. "You have only one hour. Over."

"Send the engineers," Gonen said to the stocky paratroop captain who followed him. The officer nodded and vanished in the dark. Five minutes later phase two was under way. Equipped with torches and mechanical instruments, a special engineering unit began to dismantle the huge radar station that had been built on an artificial hill in the center of the camp. The smaller components were swiftly packed and stuffed into large wooden crates. But most of the electronic equipment was stored in two oblong metallic structures, looking like ship-cargo containers and attached to each other. The engineers sawed them apart and expertly tied steel cables around them. When clearance was given, two heavy Sikorsky CH 53 helicopters appeared from the other side of the gulf. While still hovering over the base, they lit all their projectors and began to perform a strange ballet over the radar hill, trying to grip the steel cables with the hooks of their cranes. Several engineers jumped on the electronic-filled containers, caught the hooks, and adroitly fastened them to the cables. Like prehistoric birds escaping with their prey the choppers gained altitude and sailed to the east, the precious booty dangling under their clumsy bellies. Down by the hangars sweating, swearing paratroops were still running back and forth, feverishly loading crates of papers and instruments into the French helicopters. Several of the Super Frelons made three or four runs to Israeli-occupied Sinai and back.

At about 3 A.M. it was all over. The exhausted paratroops climbed into the aircraft, which took off in rapid succession. As they gained altitude, the soldiers, forgetting their fatigue, burst into loud singing, accompanied by enthusiastic hand-clapping. They were exultant, and with good reason. They had just completed the most extraordinary commando operation in the history of the Israeli Army: the stealing of a whole, new, top-secret radar installation.

At the Israeli Air Force base of Bir-Gafgafa, in the Sinai, desert winds howled, blowing clouds of sand on the concrete runways. The night was dark and moonless. Leaning on a jeep, two men clad in heavy windbreakers watched silently as the jubilant paratroops alighted from the helicopters. One of them pulled down his desert goggles and let them rest on his neck. A black patch covered his left eye. It was a trademark recognized around the world, as was the lean, strong face that surrounded it. The man was Israeli Defense Minister Moshe Dayan. His companion was a small, silver-haired man, with a prominent nose and placid blue eyes. He wore black boots, and his black beret was neatly tucked under his epaulet. On it were printed in combat-green color two fig leaves and a sword crossed with an olive branch, the insignia of the highest rank in the Israeli Army: lieutenant general. He was Commander in Chief of the Army, General Chaim Bar-Lev. In spite of the gusts of cold desert wind he managed to light a fat cigar. Havanas were known to be his major vice.

He let out a contented puff of smoke. "Shall we welcome the boys?" he asked. He had a slow, phlegmatic voice that inspired a feeling of security.

"In a moment," Dayan replied. "I want to see them unloading first."

"They almost had an accident over the gulf," Bar-Lev said. "The damn radar container weighed more than four tons, and for a moment we thought the chopper wouldn't make it. We ordered the pilot to drop it in the sea, but he just kept going. As soon as the men are ready, we'll have all the equipment sent to Five Forty-seven for assembly and study."

"And when will you have any answers?"

Bar-Lev weighed his words carefully. "I suppose it won't take too long before we find a way to overcome this particular type of radar. Since the Six-Day War we had no trouble in jamming their French and Russian radars. But after they mounted this new model at Marsa, I was worried. As I told you then, we'd never seen anything like it before—different design, different antennae—everything. You remember the Air Force estimate? This radar could block the access of our jets to Cairo and stop all the long-range bombing and aerial surveillance projects. But we'll find out now what makes it go and what makes it stop."

They were interrupted by a group of young paratroops who had spotted the black patch. In the informal atmosphere of the Israeli Army, especially under combat conditions, soldiers felt no restraint in addressing a minister or a commander in chief.

"Well, sir, what do you think of the operation?" a tall, blue-eyed sergeant asked Bar-Lev. His hair was disheveled and his uniform wrinkled and dusty.

"First-class performance," the Commander in Chief drawled. "Couldn't be better. James Bond should start looking for a new job."

Chuckling, Dayan adjusted the thin string that held his eye patch in place. It was a familiar gesture. "I knew all along that it would be a success. Bar-Lev wanted to dispatch spies all over the world to get the plans of this new radar. I said to him, 'Chaim, the hell with spies. There's only one way to handle these kinds of things—lift them!' "

With an outburst of laughter the group moved to one of the big hangars, where an impromptu breakfast was served.

Before going in, Dayan pulled aside his a.d.c., a thin, slightly stooped lieutenant colonel who wore a perpetually amused look on his face. "Amir, call the censorship office right away. I want total secrecy on that operation. Not a word in the press. We'll leave it to the Egyptians to react."

The officer nodded and left.

But the secret couldn't be kept more than three days. The rumors swept the country like a brush fire. On January 4, Melvin Stafford, the zealous correspondent of the "Sunday Magazine," picked up the scent. Breaking censorship regulations, he flew to Cyprus and from Nicosia cabled the sensational story to London.

The next morning the audacious "radar hijacking" made headlines all over the world. For the second time in a week the Israelis had surpassed the Baghdad thief. A few nights earlier, on a cold, foggy Christmas evening, they had defied the one-sided French embargo and stolen the five missile boats the French had built for them from the Cherbourg shipyards.

PART ONE

The Plan

1

January 6, 1972

The Commission meetings were held once a week in a middle-sized conference room on the top floor of a rather shabby house in central Tel-Aviv. The building contained several departments of the Mossad—the Israeli security and intelligence agency, roughly equivalent to the American CIA. Overlooking the Dizengoff Plaza, the house was conveniently situated. It had its own underground garage, connected by two elevators to the top floor. Visitors would enter through an ordinary-looking door into a small foyer. After a thorough search by two armed guards in civilian clothes, they would then be admitted to the conference room. The room was ordinarily shut off by a heavy steel door, laden with locks and controlled from inside by closed-circuit TV. Right behind the third guard, who also checked the identity of the visitors, stood a small cubicle. This cubicle held an electronic switchboard whose phone lines were directly connected to the offices of the Prime Minister, the Ministers of Defense and Foreign Affairs, the Chief of Staff, and the various secret services.

The conference room itself was modestly appointed. The cream-painted walls were bare, except for a faded color photograph of Ben-Gurion that somebody had forgotten to remove when he left office nine years ago. A large window on the western wall would have offered a glorious panoramic view of Jaffa Bay were it not permanently covered with a heavy curtain that had been snow-white when the state was born a quarter of a century ago. A rectangular table surrounded by six chairs stood under two powerful neon lamps. Other chairs lined the walls. When the Commission was in session, the heads of the intelligence community would sit around the table; their aides would take their places along the walls. A portable green board, a projection screen, and a large assortment of maps of the Middle East were kept in an adjacent cupboard. This was done by explicit order of the Old Man. Pedantic in the extreme, he would never allow any person or item in the room that was not, as he put it, "indispensable" to the matter at hand.

But this morning everything and everybody was indispensable, or so it seemed. At ten minutes before eight the meeting room was boiling with activity. Two young majors in khaki uniforms were putting the final touches to a detailed sketch of the Marsa base. This sketch was drawn with varicolored chalk on the green board. Another officer was hanging a large map of the Middle East on the opposite wall. Red- and blue-dotted circles covered the map. Several civilian and military aides were sitting along the walls where they intently scanned voluminous files and plastic map-folders. In one corner four senior officers of the Air Force were conversing in low voices. Joe Gonen was among them.

A few minutes before eight, three middle-aged women wearing white aprons entered the room. They brought with them several trays laden with soft drinks, dry cakes, fruit, and jugs of black coffee. Then they hastily retreated, just before another door at the back of the room opened and the Old Man stepped inside. It was exactly eight o'clock.

He was small, stocky, but broad-shouldered, solidly supported by rather short legs. His mane of pure white hair, carefully combed to one side, crowned a large, clear forehead. At first glance he looked like a kindly grandfather or retired scholar, but the coldness of the shrewd blue-gray eyes made one immediately abandon any such illusion. He was a tough, determined old man, and it was plain that he could be an implacable enemy. Head of the Mossad and Chairman of the Commission of Directors of the intelligence community, he was the most powerful man in the shadow world of the Israeli secret services. His name and functions were a state secret. He was a kind of legend to his men and to the few people outside the services who knew about his position. A master spy and secret warrior since the day he first landed in Palestine, smuggling a revolver in a loaf of bread, Russian-born Jeremiah Peled had sedulously climbed to the top of the secret services. Ten years ago Ben-Gurion had appointed him Director of the Mossad and Chairman of the Commission consisting of the heads of all the secret services. Now his subordinates addressed him by his biblical name, Jeremiah, but wondered whether he'd had an ulterior purpose in choosing his Hebrew family name, Peled, which means steel. None of them, though, could remember when or why they had started to call him the Old Man.

A kind of electric current swept through the crowded room when he crossed it in quick, short strides, greeting everyone with a perfunctory nod, and sat at his usual place, banging rather than putting his bunch of keys on the dark oak table. They said he had once executed a traitor to the Haganah with his bare hands, an informer of the British police during the bitter underground fight against Britain's rule in Palestine. Nobody could tell for sure whether the story was true. Everybody, however, was certain that if Jeremiah believed it was "indispensable"— but only in that case—he would have killed him without hesitation.

The directors of the other secret services took seats around the table without concern for protocol. On Jeremiah's right sat a thin man of about forty-five, wearing a general's uniform: Aharon Yariv, head of the Aman, military intelligence. On his left sat Arthur Davidi, chief of the Shin Bet, the internal security service. The senior police officer already whispering in Davidi's ear was Nitzav Uri Oppenheimer, director of the special branch of the Israeli police. Oppenheimer and Davidi had worked together, mostly in counterespionage operations. The head of the fifth branch of the secret services was Joseph Gilat, director of the Research Department in the Ministry of Foreign Affairs.

Though the sixth chair at the table was usually vacant, this day it was occupied by a taciturn, bespectacled man, dressed in dark suit and tie. He was Dr. Jacob Herzog, one of the most brilliant men in the country and Prime Minister Golda Meir's closest adviser. If nothing else, Herzog's presence made it clear that someone high in the government attached great importance to this gathering of the Commission.

Jeremiah looked around him sternly. That was enough; everyone came to attention. "As you know, our scheduled meeting was to take place tomorrow," he began. "I have asked you to convene this morning because something very serious has been discovered as a result of the raid of our commandos on Marsa. But before I go into detail, I'll ask General Yariv to report about the consequences of the operation on the Egyptian side."

Yariv, the director of military intelligence, had the habit of wearing sunglasses to protect his eyes. In the artificially illuminated room he looked like a mafia don, but he was poised and his exposition was clear and succinct.

"One could expect," he said, "that after such an obvious humiliation as the Marsa raid, the Egyptian Government would be furious. This time, however, they reacted with unprecedented violence. I can confirm the rumors that started circulating early yesterday morning. By personal order of the Minister of War, countersigned by President Sadat, three senior officers were court-martialed. They were General Ali El-Mohsan, Commander of the Second Military Zone, First Egyptian Army; Colonel Ibrahim Shanti, Commander of the 56th Infantry Brigade, in charge of the defense of Marsa and Ras-Banas; and Air Force Colonel Gani el Madawi, responsible for the aerial defense system in that particular region. They were found guilty on charges of criminal negligence and were executed immediately."

"In secret?" asked Davidi, chief of the Shin Bet, the internal security service.

"Not exactly. After the execution a report about the trial and the verdict was circulated among all the senior officers of the Egyptian Army—about nine hundred colonels and generals. It was graded top secret, and the press didn't mention it. The report was a warning that something like that must never happen again. The General Staff has the feeling that the Egyptian Army has become the laughingstock of the world."

"We should publish the story about these executions," Davidi suggested.

"The men from psychological warfare agree," Yariv replied. "But we shouldn't leak it directly. It's too risky. I think that the Rome station of the Mossad should dispatch the Egyptian Army report through the usual chain to our man in *L'Orient-Le Jour* newspaper in Beirut. Coming from them, the story will be more credible and our sources will be protected."

Joseph Gilat, from the Ministry of Foreign Affairs, interrupted, "But why Rome? Shouldn't we—"

Jeremiah Peled was moving restlessly in his chair. "We have more important matters at hand," he muttered. "Aharon, if you have finished, I'd like to say something." Yariv nodded and smiled. Everybody knew he was Peled's favorite, and he couldn't care less about the Old Man's brusque manner.

Peled came straight to the point. "Some of you may have been surprised by the fact that we didn't take any Egyptian prisoners—in particular technicians who could have easily explained the functioning of the new radar to us. If we didn't do that, it was for a very special reason. All the personnel in the camp we captured were Russian!"

The listeners gasped. Only Yariv, Herzog, and Gonen remained quiet. They already knew.

"Russians?" Davidi looked puzzled. "Manning a radar station? What for?"

Peled glanced at him obliquely and continued, "The camp was protected on the outside by Egyptian forces. But no Egyptian was ever allowed to enter it. We had it all wrong. Marsa was a purely Russian base. We know, of course, about the existence of several Russian bases, mostly Air Force, which are strictly out of bounds for the Egyptians, but we didn't know about any radar installations. Now we had a second surprise after our people started to examine the captured electronic equipment. Lieutenant Colonel Gonen, of Air Force intelligence, will tell you about it."

Gonen walked with an almost imperceptible limp to the green board. He was a blond, handsome pilot in his early thirties, and the limp was a result of the direct hit that had blown his Mirage III-C to pieces over the Nile delta on June 5, 1967. He had managed to activate his ejection seat and miraculously survived. After two days of hiding in a palm grove from an hysterical mob of fellahin armed with shovels and axes, he was rescued by an Israeli helicopter. But it was too late to completely cure the injury to his leg. He went through a series of painful operations, and finally the doctors had to tell him that he would never fly again, which accounted for the thin, bitter lines on the sides of his mouth and for his almost superhuman ambition to distinguish himself in his new career. It had not been easy for Joe Gonen. Flying had been his great passion. Fortunately, the world of intelligence intrigued him. After he had successfully completed several perilous missions in enemy countries, people stopped calling him "the flying playboy." He played a vital role in the Marsa operation, and when he took the floor the old foxes of espionage listened to him with respect.

He said slowly, "We expected to find a radar station in Marsa, but we discovered something entirely different: an electronic installation, which is, beyond any doubt, part of a control and guidance system for intermediate-range ballistic missiles."

For the second time this morning a gloomy, awed silence descended upon the room.

Gonen calmly laid the facts before the Commission. He pointed out the various buildings and hangars represented in the sketch of the Marsa base and explained their functions. The radar installation, he said, seemed to be a part of an entire infrastructure built by the Russians in several places in Egypt. He could not tell whether the missiles themselves had been put in position or whether they had been assembled at all. It was quite possible that the missiles had not yet arrived in Egypt. Actually, the installation at Marsa was not operational, and many electronic components were found in their original cases. The missiles were undoubtedly going to be equipped with nuclear warheads. Nevertheless, he was almost sure that they were not there to be used against Israel. "Their range is too long for that," he pointed out. "If they want to hit us, they can use the Scud rockets that they have been supplying to Egypt for years. They have a range of three hundred and fifty miles, and can be equipped with atomic or conventional warheads."

He went on to explain that maps and documents seized on the spot showed the supposed trajectories of the missiles would reach the Arab oil-producing countries. Moving to face the large Middle East map hanging on the opposite wall, Gonen indicated the red and blue circles representing the estimated range of the IRBM's. "We think they want to threaten Saudi Arabia, Kuwait, Qatar, Bahrein, Iraq, Libya, Algeria, and some smaller sheikdoms in the Persian Gulf. We can't tell yet why, and we can't tell when this plan might become operational. We don't know whether the Russians have already started building their launching bases; maybe they're camouflaging them. In the documents we found several hints about 'D day' and 'When Egypt moves,' but they were vague and incomplete."

The Old Man glanced around the table. "I gather that all of you understand what this discovery means. Soviet Russia is secretly building IRBM bases in Egypt, maybe even without the knowledge of the Egyptian civil and military authorities. At a certain moment in the future she'll be able to threaten any oil-producing Arab country in the Middle East. This plan is in a way connected with an Egyptian move. We still don't know what kind of move, but I couldn't exclude an attack on Israel. Such an attack could furnish a pretext for Russia to go on with her own plans."

"What do you intend to do about that, Jeremiah?" asked the Director of the Shin Bet.

"I think this matter does not concern us alone," Peled replied. For a moment he was silent. Then he looked at his watch. "There is an emergency Cabinet meeting at four P.M. At seven thirty I am boarding a nonstop flight to New York. I have already cabled the Director of the CIA."

2

January 9, 1972

The director of the CIA stepped out of the unobtrusive light blue sedan he had driven himself through the west entrance of the White House. Four of his top aides emerged from a second car. It was a crisp, sunny morning in Washington. Peter Wilkie glanced around before entering the West Wing. Satisfied that there was no reporter in the vicinity, he shook the hand of the young security officer who was waiting for him and then followed him through the corridors. As the years went by, he had developed an irrational phobia for journalists, whom he considered irresponsible and unnecessary. Today especially he wanted to avoid a chance encounter with the press. He had taken unusual precautions coming to the White House, and insisted that all the other members of the National Security Council and the U.S. Intelligence Board do the same. But he would bet that on the first page of tomorrow's *Times* he would find the usual short item announcing that a top-secret joint meeting of the NSC and the USIB had been urgently summoned by the President at Wilkie's suggestion. He sighed. He just hoped that nothing about the reason for the meeting would appear in the papers. He made a mental note to ask the President's permission for some cover story—Vietnam, or Chile, or something.

The President looked particularly tense and preoccupied this morning. He was the last to enter the room, accompanied by the Secretary of State and his omniscient adviser for national security affairs. All the other members of the National Security Council and the U.S. Intelligence Board, the Secretary of Defense, the Army chiefs, the directors of the FBI, the DIA, and other national and military agencies were already there. Peter Wilkie waited for the President and his entourage to be seated, and then took the floor.

"The subject I want to report about is Soviet penetration in the Middle East," he said, determined to play down the story as much as possible. He started with a detailed description of persistent Soviet efforts in recent years to gain a foothold in the Middle East, especially in Egypt, Iraq, and Syria. He explained how the Arab-Israeli conflict was cunningly used by the Russians in order to deepen and enlarge their hold in those countries. An integral part of the Russian penetration had been the establishment of air and naval bases, mostly in Egypt; they were kept strictly out of bounds for Egyptian personnel. Wilkie consulted his papers. "Today in Egypt, itself, the Russians have placed twenty-two thousand military 'advisers.' The advisers include instructors to the Egyptian Army, technical experts, crews manning anti-aircraft missile bases, and also pilots who participate in sorties with the Egyptian Air Force against Israeli planes. Those pilots fly their own Soviet planes from their own autonomous bases. The planes, however, are painted in Egyptian colors. There is a standing order to the Soviet pilots to avoid, as far as possible, any encounters with the Israelis over the Sinai peninsula, because of the risk of being shot and captured by them. That could be sufficient proof of their participation in the Arab-Israeli war, and Moscow fears the American reaction.

"Until recently," Wilkie admitted, "we did not have a clear evaluation of the real aim of the Soviets in the Middle East. We wondered if they just wanted to spread their influence over the area or create pro-communist governments and obtain military bases. Maybe even take over direct military control in the Middle East and isolate Turkey and Iran, which endanger Russia's soft underbelly." He paused. "Lately, however, two very disturbing pieces of information have reached us, one of a political and one of a technical character. They shed new light on the situation.

"The political report reached us in a very ... hum ... unusual way, and we were not sure that the source could be trusted. It implied that the next goal of the Soviet Union in the Middle East was to gain complete control over the sources of oil in this region."

"But how?" asked the Secretary of State. He nurtured rather intense feelings of dislike and distrust toward Wilkie. Even if he had tried to conceal them, he could not have done so. They were eloquently spread all over his face and in the cold, stinging tone of his voice.

"That is the question we asked ourselves, Mr. Secretary," Wilkie answered patiently. "We tried to check the information through some of our best sources, without success. Nobody could confirm it. And suddenly, yesterday, a technical report was rushed to us from Tel-Aviv that corroborated the Russian story."

The Director of the CIA described to his audience the Israeli raid on Marsa and the stunning discovery of the maps, the plans, and the missile-guidance installation. "The Israelis say that all the Arab oil-producing countries will be in the range of the Russian IRBM's once they are operational. According to them, that could take about two more years. If our assumption is correct, the Russians will be moving very slowly. They understand that arousing the Egyptians' suspicions prematurely might jeopardize the entire project."

"Do you trust the Israeli reports?" It was the Secretary of State again.

"Absolutely," Wilkie snapped. "They sent us photographs of the maps and blueprints, and our man in Tel-Aviv was flown to Sinai to see the equipment for himself."

"Did you reach any conclusions about the master plan of the Russians?" asked the Secretary of Defense.

"Nothing final yet," Wilkie answered cautiously, looking quickly at the President, "but our experts believe the general pattern is fairly clear. The basic assumption of the Russians is that the United States would not run the risk of a world war because of the Middle East. They therefore feel free to act. In the last three years Russia has been patiently, but repeatedly, encouraging Egypt and Sy-

ria to prepare for a new war in order to win back the territories lost to Israel in the Six-Day War. We believe that
when the war starts—in two or three years—the Russians
might intervene on a limited scale, sending small units to
help or advise the Arabs. Actually, those forces would be
used for manning and arming the missile bases in Egypt,
which will be completed by then. Israel might be
destroyed. An immediate military threat against the oil-
producing states would follow, and would force them to
surrender to Russian domination in the area. The West
would suddenly awake and find out that the oil supply
was under Soviet control. That means that the free world
would depend for its survival on Russian goodwill."

A silence fell on the room.

"It is a terrible political weapon," Wilkie added, "and
we might become the victims of the biggest blackmail of
the century. We might be brought to our knees by the
Russians."

"Or forced to fight back," the Defense Secretary said
slowly.

Following these revelations Wilkie was bombarded with
questions. Under the cross fire he admitted that the threat
of nuclear missiles against the Arab countries might not
necessarily be a direct Soviet threat. "It might be disguised," he said, somewhat on the defensive. "One of the
possibilities we have to bear in mind is that during the war
in the Middle East a pro-Soviet junta could seize power in
Egypt and receive—'formally'—the missile bases under its
control. The confrontation then might be presented as a
purely inter-Arab dispute, and the West would have no
pretext to intervene."

"But what about Egypt?" asked General Carter, Chairman of the Joint Chiefs of Staff. "Would she cooperate?
What if we inform the government now of the missile
buildup?"

Unexpectedly, it was the President's adviser for national security affairs who rose to answer for CIA Director Wilkie. He carefully adjusted his glasses. "We believe
that the Egyptians do not know anything about the Russian enterprises. But even if it came to their attention, I

don't think President Sadat would react firmly. He has gone too far in his pledge to regain the occupied territories. At this point he can't afford to lose the massive Soviet military aid. Even if we bring him the information on a platter, he will probably bury his head in the sand and pretend not to hear and not to see anything."

The President was grim. "One element in their estimate is correct, I must say. The United States will not risk a world war because of the Middle East."

The military did not give up. "Couldn't we intervene in Moscow," General Carter asked, "and demand that the Soviets immediately dismantle the missile installations?"

"They will simply refuse to do so," the President's adviser replied gloomily, "and the result will be a painful humiliation for us. This is not 1962, and Egypt is not Cuba."

"Then why don't we just make the story public?"

"Because we will be playing straight into the hands of the Russians. If we are not determined to take action, and I'm afraid we are not, then the publication of the story will be a kind of admission on our part that Egypt has become a Soviet base."

"But we must decide to do something!" General Carter was fuming.

The President moved uneasily in his chair. "I know, General. Something will be done." Then he added cryptically, "But for the moment—let's ponder and consider."

He stood up. The meeting was over.

In the Oval Room, the President and the Director of the CIA conferred privately for some minutes.

"Any suggestions, Peter?" the President asked Wilkie.

"The Israelis seem to have a plan, sir."

"The Israelis? Did you talk to them?"

"The chief of their secret services is here with some aides. He brought me the Marsa file and suggested a joint operation."

The President did not look happy. "I don't know . . ." he said vaguely. "I don't like it . . . I wouldn't like anything too close. No commitment, I mean."

"Not at all, sir. We don't know what their plan is, nor how they intend to carry it out. Our part is quite minor and marginal at this stage. I just need to make some phone calls."

"O.K." The President shrugged. "Don't get us too far involved, Peter. We're on very thin ice here, you know."

Back at his office in Langley Woods, Wilkie dialed a phone number on his direct line. "Jenny? . . . It's been a long time, and—"

The moment she recognized his voice, she slammed the receiver down, her beautiful features distorted in anger, and swore a furious oath. She would never go back.

In downtown Washington one of the members of the U.S. Intelligence Board walked into a public phone booth. He dialed a New York number. The voice that answered was very careful. The man who phoned whispered urgently into the mouthpiece.

3

January 11, 1972

There were only a few passengers on the weekly Lufthansa night flight to Munich. Jeremiah Peled ceremoniously shook the hand of the CIA liaison officer who had come to see him through formalities at Kennedy Airport and marched quickly to the departure lounge. He casually glanced out of a window. It was still snowing—a slow graceful descent of large, soft white flakes. Caught for a second in the multicolored lights of the airport, the myriad falling snowflakes gave him a fleeting sense of serenity. In the interior of the Boeing 707, he went straight to his seat: on the aisle, one row before last, economy class. No earthly reason would make him travel first class; since his pioneering days in the impoverished kibbutz in Galilee he'd had an aversion to all forms of luxury. From old habit he tucked his attaché case beneath his seat, took off his heavy blue coat, sat down, and fastened his seat belt. That's the way he liked to travel: alone, without having to waste his time in idle talk with one of his men or with some government official who knew his true identity and wouldn't shut his mouth for hours, trying eagerly to impress him. And maybe it was for a reason he wouldn't admit even to himself: under his tough shield he was a shy man, who felt rather uncomfortable in other people's presence, and was most at ease when he was by himself.

His last meeting with Wilkie had been just what he had expected it to be. Wilkie was sympathetic to his country's welfare, Peled knew, yet he had promised to cooperate not out of affection for Israel but because he understood that the Mossad could do it alone, without the CIA's help

25

or permission. By extending a helping hand Wilkie could at least make sure that the American end of the operation would be completely under his control.

Peled was startled out of his thoughts by the mellifluous voice of the hostess over the loudspeakers, greeting the passengers in English and German. His trained eyes wandered around, appraising and classifying the other passengers. They rested for a moment on the man sitting across the aisle, one row ahead of him. He was in his fifties—bald, stout, heavy-jowled. He was sweating profusely, and repeatedly mopped his forehead with a large white handkerchief. A pile of German newspapers lay on his knees, and as a redheaded hostess with a flashing smile bent over him his newspapers and magazines spilled on the floor. From between the folded pages of the respectable *Die Welt* a vulgar pornographic review slipped out, two naked girls hopelessly entangled on its glossy cover. The beefy neck of the man turned purple, and he hurriedly gathered his papers in embarrassment. The Old Man couldn't help but smile.

The powerful Rolls-Royce engines roared furiously. In a few minutes the big jet liner darted forward and took off toward the gently snowing winter clouds. Peled closed his eyes. The take-off triggered a wave of vivid memories that surged out of his past. All those flights, alone, using aliases, on dangerous missions, which sometimes were crucial to the very existence of his country. He remembered his hasty departure for Europe, almost ten years ago, when Israel had been surprised to learn that hundreds of German scientists and technicians were in Egypt, secretly building medium-range missiles, armed with nonconventional warheads. Panic had swept the little country, threatened with a terrifying annihilation by cobalt and strontium radioactive bombardment. He had just been appointed head of the Mossad. In a crash program he had rushed to Europe at the head of his operational unit. In three weeks' time, heedless of the risks, his team had succeeded in locating and raiding the nerve centers of the organization in Europe and getting hold of all the documents, the suppliers' addresses, and the lists of scientists. In six months nobody would supply a milligram of cobalt to Cairo and dozens of German scientists, frightened by mysterious bomb attempts on their lives, were leaving Egypt. A year after the alert had been given, Egypt's President Nasser had to abandon the project and close the rocket factories in Heliopolis.

And another flight, even earlier, when he had gone to the Argentine to capture Adolf Eichmann. He could never forget that shocking moment, in an unfurnished room in the cellar of the safehouse on the outskirts of Buenos Aires, when his prisoner, a bald, thin, bespectacled man, had suddenly broken down and said, "I am Adolf Eichmann. I know, I am in the hands of the Israelis." His first urge was to strangle the Nazi monster. Didn't Eichmann proclaim at the end of the war that he would "jump laughing into [his] grave, satisfied to have killed six million Jews?" Instead Peled had run out of the room into the cold, dark garden and collapsed, his trembling sweating body unable to sustain him. A week later he was sitting, unruffled, across the aisle from Eichmann, whom he had smuggled aboard an El Al plane in a steward's uniform, in order to bring him to trial in Israel.

And then there had been that lonely flight to Switzerland, to meet and convince an Iraqi pilot to defect to Israel with his priceless MIG-21 jet fighter, never before captured and examined by the West; that perilous trip to Egypt, under a NATO cover, to encourage a pro-Western opposition group at the highest level of the Army; and more recently, his last-chance flight to Washington, on the eve of the Six-Day War, when he had to persuade the U.S. Government that Israel would have to strike first if it wanted to survive.

It was always a question of survival. When he had first come to Palestine in 1929, he arrived in the middle of a bloodbath as Arab mobs murdered hundreds of Jews in Jerusalem, Safed, Tiberias, and butchered the small Orthodox Jewish community in Hebron. He had paid his personal toll of blood and tears for the survival of Israel when his only son, Omri, had fallen in the Battle of Jerusalem, during the War of Independence. His wife,

Myriam, had not outlived Omri long. After she died, he devoted himself to his job with a kind of blind rage. It was said that he was never the same again, but he couldn't remember that he had ever been different.

And now he was once more on a fateful mission, while his faraway country, serene and confident after the Six-Day victory, was still unaware of the deadly danger lurking on its borders. He was going to launch the most hazardous operation in his career. But the key to start things moving lay in his scheduled meeting with a man, a German, ten hours from now. He was an old man, this German, retired four years, but his name was still one of the most eminent in the shadow world of espionage: General Reinhard Gehlen.

He had known Gehlen for many years. The first time he had heard his name was in 1947, a year before the state of Israel was born. A Russian Jew, an officer in the Soviet secret service, had defected in Germany and was hastily shipped to Palestine by the underground network of the Haganah. When questioned by Peled, the defector said that he had been sent to the American sector of Germany to find Reinhard Gehlen. Noticing that Jeremiah and the other Haganah officers seemed perplexed, he told them a curious story. Gehlen, he said, had been one of the most gifted intelligence officers in the Wehrmacht during the war. A small, lean man with sly eyes and a natural gift for conspiracy, he had risen like a meteor in the Abwehr—the intelligence service of the German Army. Appointed major in March 1939, he was general in December 1944. With extraordinary patience and skill he had succeeded in establishing a highly efficient spy network in the Soviet Union. His spies included senior officers, government officials, and famous journalists. There were rumors that he had even managed to infiltrate the MVD, the Soviet security service directed by the notorious Lavrenti Beria.

During the war, the Soviet defector continued, Gehlen's network had supplied him with invaluable information. All the efforts of Soviet counterespionage to break up the organization ended in failure. By the time the war was over, Gehlen's name was at the top of the Soviet "Wanted" lists, but he had disappeared without leaving a trace. For some time the Russians believed he might be dead, or that he had escaped to a remote continent. At the end of 1946, however, they discovered that Gehlen and his organization were very much alive. Shortly after the end of the war the cunning little General had surrendered to the Americans and offered them a deal: he was ready to put at their disposal all of his files, his knowledge, and his dormant networks in the Soviet Union if they would agree to help him reactivate his espionage organization. The Americans had agreed. In August 1945 they had secretly brought Gehlen and his closest aides to Washington. A year later Gehlen was back. The phoenix had risen from his ashes, and the most dangerous master spy again had his sensitive antennae focused on the best-protected secrets of the Kremlin. Beria had decided to dispatch his cleverest spies, his toughest agents, to Germany, to find and destroy Gehlen and his men. "That's how I reached Germany and escaped to Palestine," the Jewish officer said, ending his story.

Some years later, when the Federal Republic of Germany was established, Peled had heard of Gehlen again. He had built a fine secret service, which was officially named the BND (Bundesnachrichtendienst—Federal Intelligence Service), but which was better known around the world as "the Gehlen organization." It was still the best in the world at gathering intelligence inside the Soviet Union. The moles Gehlen had planted with such care in Russia in the forties were regularly rendering first-rate information. By the end of the fifties the Gehlen organization had established contact with the Israeli secret services on the initiative of German Chancellor Konrad Adenauer, who felt that his country had to do everything possible to pay its heavy moral debt to the Jewish people. Peled met Gehlen several times. They didn't become friends, but they developed the deep respect and esteem for each other that characterize relations between top professionals. In 1962 the KGB, the Soviet secret service that succeeded the MVD, attempted to use the close relations

between the Mossad and the Gehlen organization for its
own purposes. The Russians tried to infiltrate their best
Israeli spy, a high government official by the name of Dr.
Israel Beer, into Gehlen's headquarters in Pullach. Gehlen
didn't suspect anything. Dr. Beer was cordially received
and briefed. But on arrival in Israel he was picked up by
the Old Man and finished his days in prison.

Some years later a top Soviet agent captured by the Israelis broke down under interrogation. In speaking about
his past he revealed his part in the establishment of a
pro-communist spy ring inside the headquarters of the
Gehlen organization. Peled promptly relayed the stunning
information to Gehlen. A quick series of arrests followed,
and the network was crushed. The Germans were deeply
impressed and grateful to the Mossad, for the communist
spies could have destroyed their organization.

Gehlen certainly remembered those episodes, Peled
thought. But would he agree to do what I, what the state
of Israel, would ask of him?

He opened his eyes. The gray light of dawn tinged the
oval windows with an eerie color, and the huge plane
started its descent toward Munich.

In the sleepy airport a young man greeted him. He
didn't waste time with questions about the flight, the
weather, and other banalities. "The car is outside," he
said. "One of the boys is waiting with the motor running.
Papers, maps, everything is ready." Peled stepped quickly
toward the exit. His face showed no reaction when he saw
two more of his men discreetly watching the arrival area.
One was munching a sausage by a night-and-day *schnel-
limbiss Kiosk;* the other was immersed in the *Süddeutsche
Zeitung* by the outer door. He knew that they had the
place covered. At the slightest alert they could be on their
knees, shooting to kill, while the young man who followed
him would whisk him, in a matter of seconds, through a
reconnoitered and rehearsed escape route. He didn't like
all that stuff, but knew it was necessary. Germany was full
of Arabs, and the Al Fatah terrorist organization had
trained people in every major city.

The agent at the exit casually walked out through the

glass and steel doors, completely shielding the Old Man, who emerged scarcely a yard behind him. He took some steps on the slippery, frost-covered sidewalk, then moved aside, just enough to allow Peled to get into the right front seat of the black Mercedes. The car moved forward smoothly, without any futile tire screeching, which would only attract attention. The agent with the newspaper was picked up by a modest BMW gray sedan with two other people already inside. They followed Peled's car.

It was the second agent, left in the entrance hall of the airport, who noticed the heavy stranger hurrying outside half a minute after Peled, and with surprising swiftness jumping into a blue Opel Kadett that had suddenly appeared out of a long line of waiting taxis. Without losing his composure, and still chewing his *Würst,* the Israeli slipped a coin into a public phone by the *Kiosk.* He gave a short description of the car and the man, not forgetting to mention that the suspect was mopping his perspiring forehead with a large white handkerchief.

Less than two hours later the black Mercedes carrying Peled stopped before an impressive gate, artistically composed of long, thin lengths of wrought iron. The place was breath-taking: All around, the huge mountains of Bavaria rose majestically under a colorful blanket of green conifers and deep, freshly fallen snow. He got out of the car. A man in a sheepskin coat, thick galoshes, and a fur hat detached himself from the gatepost and came forward to greet him. It was Reinhard Gehlen.

Inside the spacious mansion the two men sat on comfortable leather armchairs by the glowing fireside. The Old Man politely declined the traditional *Schnaps* but thankfully accepted a mug of black coffee served by a smiling, self-effacing elderly woman. When they were alone, Peled did not waste time with niceties.

"We need your help," he said. "Israel is in danger."

Several moments passed before Gehlen answered. "They still call it 'the Gehlen organization,' " he said with a twinge of nostalgia, "but you know that I have been retired for nearly four years. Of course, I'll always be at your disposal and gladly give you my personal assistance.

But why should you need me? You have one of the best
services in the world, and your sources in Egypt and Syria
are the dream of any master spy on earth."

Peled looked at him searchingly. The man had grown
old—he was about seventy now—but still sat erect in his
chair, chest forward, head high, like a classic Prussian officer. His mustache had become thin and white, and his
head was almost bald.

"It is not Egypt or Syria that I fear," Peled said with a
wry expression. "It is the Russians."

The shadow of a smile flashed on Gehlen's thin lips.
"So that's why you came to me," he said. "I should have
guessed it when I got your telegram."

Peled looked at him with mock irony. "Oh, I am sure
you guessed it, all right."

Again the smile touched Gehlen's face, but he said
nothing.

"I won't beat around the bush," Peled said. "We desperately need some top-grade inside information from the
U.S.S.R. We have no agents there, and you know it. We
talked to the Americans. They are as much in the dark as
we are. That's why I came to you. You're the only one
who can help us." He paused. "I don't want to over-
dramatize, but it might well be a matter of life and death
to my country."

For the first time Gehlen looked straight into the eyes
of his guest. "I know what an effort it must be for you to
come here and talk to me, a German general who,
Abwehr or no Abwehr, has fought for Hitler. I would like
to help you, but how can I? My famous organization inside Russia is no more than a legend now. My spies, my
informers, are all either dead of old age or by the careful
aim of the KGB firing squads. Don't forget—it was thirty
years ago. If you ask me about our actual networks—
sure, we have more recently recruited spies—but even I
don't know anything about them." He added bitterly,
"They don't brief me anymore. Maybe you should contact
the BND directly, but I doubt . . ." His words faded
away.

"I don't want to be indiscreet," Peled said slowly, "but

4

February 11 - May 19, 1972

As it had on every day, the black shining Zil limousine stopped at the entrance of an ugly modern apartment house on the fashionable Kutuzovsky Prospect. The time was exactly 8:35 A.M. The militiaman at the entrance watched indifferently as the young man in gray clothes emerged coatless and bareheaded into the biting Moscow cold and quickly ran inside. Two minutes later he was back, followed by a tall, heavy-set man wearing a thick overcoat and a soft felt hat. His blond sideburns were turning white. He wore rimless spectacles on expressionless eyes; his slightly upturned upper lip gave his frozen features a constant expression of disgust. The militiaman clicked his heels and saluted. KGB Chairman Yuri Vladimirovich Andropov nodded curtly and was ushered into the back of the limousine by the uniformed chauffeur, while his young bodyguard took his place in the front right seat. Andropov laid a thin brown leather briefcase beside him and took off his hat. "To the office, Piotr," he said quietly to the chauffeur.

Fifteen minutes later—traffic was quite heavy this morning because of the falling snow—the limousine drew to a stop in the inner court of 2, Dzerzhinsky Square, only two blocks away from the Kremlin. Responding with short nods to the armed guards who jumped to attention as he passed, Andropov crossed the inner court, not casting even a peripheral glance at the gloomy gray complex of Lubyanka prison, which stood on the other side of the yard. He had long ago become used to the fact that three of his predecessors—Henrikh Yagoda, Nikolai Yezhov ("the bloody dwarf"), and Lavrenti Beria—had been tortured and shot in its execution chambers. He entered the old section of his headquarters—better known as "the Center" of the KGB—through a heavy wooden door. It was a gray stone building, dating back to the beginning of the century, when it had been the headquarters of the All-Russian Insurance Company. Since the founder of the Soviet secret service, Feliks Edmundevich Dzerzhinsky, confiscated the house in 1918, it had remained the nerve center of the service, despite the frequent changes in name and function that occurred over the years—from Cheka to GPU, then NKVD, MVD, and today KGB— Committee for State Security.

Andropov and his bodyguard marched through the green-walled corridors, illuminated by white shaded oval lamps hanging from the ceiling at regular intervals. Their steps echoed on the bare wooden floor. They crossed into the new part of the building—a heavy-looking, massive nine-story structure that had been built shortly after World War II by political prisoners and captured Germans. An old-fashioned elevator took them to the third floor. The bodyguard helped the Chairman take off his coat and hat, and vanished into an adjacent room while Andropov, in a conservative, well-tailored suit, entered his private office.

It was a large, beautiful room, richly furnished and decorated with taste. The thick Persian carpets on the floor, the dark mahogany wall panels, the deep, comfortable sofas, the huge windows overlooking the lively Marx Prospect, gave one the feeling that he was in the office of a prosperous Western businessman. Only the portrait of Dzerzhinsky on the wall and the row of six telephones on the large redwood desk betrayed the real character of the place. Andropov liked his office, and stubbornly rejected his aides' suggestions to move to the new glass and steel modern compound, hidden in a pine forest outside Moscow. The building was going to be completed next summer, but the Chairman had already decided that only the First Chief Directorate (Foreign Operations) would move there. He explained his decision to stay at Dzerzhinsky Square by its proximity to the Kremlin.

This morning several people were waiting for him in his

office. They all rose when he entered, but he smoothly asked them to be seated again. His voice was quiet and cultured, and his manners were pleasant. Only the lusterless eyes suggested that here was a wolf in a lamb's skin.

All six of his deputies were present: Tsvigun, Pirozhkov, Pankratov, Malygin, Tsinev, and Chebrikov. He had also summoned Mikhail Tsymbal, Deputy Director of Foreign Operations; Razumov, Chief of the Planning and Analysis Directorate, and General Lev Ivanovich Yulin, Director of the Eighth Department (Middle East), First Chief Directorate. Quite exceptionally a GRU liaison officer, military intelligence, Colonel Mnoushkin, was allowed to assist at this extraordinary meeting.

Andropov leaned back in his swivel chair and waited for his secretary, a nervous-looking black-haired young man, to put a thick brown file in front of him before hurriedly leaving. "Comrades," he said, "I'll ask General Yulin to report on the latest developments concerning the Aurora project."

General Lev Ivanovich Yulin was a small, gray-haired man with sharp features and narrow, wise eyes surrounded by a web of tiny wrinkles and deeply sunken under bushy white eyebrows. He had been a secret service officer almost all his life, and felt at home in this world of conspiracy, danger, and betrayal. He had been recruited at the age of nineteen by the henchmen of Henrikh Yagoda, head of the NKVD, who was then deeply involved in the bloody purges of the thirties and was searching for fanatic, unscrupulous young men ready to die—or rather to kill—in the name of the Revolution. Young Yulin had proved he could be both vicious and unprincipled. Nevertheless, he wanted a different kind of undercover work. The opportunity came during World War II, when he was able to establish his renown through numerous dazzling operations behind enemy lines. After the war ended, he transferred his activities to America and Western Europe. Often assigned to special missions for the MVD, the NKVD, and the GRU, he took part in several of the most spectacular espionage operations of the cold war era. In the fifties he came to the Middle East for the first time and discovered there a field of activity that suited his talents and tastes perfectly. At the head of the special operations group he had personally recruited and trained, he started to plan and carry out daring espionage exploits all over the Middle East. Soon he was appointed head of the Eighth Department, but continued to lead his men in perilous operations in Israel and the Arab countries. Risky, well-planned enterprises were like opium to him, and he hated paperwork. As the years went by, he was justly proud of the many successful coups he had conceived and carried out: the breaking of the CIA offensive in Egypt in 1955; the behind-the-scenes planning of murders, political blackmail, ministers' corruption, and financial maneuvering that brought a pro-communist government to power in Syria in 1958; the infiltration of General Kassem's regime in Iraq a year later; the gradual take-over of the terrorist Al Fatah movement by pro-communist elements after 1968. He had personally succeeded first in compromising, then blackmailing, several eminent Israelis, who were left with no other choice but to supply the KGB for many years with highly reliable information about Israel's military might and the political trends of her leadership.

At fifty-eight he was regarded as one of the best KGB officers, with a good chance to reach the top in the next few years. Yet he stayed on at his current post. A field operator, gifted with a legendary intuition and a shrewd, scheming mind, he stubbornly refused to leave his department for a higher assignment.

This morning's meeting had been convened at his request. His expression was passive and his strong voice neutral as he leaned forward and started to speak, without consulting the file on his knees. "More than a month has passed since the Israeli commandos performed an aggressive penetration of Egyptian soil and captured our installations at Marsa. Yet not a word has been officially published by the government of Tel-Aviv. We know all that Army and government officials have told journalists, off the record, that the information published by the 'Sunday Magazine' was more or less correct, and they have captured a new type of radar, which is still being exam-

ined. In a paradoxical way these informal leaks have so
far lulled all the possible suspicions of the Egyptian Government. As all of you certainly remember, when we
launched the Aurora project we informed Egypt that
Marsa would be used for experimenting with a new type
of radar before it was turned over to their aerial defense
system.

"Somebody could have been tempted to think that the
Israelis have failed to discover the real function of the installations. Unfortunately, we have received positive proof
to the contrary. We know that a few days after the raid
the Director of the Mossad, Peled, flew to Washington
and submitted a full report about the equipment and
documents captured at Marsa. A meeting of the National
Security Council was convened, but no action was decided
upon. Our source says they are still very much in the dark
about our intentions." Yulin put on his thick glasses and
for the first time glanced at his papers. "The source says
that 'the President and his counselors put on a poor show
of their impotence and admitted they couldn't do anything
to block our projects, not even inform the government of
Egypt.' "

Yulin looked around him as if to make sure that everybody had understood. "On the other hand, the Mossad
Director was followed from Washington to New York,
and thenceforth to Munich. He drove straight to Gehlen's
residence." He paused again. "You know well, comrades,
what that means. He could ask Gehlen for only one piece
of information: his contacts in this country. I believe that
the Israelis want to get information on the Aurora project
from inside the U.S.S.R. We must be very careful. This
. . . this unfortunate accident could completely destroy our
Egyptian endeavor."

Razumov, the Chief of Planning and Analysis, looked
at him with a half-smile. "I see that you are worried, Lev
Ivanovich, and I understand perfectly why. Yet if we try
to analyze the situation, it all boils down to the fact that
the Israelis and the Americans know something about
Aurora but are unable to react. Isn't that right? If we
succeed in handling the Egyptians, we might proceed ac-

cording to plan. You, yourself, said that the Americans are unable to react."

Andropov nodded in approval. "The decision of the Politburo still stands," he said. "We shall continue the construction of our installations in Egypt. We shall double the camouflage and security measures. We must also protest to the Egyptian Government the poor vigilance of their soldiers around the Marsa base and demand that the guard of our other bases be reinforced. I suggest even to make them visit one of the bases where nothing is happening, on the pretext of showing them the security measures we, ourselves, are applying. They'll feel flattered, and we'll foil in advance any Egyptian request to visit all our bases, which could precipitate an unpleasant confrontation."

Yulin did not seem convinced. "We could continue as if nothing had happened if it were a matter of weeks, maybe months, Comrade Chairman. But in this case we still have work for a year or two, at least."

"Couldn't we speed up the whole project?" Andropov asked. "We could order the Army to start shipping those missiles immediately and to simplify the design of the launching sites. What about our friends there? When would they be ready to take over?"

"Not yet, Comrade Andropov," Yulin answered promptly. "We must be very careful this time. We all know what happened last May. Our people were too impatient, and the result was that President Sadat wiped out the entire organization and sent everybody to jail: Ali Sabri, Sharaf, Gomaa, Fawzi ... Our last hope is General Salem."

"Well, what about him?" Andropov was becoming impatient.

"He is a good man, comrade, but our estimate is that he will be able to overthrow Sadat only after a victorious war against Israel. Only then will he have the Army and the people on his side. But they need quite a long time until they are capable of fighting a war. That's what I meant when I said one or two years. I don't think we can risk anything before the war."

"Yes," Andropov agreed thoughtfully. "I will report that to the Politburo. To sum up the situation now: the enemy has by accident obtained some vague notion of what is going to happen. He can't act on the basis of that knowledge. Therefore we must expect a combined Israeli-American secret operation. We must find out exactly what the Israelis did discover. We must also find out what they intend to do. They might already be preparing a military plan to destroy our bases. The only way they could do it is by an air strike. We must, as first priority, infiltrate the Israeli Air Force."

"That will be very difficult, Comrade Chairman," Yulin warned. "Since we closed our embassy in Tel-Aviv during the Six-Day War, we have almost no contacts there."

"No sleepers?" Andropov asked coldly, thinking of all the agents he and his men had trained and placed in foreign countries in a long-range plan and left inactive for years until they had built foolproof covers for themselves.

"Yes, several," Yulin admitted, "but they are in no position to approach the Air Force. The Israelis are going to be much more security-minded now, and any unusual approach might jeopardize Aurora."

"Try the American side of it then," Andropov suggested. "The Israelis report regularly to the Pentagon about their projects, training, *et cetera*. Any new operational project will result in orders of new equipment for their Air Force, and Razumov here, will do the deduction work for us. Try both sides, Yulin, agreed?"

"Yes, comrade. And what about Peled's meeting with Gehlen?"

"We'll do something about it," Andropov replied abstractedly.

The meeting was over, and the men got up to leave. For a moment General Yulin remained seated, looking perplexed and worried.

Andropov was not so calm and confident as he appeared. That same afternoon, he was ushered into the office of the First Secretary of the Communist Party, in the Kremlin. The Secretary quickly summoned the Premier and the Ministers of Defense and Foreign Affairs. "This Marsa raid might bring an end to project Aurora," Andropov informed them. "There is proof that in the last few weeks the Israeli and the American secret services have been engaging in unprecedented activity in the Arab countries, especially in Egypt. They are determined to find out exactly what our intentions are. And they'll find out— if we don't stop them *now*."

"Do you have any suggestions?" Marshal Andrei Grechko inquired acidly. The Minister of Defense couldn't become accustomed to the idea that the KGB could impose its views and its policy on the mighty Soviet Army whenever it wanted.

"Yes, I have," Andropov answered tartly. "I think that we must carry out a huge smoke-screen operation. We have to convince the Israelis that we have been forced to abandon our plans. The only way to do it is for us to leave Egypt!"

"Leave Egypt? What do you mean, Yuri Vladimirovich?" The Foreign Minister sounded alarmed.

"I mean that we have to maneuver Egypt in such a way that she will expel most of our twenty-two thousand experts and military personnel from her territory. News of a very serious crisis between Egypt and the U.S.S.R. will be spread. Sharp diplomatic notes will be exchanged. This will convince the Israelis that our plans have been abandoned. Actually, the preparations for project Aurora will continue secretly."

"It sounds most unwise," the Foreign Minister said. "Endanger all our relations with Egypt, pull out those thousands of Soviet officers that were brought there. And all that for what?"

"Precisely," Andropov replied. "The stakes are high. I don't think you should worry. You know as well as I do that in a year or two the Egyptians will launch their war against Israel. They will need arms, planes, spare parts, international backing. They will come begging to us then—experts or no experts—and then we shall carry out Aurora. It might be the final blow to the West. Without oil all of Western Europe and America will be at our mercy."

"Yes, we know that," the First Secretary said bluntly.

"So, Leonid Ilyich?" Andropov looked at him challengingly.

The Secretary was silent for several moments. "I shall call an extraordinary meeting of the Politburo for tomorrow morning," he said finally.

Karol Thaler, the London correspondent of UPI, who had become famous for his inside information on the Soviet bloc, was the first to publish the sensational news on May 19, 1972. RUSSIAN EXPERTS LEAVING EGYPT read his first flash on the tickers of thousands of newspapers over the world. Thaler went on to tell of "unconfirmed rumors" about a quarrel that had erupted between the governments of Soviet Russia and Egypt. Following the Soviet refusal to supply Egypt with advanced MIG-23 jets and sophisticated missiles, President Sadat had decided to ask most of the Russian experts to leave Egypt with their families. Russia was hectically preparing an airlift for the transport of many thousands of its officers, their wives and children.

During the next few days the rumors proved to be correct. Any foreign journalist in Egypt could witness with his own eyes the hurried exodus of the Soviet military advisers. One could see them with their families in the souks of Cairo and Alexandria, buying souvenirs before their departure; boarding buses bound for the military airfields, where heavy Tupolev and Ilyushin planes were taking off around the clock. Other Russians, mostly families with small children, jammed the port of Alexandria, waiting for Russian and Polish ships to carry them back home. In an exchange of dry official communiqués between Moscow and Cairo it was announced that most of the Soviet experts, having completed their assignments in Egypt, were leaving the country. Only several hundred technicians were staying behind for a limited period of time.

Israel was euphoric. Distinguished scholars and commentators explained to the relieved nation that Soviet penetration in the Middle East was at an end, and that the U.S.S.R. had suffered its most humiliating setback in the Middle East. President Sadat of Egypt, they pointed out, having lost his principal ally, could no longer dream of a war against Israel, and had to start negotiating now. The subject was discussed at length in the Israeli Government, which adopted the view that the Russian danger in the Middle East was over for the time being. In the meetings of the Secret Services Commission similar views were expressed by several of the directors of the intelligence community. The same opinion could be heard in Washington.

Andropov's plan had indeed been a stroke of genius. It almost achieved its goal. Almost, but not completely. For while all his colleagues were jubilant, celebrating the end of their troubles, one man—Jeremiah Peled—carried on his operation with bulldog stubbornness.

PART TWO

The Name

5

August 28 - November 12, 1972

It was past midnight, and Senhora Maria Jacinto Ribeiro, owner of the Cangaceiro bar in São Paulo, was becoming more worried by the minute. A stout mulatto in her early fifties, she was nervously twisting her rose-colored handkerchief as she glanced at the two Germans sitting at table 17. They were drunk, shouting, laughing noisily, thumping their heavy fists on the table and eagerly pinching the bottoms of the frightened waitresses. Not that Senhora Ribeiro was against pinching waitresses' bottoms, especially if that helped the customer judge the quality of the girls and order one for himself in the quiet rooms conveniently located across the entrance hall. She, herself, had experienced such harmless adventures when she started her career, thirty-five years ago, as a graceful, slim, small-breasted girl in the "salon" of Alcido Costa, in the favela of Rio. That was a part of the game. But those two Germans were really going too far tonight. They had already each drunk a dozen beers and were bellowing for more. With boisterous laughter they were throwing the heavy glass mugs behind their backs, which then shattered on the tile-covered floor. Most of the other customers, afraid to intervene, had hurriedly paid their bills and left. Senhora Ribeiro's bouncer, Cicero, a mountain of a man with an iron fist, had been missing since Sunday. There was nobody to stop those wild estrangeiros while there was still time. She knew the scenario only too well: soon they would start challenging and insulting the few remaining customers, a brawl would begin, they would turn the place into a shambles, and she would have to call the police. That was her main worry. With all these waitresses and rooms in the back and some other illegal practices, a visit from the police could be disastrous. *"Minha Madre,"* she murmured fervently, addressing the Virgin Mary in the most inappropriate of places, "I pray you, do something."

A waitress shrieked when one of the Germans, a thickset little man with a brown mustache and a bald, eggshaped skull, slapped her bottom smartly, making her spill half of the beer she was trying to put on the table. It triggered another burst of laughter. The second man, big and broad-shouldered, with tousled blond hair and a greasy smile on his heavy-jowled red face, started a loud German beer song. His companion joined him, and in a moment they were howling in their hoarse voices, slapping each other on the back, and beating their feet on the shattered glass that covered the floor.

Suddenly one of the customers firmly put his glass on the bar and walked straight to their table. He was tall, thin, and blue-eyed, neatly dressed in a blue suit. Until now he had drunk his beer quietly and seemed indifferent to the disturbance at table 17. He bent over the inebriated strangers. "Could you please be quieter?" he said in German. His voice was calm and cold. "You are disturbing everybody here. This is not a pigsty."

The singing stopped abruptly. "Look at the bastard, Klaus," the small, plump German croaked angrily. "He won't let us sing. Who the hell does he think he is?" Klaus got up menacingly, kicked back his stool, and moved toward the intruder. He was much taller than his adversary, and under the sleeves of his beer-stained dandyish blazer one could see the tightening of big, powerful muscles. With unexpected swiftness for a man of his build and his inebriated condition, he swung his right hand, and his enormous fist landed with crashing force on the unprotected face of his challenger. Literally catapulted into the air, the man in the blue suit fell against a table, overturning it in his fall, and remained motionless for a moment amid fragments of glass and spilled drinks. Klaus again burst out in a hoarse laugh, while screaming waitresses ran for shelter behind the bar. Several other customers retreated hurriedly toward the exit. *"Minha Madre!"* Senhora Ribeiro cried, and crossed herself rapidly several times with a trembling hand.

The man on the floor dizzily got to his knees, and finally succeeded in pulling himself up to a standing position. With his sleeve he wiped away a tiny trickle of blood that appeared in the left corner of his mouth. He took one step forward, swayed back and forth, bent his head, and moved toward his assailant.

"If you want more, you're welcome," Klaus roared, and raised his formidable fist again.

That was the last thing he did. With a lightning jerk of his left arm his opponent blocked the upcoming blow, then viciously hit the unprotected stomach of the surprised giant with his right fist. Klaus gasped and bent forward with pain, clasping his belly with both hands. In rapid succession two sharp blows landed on his jaws. He stumbled back and fell down with a thud, only to be lifted by the lapels of his blazer and be dealt a cruel jab under his left eye. The man let him fall back and turned to his terrified companion. "What about you?" he asked, breathing heavily. "Care to join your friend?"

The frightened little man, who had temporarily lost the faculty of speech, shook his head vigorously to assure him that he didn't care at all to join the spread-eagled, immobile Klaus.

"Then get the hell out of here!"

The little man nodded a hurried acquiescence.

The man in blue walked back to the bar and picked up his drink. Several people clustered around him, to congratulate him on his fight. He was a foreigner too, but he was *macho*. Senhora Ribeiro smiled flirtatiously at him, sent the girls to clean the mess, and inquired if he would like another drink. "On the house, of course." He smiled and started to answer in Portuguese when he saw the fear in her eyes again. He pivoted swiftly to find Klaus facing him. But a glance at the limp hands dangling at the big man's sides made it plain that he had nothing to worry about. Klaus's left eye was almost closed, and the flesh around it was becoming violet, almost blue. The loosejowled face was humble, appeasing, and so was the tone. "I meant no harm, Mein Herr," the hoarse voice said, still heavy under the effect of alcohol. "I and my friend, there"—he pointed a shaking finger toward the little egg-skulled figure at table 17—"we want to apologize. We didn't want to disturb anybody. We are sorry. Shake hands, all right?"

He hesitated a moment, then shook hands with Klaus. "My name is Lemming, Klaus Lemming," said the big man, "and my friend, there, is Anton Kunda. We'll pay for all the broken glasses. Right? Now please come and have a drink with us—to show there are no bad feelings. You are a good fighter; we want to drink to your health, *ja?*"

The man in the blue suit eyed him for a moment. He shrugged. "All right," he said. "I'll come."

"Wunderbar! Come, please. We are celebrating tonight. A big business deal. So, you know. We shall be honored, Herr—Herr—"

"Bauer, Hermann Bauer," the thin man replied, and walked to table 17, gently but firmly removing the heavy hand that Klaus Lemming had laid on his shoulder in a too friendly gesture.

Lemming and Kunda did their best to please their new friend; however, they were too drunk for that. The best thing Bauer could do for them was to shove them in a taxi and send them back to their hotel, but not before they made him promise he would be their guest for dinner on the next evening. And so, at exactly 8 P.M. on August 30, Hermann Bauer stepped into the marble and plush lobby of the magnificent Hotel do Brasil.

Kunda and Lemming were expecting him at the tropical bar. Sobered up and valiantly trying to behave, they were quite different from the vulgar troublemakers he had met last night. Impeccably dressed in fine dark suits, they even would have managed to look respectable were it not for Lemming's black eye. They led him politely to the exquisite French restaurant on the top floor. Over a bottle of expensive burgundy, Kunda told him about themselves.

He was from Frankfurt; Lemming had been living in Montevideo, the capital of Uruguay, for twenty years.

They were both on a tour of the South American capitals, Kunda explained, to investigate the possibilities for promoting a huge travel agency, which was to organize group tours from Germany, Austria, and Scandinavia through all of South America. The agency had recently been established by a group of their friends in Frankfurt, and a "West German millionaire" had invested an important sum that was going to be their working capital for the first two years. Kunda was to head the Frankfurt office; Lemming was the principal agent for South America. Yesterday they were in high spirits because they had just signed "a fantastic deal" with Varig, the national airline of Brazil.

"Do you have a name for your agency?" Bauer asked with sudden interest.

"Of course," Kunda replied, and produced from his pocket a business card with his name as manager of "Sombrero-Reisen," Frankfurt. "People like those exotic names," he said with a grin.

"I ask you because we might meet each other in our business," Bauer explained. "You see, I have been living in Brazil for twenty-four years. I moved to São Paulo only a few months ago and opened an air-taxi service here. We have some light planes—two Cessnas, two Islanders. We charter them often to small tourist groups for flights to Paraguay, to the Mato Grosso, and even for several-day tours of all Brazil. Maybe we could do some business together."

"Well, I don't know," Kunda answered vaguely, nervously adjusting his dark glasses. "You see, we have everything fixed already: contracts, agreements, and so on."

"But you haven't been in touch with any service like mine?"

Kunda looked quickly at Lemming. "I'm not sure that your service is exactly in our line of things," the big German said awkwardly.

They ate the rest of their meal in silence. The almost instinctive refusal of the two travel agents to consider his casual offer offended Bauer, but he said nothing. He gulped down his *cafezinho,* got up abruptly, and shook hands with the two men before they could even offer to accompany him to his car. "Have a pleasant stay," he said curtly, then seemed to change his mind. "How long are you staying in São Paulo?"

"Oh, some more days," Lemming replied absently.

"Well, good-bye, and thanks for the excellent dinner."

On leaving the Hotel do Brasil, Bauer behaved as though he would never see his new acquaintances again.

But the next day it was Bauer who phoned them. He'd had to leave a little early last night, he said, but would they do him the honor of attending a dinner party at his house on the beach? His wife and sons would be delighted to meet them. They agreed, and didn't regret it. It was a relaxed evening in the open air, under the royal palms in Bauer's garden, with the soft waves of the Atlantic lapping lazily at their feet. They almost didn't talk about business, except for a casual remark by Bauer. "I checked you out," Hermann Bauer said, chuckling. "I talked to the manager of Varig in São Paulo, a good friend of mine. He said they had screened your agency before they signed the contract and that you are very reliable. They predict a brilliant future for Sombrero-Reisen." Kunda and Lemming appeared flattered.

The dinner party was followed by several beach outings at the ocean, other dinners, and a delightful trip to the "German province" of Santa Catarina. They flew there on a sunny morning in one of Bauer's Cessnas and came back late at night. Bauer drove them back to their hotel, but before they got out of the car Kunda, who was sitting in the back, leaned forward and put his hand on Bauer's shoulder. "Hermann, will you come and have a drink with us? We leave tomorrow, and I'd like to talk to you."

They found a place in a secluded corner of the bar. Kunda looked thoughtfully at Bauer.

"May I ask you a question? A personal one, I mean."

"Sure," Bauer said, surprised.

"We've spent a lot of time together during the past week. We've talked about a lot of things. But every time we touched the subject of what we did in the war you shut up like a clam. Why, Hermann?"

"It is a subject I don't like to discuss," Bauer said distantly. Then he added, "As a matter of fact, I could ask you the same question. You didn't disclose what you did during the war either."

"Maybe for the same reason as you," Lemming interjected enigmatically.

Bauer looked at him sharply. "What do you mean?"

"Come on, come on," Kunda said soothingly. "You checked on us, but we checked on you, too. You lived here in Brazil for twenty-four years. You told us that yourself. Incidentally, there are many Germans in this country and all over South America who immigrated here during the years following the war. They just felt that Germany was not safe anymore. They felt that their country had been betrayed and that they were being hunted now for what they did or did not do."

"I am not ashamed of anything I did!" Bauer's voice became strident.

"Neither are we, Hermann," Kunda retorted promptly. "You were in the German Army. You escaped to Brazil. You are more or less known to some of our friends. These are the facts."

"What kind of friends do you have here?" Bauer was strung taut as a chord.

"Good men," Kunda answered, then added pleadingly, "Look, let's be frank. I wouldn't have talked to you like that if I had not gotten the green light from my people. I was an officer in the SS during the war, and so was Klaus. And so are most of our partners in Sombrero-Reisen. You can just call it a friends' organization, to help themselves and to help others if there was need. Our chief financier was also with us during the war. We are quite safe today, aren't we, Klaus?"

Klaus nodded slowly.

"You can check the records of the SS officers. You won't find any Kunda or Lemming there. Our former names have long been buried and almost forgotten. And so have those of all our friends. I wouldn't ask you whether Bauer is your true name. That's your secret."

Bauer made as if to answer, but Kunda raised his hand.

"Please. You might have understood that, until now, the main reason for our reluctance to talk business with you was that we have a primary rule in our organization: not to accept any outside people, just our own. We want to be sure, that's all. Many of us, including Klaus and myself, are still sought by Israeli avenger commandos and the German police. Our boss spent half his life in hiding, until he could get a foolproof new identity. Now I have the impression that you are one of us. Our friends here say that your financial situation is quite troubled. Your air-taxi service is not doing well, and our agency could be a bonanza to you."

Bauer said nothing.

Kunda went on softly, "If you are still interested, I'll talk to our friends back in Germany. You would make a wonderful director of our Brazilian office."

Bauer looked him straight in the eyes. "I am interested," he said. Then he added, "You don't have to worry. And you know what I mean."

Kunda got up from his place and pumped Bauer's hand vigorously. "Good! I'm flying back to Frankfurt. I'll let you know. In a couple of months we are going to have a meeting of all our chief executives in South America—in Brazil or Argentina, maybe Uruguay. You'll meet the boss himself. I am sure it will work out."

In his turn Lemming also shook hands with Bauer. "No hard feelings about the eye, my friend." He smiled. "It's completely over now. I hope you get into our business. It's going to be a gold mine. I know it."

At the end of October, Hermann Bauer received a registered letter from Frankfurt. A colorful sombrero was painted on the envelope, under the inscription "Sombrero-Reisen," followed by a long series of addresses, post office boxes, and telephone numbers from all over Germany, Norway, Sweden, and Denmark. He slit open the envelope. Inside there was a very cordial letter from Anton Kunda. He was happy to inform him that "the big boss" was in favor of his joining the agency. The meeting they talked about was going to take place on November 13, in Montevideo. Enclosed was an Air France round-trip ticket to Montevideo. A reservation in Bauer's name had been made starting November 12 at the Hotel Victoria. "We'll be delighted to see you again. Klaus and I send you our warmest wishes and our deep respects to Frau Bauer."

Bauer smiled with satisfaction as he read the letter. It had been quite difficult, but he had made it. He picked up the telephone receiver and dialed a number. That same night, in a shabby café on the beach, he conferred for a long time with two men and listened carefully to their instructions. Before he left the place, one of them gave him a list of names and phone numbers.

"Memorize and destroy," he said. "A phone report every twelve hours. The last phone number is in case of emergency. Our people there will be close at hand, just in case it is a trap."

On November 10 he received a cable: EXPECTING YOU MONTEVIDEO THURSDAY REGARDS ANTON.

Later Bauer boarded an Air France plane for the capital of Uruguay. In his pocket he had a .38 Colt Police Special. Just in case.

6

November 8 - November 13, 1972

On November 8, Rolf Roeder, bearer of Austrian passport 726161, arrived in Montevideo. He checked into the Gloria Palace Hotel and rented a green Volkswagen. He spent most of the following days in his hotel room, and in the evenings went out alone and returned alone.

On November 9, Otto Klein, bearer of German passport 2.778.905, arrived in Montevideo. He checked into the Hotel Uruguay and rented a Fiat 124.

On November 11, Rudy Buehler, German passport 995.971, arrived in Montevideo. He checked into the Hotel Nogaro and hired a white Ford Cortina.

On that same day Anton Kunda arrived from Frankfurt, via Lisbon and Rio, by Varig. He was met at the airport by Klaus Lemming, who drove him to the Hotel Victoria and there gave him the keys and papers of a rented black Volkswagen.

"Is everything O.K.?" Kunda asked.

"Yes. Hermann is coming tomorrow, so we can stick to the original date of November thirteen. He will meet our people in a house I have rented in the Calle Bolivia at Morales, by the beach. It is a quiet place, and we won't be disturbed."

"Yes," Kunda said, but he frowned.

"Are you afraid of a trap?" Lemming asked.

"I don't know," he replied. "Until now Hermann hasn't given us any reason for suspicion. You never know, of course."

"Can we do anything?"

"Keep an eye on him. Send somebody ahead of me to the airport when he arrives, to check him for arms. And put a tag on him if he leaves the hotel. That's all we can do. Could you monitor his phone calls?"

"No. Impossible." Lemming was certain.

On November 12, Bauer landed in Montevideo. Called on the loudspeakers to the information desk, he was told that a Señor Kunda was waiting for him in his car outside the terminal. He turned to the exit, carrying a small overnight bag. A young man in a hurry darted past him, slipped, and brushed against him. He apologized absently and continued to run toward the exit, reaching the huge glass doors some thirty seconds ahead of Bauer. He looked at Kunda, who was standing by his Volkswagen, and his lips moved without a sound. "Gun," the silent lips said. Kunda's face remained impassive under his dark glasses.

A moment later Bauer's familiar, erect figure emerged from the terminal building. Kunda waved to him, and they shook hands warmly. He drove Bauer to the Hotel Victoria, but declined his invitation to go out that evening. "I arrived from Frankfurt last night and still haven't adjusted to the time difference," he explained. "I feel like a drunk, and my head is splitting."

"When shall we meet, then?" Bauer asked.

"As agreed. Be ready tomorrow at about a quarter to one. We'll have a late lunch with all our people. Most of them are already here. The boss arrives tonight."

"Where is the meeting?" Bauer tried to make his voice sound casual.

"At Lemming's house."

"Where?" he insisted.

Kunda looked at him for a moment, then smiled, took a slip of paper out of his pocket, and read the address aloud.

On November 13, at 12:30 P.M., Bauer dialed a number on the direct line from his room. "I have an appointment at one p.m. in the Casa Cuvertini, Calle Bolivia. If I don't come back or phone by two thirty, you move in."

The streets in the quiet residential suburb of Morales were deserted. It was late spring in Uruguay, and the air was already humid and stifling. The southern sun seemed to melt the black asphalt. Most shops were closed, and people had barricaded themselves behind tightly drawn shutters for a few hours of blessed Latin siesta.

The black Volkswagen drew to a stop in the Calle Bolivia, at the entrance to the Casa Cuvertini. A green Volkswagen and a white Cortina were parked across the street.

"This is the place," Kunda said. Bauer got out of the car and glanced around. There was nobody in sight.

"Will you lead the way?" he asked politely. Kunda noticed the tiny beads of perspiration on his forehead and the involuntary tightening of the jaw muscles. The man was in a state of high tension.

He stepped forward and rang the bell. Quickly approaching footsteps sounded from inside. The door opened and there was Lemming, beaming with pleasure. "Hermann! Welcome! Come in, come in."

Bauer stepped inside. "Hello, Klaus, how—"

Everything happened at once. At the same second the door was slammed shut, somebody jumped on Bauer from behind and gripped his body with a crushing hold, immobilizing his hands. Two other men, who had been waiting in the dark corridor with guns drawn, sprung at him, aiming their weapons at his head and chest. Lemming's huge hand crashed on his mouth, almost suffocating him.

"Don't move! Don't touch your gun!" Kunda's command was harsh. "We know you carry a gun."

Without looking at his face Kunda frisked him and relieved him of his weapon. Handcuffs clicked on his hands and ankles. His mouth was expertly gagged. He couldn't move. Lemming and the man who had caught him from behind carried him inside and put him in an armchair, in the middle of a big, shabbily furnished living room.

"If you behave, you won't be killed," one of his captors said in German. "Listen carefully. I repeat: if you behave, you won't be killed. You will be set free—not immediately, but in a reasonable period of time. Your family will be notified that you are alive. If you heard and understood what I said, move your head."

Bauer nodded once.

"This is an isolated place. Even if you shout, nobody will hear you. These two men will have you covered with their guns all during the interrogation. Any suspicious movement on your part will result in your death. Now, if you agree to cooperate and not attempt anything, we'll remove the gag and handcuffs."

Bauer nodded again. Silently Kunda and Lemming took off the handcuffs and the mouth gag.

"Have a cigarette," the stranger said. "Try not to be nervous. I repeat: we have no intention of killing you; on the contrary. Relax, Herr Bauer—or should I say Major Roehm?"

His captors waited patiently until the long string of furious curses died in his mouth. "It's a pity to waste your breath," Kunda said soothingly. "My friend told you we know who you are, but we mean no harm."

"So you did find me in the end," Roehm said bitterly. "Are you Russians, or what?"

"No, we are not Russians. We are not going to tell you who we are."

Roehm looked around him, sizing up the situation. Lemming had left the room—he must be observing the street. A house like this certainly had another exit, but there might be other people around. One of the gunmen was leaning on the sill of the closed and shuttered window. Kunda and the other one stood by the two doors leading out of the room. Kunda was armed too, but he kept his gun tucked in his belt. Anyway, he was the farthest away of all the people in the room. If he tried to get at him, he'd be shot dead before taking one step forward. They wouldn't fear the noise. Both guns were fitted with long cylindrical silencers.

"Did you tell anybody that you were coming here?" Kunda asked.

A faint glimmer of hope flickered in his mind. "No," he replied.

"Tell us," Kunda insisted. "If we did, we'll transfer you to another place. We don't want fights. We don't want to kill you. Is that clear?"

"I didn't tell anybody," Roehm said. He drew anxiously on his cigarette. The acrid smoke—they weren't American cigarettes—burned his lungs, and he coughed and cursed.

"No contacts here?"

"No contacts."

Kunda didn't talk anymore. "You can call me Hans," the tall stranger said.

"What do you want?"

"You must have guessed. We want your list, Major."

"What list?"

Hans gazed at him steadily and spoke in an even tone. "You are an intelligent man. You must have understood that we know everything about you. Our men didn't stumble on you in the Cangaceiro bar by sheer luck. You know that."

"I have no list."

"We are not going to torture you, Major Roehm. If you don't tell us, we'll just have to kill you. Think about it." Hans lit a cigarette and left the room.

Time seemed to be trickling by slowly. Roehm longed to find out what time it was, how many hours he had been here, but they had taken his watch. Another of those damn psychological tricks.

After an eternity Hans came back. "We want your list. We want to know where it is. Don't pretend you don't know what we are talking about. I think you're afraid for your safety and for your family." His demeanor was understanding, even sympathetic. "We can offer you new identities, new, genuine passports, enough money to start a new life, a home and a job in a different part of the world. You won't have to worry anymore."

"That's one alternative," Kunda intervened sharply. "The other one is clear. You don't talk—we shoot you right away."

Roehm cursed under his breath. Yes, he knew these interrogation tactics only too well: the alternate use of the promise and the menace, the carrot and the stick. They could try that if they liked. He was not going to fall for such lousy second-rate methods.

Klaus tiptoed into the room and whispered into Hans's ear. "Yes. Thank you," he said, and turned to Roehm. "There is something else. You might be interested to know that since noon your wife and sons have been in our hands."

The blood drained from Roehm's face. "I don't believe you," he said in a shaky voice. "It's a damn lie! You're trying to break me."

"No reason to lie to you," Hans replied matter-of-factly. "There was something wrong with the current in your home this morning. Your wife called the electric company. Our men, dressed as electricians, went to your house. They hold your family at gunpoint. The servants, too. They'll kill everybody if you don't talk."

Lemming came back carrying a telephone on a long cord, cradle in one hand, receiver in the other. "We didn't tell you before; we just established communication. Would you like to talk to your wife?"

Roehm passed his tongue over his dry lips. He nodded yes.

"She is on the line," Lemming said.

"Emma?" Roehm's voice was still trembling. "Emma, it's me!" Lemming's hand immediately covered the mouthpiece.

"Heinrich!" The high-pitched, terrified shriek shot out of the receiver. "Where are you? Do something! They are going to kill us all; do something! Oh, please, please, Heinrich . . ."

Her sobs still echoed in his ears as Lemming cut the communication and went out of the room.

"Bastards!" he muttered.

"We promised you: no harm to anybody. Money, new passports, security. Just the list." Hans continued to look at him without emotion.

Heinrich Roehm spoke like an automaton. "The list is in a safe deposit box in Switzerland. To get it all you have to do is enter the secret accounts and deposits department of the main Bern office of the Banques Helvétiques Unifiées. You have to pronounce a word and a number: Schwartzwald 5491."

"You saved your life, Roehm," Kunda said, honestly relieved, and called Lemming. "I want you to telephone, in Roehm's presence, to São Paulo, order our men to leave the place, and keep the line open until they are gone, so Frau Bauer—or Roehm—will confirm it herself."

A few minutes later Emma Roehm's voice could be heard in the receiver again, this time overwhelmed with relief. "They are gone, Heinrich, all of them!" There was no answer. "Do you hear me, Heinrich, they have left!"

"It's all right," he said slowly. "Don't call the police. Don't tell anybody. I'll be back"—he looked searchingly at Kunda—"soon, quite soon, I promise."

Lemming took the phone out quietly. "You saved your life," Kunda repeated, and removed his dark glasses. "Now you'll have to spend several weeks in our 'protective custody.' Don't frown. If I may say so, it's not so terrible. I rather like you, as you know. We'll get you out of here and—"

Suddenly the screeching brakes of a car rent the quiet of Calle Bolivia. From the door came Lemming's harsh cry: "They are coming! Three of them, armed!" Then they heard the thump of heavy steps and pounding on the door.

"Back exit, quick!" roared Hans. The two gunmen ran, with Lemming following. The heavy bolted door was cracking. Two shots were heard from outside as the attackers tried to break the lock.

"So you did call your friends," Kunda whispered furiously. "You fool!"

Roehm wasn't listening. It was now or never, he said to himself, and felt all his muscles tighten. Kunda took a hesitant step toward him, and then he jumped. Instinctively he dived in the direction of the open door, in a desperate attempt to escape. But he had no chance. Behind him Kunda drew his gun. The sound of the first shot made him turn and look back. The last thing he saw before Kunda squeezed the trigger again was a pained, desperate expression in the little brown eyes. Then his chest exploded and he fell, barely a few steps from the battered chair.

Before Roehm's friends, members of the secret "Das Reich" organization, broke down the door, the kidnappers had gone by the back exit to a small alley leading into Calle Colombia. In seconds the commercial van and the Volvo sedan that had been parked there turned the corner and disappeared.

When Das Reich men rushed into the villa, they found only the lifeless body of Heinrich Roehm.

7

November 14 - November 22, 1972

The next morning an aging white-haired gentleman
alighted from a chauffeur-driven black limousine and entered the central branch of the Banques Helvétiques
Unifiées, in Bern. His candid blue eyes, protected by
horn-rimmed glasses, his expensive overcoat, and well-
cultivated manners cast about him an aura of natural authority. He seemed to be someone to whom deference was
due. The clerk at the information counter was delighted
to escort him to the secret accounts and deposits department, prudently secluded on the second floor. He asked to
see the manager of the department, to whom he gave the
password. The manager then asked him to wait in his office and went to the vaults. A few minutes later he was
back and handed his visitor an old-looking, unmarked,
sealed envelope.

It contained a single sheet of paper—the secret list of
Heinrich Roehm.

Jeremiah Peled intently examined the twenty-seven-
year-old piece of paper that had already cost one man his
life. His agents had succeeded where the Germans and the
Russians had failed: first locating, then capturing Heinrich Roehm. He remembered his meeting with Gehlen,
ten months ago, and the urgent message he had
dispatched to all the Mossad stations around the world:
"Find Roehm!" But the operation had started badly, and
more than once he had felt that he was on the verge of
failure. In vain his agents had interrogated the "Nazi
hunters" in Vienna, Frankfurt, Jerusalem, and Ludwigs-
burg; in vain had they examined the long lists of Nazi

criminals at large that were on file in various archives. Their luck turned only months later, when one of his best men, posing as an ex-Nazi, had successfully penetrated a secret ring of former German officers in Paraguay. He had gained access to the files of the organization, which covered all South America. There he discovered the new name and address of Heinrich Roehm. Then came the intricate operation in São Paulo and Montevideo—and its final outcome was the single sheet of paper he now held in his hand.

It was an oblong typewritten leaf of ordinary quality. At single-spaced intervals some amateur typist—undoubtedly Roehm himself—had typed twenty-two names. The list filled approximately half of the type sheet. There were just the names. No addresses or functions, only Christian and family names, and for the military their Army ranks. Beside each name was its code appellation, which also implied the emergency method of contact—by direct approach and use of the code word.

Nothing was written about the information that each source had supplied, and there was no indication of more sophisticated systems of communication. It was obvious that Roehm had hastily prepared this list for his own use, certainly destroying the original files and limiting the document to the essentials he needed. But even in this form it was highly explosive material.

There was only one deviation from the pattern. The last name in the list, opposite the number 22, was missing. There was just the code word: Minerva 6N. Under it, covering most of the rest of the page, was a handwritten remark, again no doubt, by Roehm himself. Peled was not fluent in German, and he read it slowly:

> *I worked with Minerva for three years, from 1941 to 1944. I was his ring director. Nevertheless, I never met him and never learned his true identity. To my knowledge, there was nobody in the Abwehr, not even Canaris himself, who knew the real identity of Minerva. We only know that he is an important official in the state secret police. He had been a junior*

agent in the GPU, and later in the NKVD. It was he who established contact with us in 1939 by leaving an unsigned note in the car of our chief agent in Moscow, whose cover was a job as representative of Krupp in our trade mission. Since contact was established, Minerva supplied us with a regular flow of information by an intricate system of dead-letter boxes. We never saw him and never heard his voice. During the war we supplied him with a transmitter, and he broadcast to us in Morse. His information was mainly Kremlin inside stuff and sporadic but excellent surveys of the Ukrainian guerrilla operations behind our lines by the Red partisan division. He did not ask for money, and my guess is that his motivation was political. This impression was corroborated by the fact that his information was selective. He fed us what he wanted to, but kept back top information, which he certainly possessed.

The Old Man read it again and again, frowning, as if trying to extract from the note what was there though not written down.

"What do you make of it, Jeremiah?" asked his deputy, Mike Avivi, who was closely watching his reaction from across the large teak desk in his office. He was a chunky, jovial man with close-cut blond hair, twinkling blue eyes, and a fair complexion—the ideal candidate for a Scandinavian cover, which he often used in operational sorties.

Peled put the paper on the table. "No doubt Roehm wrote all that for his own protection," he said matter-of-factly. "Remember, he compiled this dossier in 1945. He certainly intended at the beginning to sell it to the Russians. If not, he would have joined Gehlen or contacted the Americans. Yet he was aware of the Russian methods of extracting information from people. If he fell into their hands, they might have tortured him almost to death to disclose Minerva's identity. So he put everything he knew about him on paper, to prove he really didn't know his identity. It was a kind of life insurance, in case the worst happened."

Avivi didn't seem convinced. "What life insurance are ou talking about? They would have killed him anyway. n the contrary, maybe he knew the true identity of Iinerva, and that was a trump card he kept up his sleeve r further dealing."

"Maybe he knew and maybe he didn't," the Old Man id impatiently. He didn't like being contradicted. "Any-ay, this discussion is academic. The man is dead and is is all we have. Now what are you going to do about ?"

"Give me a couple of weeks," Avivi replied. "I have al-ady assembled our experts on Russian affairs. We'll neck and double-check every name on that list. After I lked to you on the phone yesterday, I cabled the CIA to nd us their top man in this field. They agreed immedi-ely. They are even more interested in seeing the list an we are. They are sending us Snyder—you met him nce—and Lederer. They'll be here tomorrow."

"You know that I'm not very happy with their knowing l that part of it," Peled said irritably. "At least they ould promise not to exploit any name on the list before ur operation is over."

"I'll take care of that," Avivi assured him. "But I think e have no choice. We don't have any comprehensive sts of Russian officials and military top brass. The mericans can just feed most of the names into their omputers and everything clicks out."

"All right, but I'll want a full report every day."

Avivi rose to leave.

"We have very little time, Mike," Peled warned him. A week, no more. That's all I can give you."

A week later Jeremiah Peled drove to the secluded villa nat the Mossad had put at the disposal of "the Russian am." The villa was located in Herzlia, about ten miles om Tel-Aviv. Winter had descended abruptly—as sual—and a heavy downpour out of a menacing black ky violently assailed the coastal plain. The deluge was ccompanied by howling winds and thunder. Gigantic oamy waves flooded the seaside drive in Tel-Aviv, carrying back with them lounge chairs, multicolored umbrellas and round wooden tables from the sidewalk cafés. It too no more than fifteen seconds for the still superbly fit Ol Man to run from his car to the sheltered entrance of th villa, but it didn't help. He was soaked to the bones, an his shoes were heavy with reddish ankle-deep mud. H swore under his breath. He had offered the Russian tear a suite of offices in the main building of the Mossad, jus a floor below his own office, with all the necessary accom modations and equipment they needed, but the American had stubbornly refused. "We were told this was an in formal mission," Snyder had said, "and it has to be car ried out on neutral ground. Peter wouldn't allow us to go near the Mossad. He was adamant about it." The Ameri cans had also refused to use the Mossad communicatio channels, and for every cable or phone call were rushin to their embassy on Hayarkon Street. It was not so bad after all: following the Six-Day War the CIA had in stalled a scrambler on one of the hot lines linking the em bassy with the State Department.

Peled was admitted by the guard on duty, threw hi useless raincoat on one chair, and entered the living room which the team had named "the workshop." That's th way it looked, with big black and green boards hangin everywhere, names written on them in English, Hebrew and Russian. On a huge board of plastic foam wer pinned lists, cables, sheets of paper, even several radi photographs. Files, notebooks, and manuals were strew on the sofas, on the floor, on the tables. The ashtray overflowed with cigarette stubs, and paper cups with residue of black coffee were piled in one corner, alon with big empty cola bottles and beer cans. A strong smel of stale cigar smoke hung in the air. From the corner o his eye Peled caught sight of some whiskey bottles, hastil hidden behind the large window curtains. His men knew his aversion to hard liquor; he would severely punish any one he caught drinking while on an assignment. This time with rare tact, he decided not to mention it. The men ha been working around the clock for almost a week, and h knew American drinking habits. He let it go with a mild

bout him as we were at the beginning. For once, the omputers didn't help."

"Yes, yes!" Peled waved his copy of the list impa- ently. "But there is still another name. What about im?"

"Ah, this one, the only one you didn't cross out, ight?" Avivi smiled broadly and looked at Snyder.

Snyder smiled too. "With this one I think you have hit he jackpot, sir. You've got your man."

Peled didn't take part in the general exhilaration. What do you mean? Get to the point, please."

"Go on," Avivi said to Snyder. "You tell him. It's your aby."

"Yes," said Snyder, beaming. "You have him on your ist. Major Lavrenti Blagonravov. I had the feeling that I new the name, and I cabled Washington about him. It vas simple, as a matter of fact. Today the man is Lieu- enant General Blagonravov, one of the top officers in harge of the Soviets' missile program. He was assigned to heir strategic missile project from its start, when they vere still working with the German scientists they had idnaped after the war. He supervised the building of heir first rockets, the R-10, R-11, and R-14. He escaped niraculously when that explosion took place in Siberia. You remember the A-32 exploding on its launching pad nd wiping out seven generals and dozens of officers, cientists, and government officials. He was de Gaulle's uide on his official visit to Baikonur in 1966. He partici- ates in all the top-level meetings in the Kremlin when nissile and nuclear subjects are discussed. We know that e is consulted at length before each session of the SALT alks."

Peled couldn't control his growing excitement. "That's antastic!" he exclaimed. "He must be our man."

"If there is a secret, he'll know it," Snyder said. "And I ave some more news for you. Washington informs me hat lately he travels to Egypt quite often."

"Have you all that in writing?" Peled asked. He tried to uppress this feeling of joy that was surging inside him.

The most difficult part of his operation was still ahead.

Snyder brought him two closely typewritten sheets. "That's all the information we have on Lieutenant General Blagonravov." Then he detached from the foam board the photograph of a serious, square-headed officer, his face cast in the traditional stoic attitude Russian generals adopt before the camera, his large chest covered with a few dozen medals. "This is your man."

"This is our man," Peled repeated slowly. He rose. "My friends, I can't tell you how grateful I am." Then happily smiling at Avivi, he said, "Mike, tonight, a dinner party in my house. You bring the food from the best restaurants. You'll be my guests." Stopping by the door, he added, "And you can bring those bottles from behind the curtain. Buy some more—and put them on my personal account. We'll drink to Lavrenti Blagonravov's health tonight!"

Avivi was astounded. The Old Man has gone off his rocker for sure, he thought.

But before Peled drank to Lavrenti Blagonravov's health, he had more important business to attend to. In the late afternoon he summoned four people to his office. Two of them, Raphael Dori and Dan Brandt, were employees of the Mossad and considered to be the stars of the Research Department. The third, David Ron, was a senior police officer, reputed to be the best police investigator in the country. He had joined the force after a brilliant career in the Shin Bet. He had a tidy, incisive mind and good intuition, and he had solved a large number of crimes. After Ron had left the secret service, Peled refused to delete his name from his lists. He was now and again "borrowed" by the Mossad for several undercover missions abroad. The fourth man was Professor Joseph Heller, lecturer in contemporary history at Tel-Aviv University. He was a former member of the Mossad, and had displayed extraordinary intellectual capacities in planning and carrying out unconventional operations. The four men, in spite of their different backgrounds, had already worked as a team on several occasions in past years.

Peled invited them to sit down. "Recently we have succeeded in obtaining, by somewhat unusual means, a list of people who were German spies in the Soviet Union during World War Two." He didn't tell them how he got the list or why he needed it, and they knew him too well to ask. "From all the names that were on the list, only two were of any interest to us. One was a Soviet general, Lavrenti Blagonravov. We'll take care of him. The second was a mysterious high-placed official of the Soviet secret service whose code name during the war was Minerva 6N."

He circulated photocopies of Roehm's list among the four men. "Read carefully the handwritten note about Minerva," he said. To Raphael Dori, who did not read German, he handed a translated copy of the list. Heller was the first to speak. "I think I can guess what you're going to tell us, Jeremiah."

The Old Man smiled. "Of course. The four of you are the best research team I can recruit in the whole country. I want you to leave everything you are working on and concentrate on one question: who is Minerva? I have already talked to the Inspector General of the police force about you, David. Beginning tomorrow morning you are at my disposal. As for you, Joseph"—he turned to Professor Heller—"the work I'll assign to you may take many months. I know that the academic year has just started. If you can find a solution by yourself—fine. If you wish, I can have the Minister of Education, or even the Prime Minister, call the university rector and convince him to put you at the disposal of the government. In any case, I need you and I won't take no for an answer."

"It's all right, Jeremiah," Professor Heller said while lighting his briar pipe. "You don't have to convince me. We'll think of something."

"Very well, then." Peled beamed with satisfaction. "About Dori and Brandt there are no problems, of course. You just tell your boss that I requisitioned you.

"Now, about your assignment. You must find out who

Minerva is. This is of the utmost importance. Do a little
preliminary work here, then go to Europe. Go to all the li-
braries, research institutes, documentation centers. We'll
get—and don't ask me how—the full list of top Soviet officials of the KGB and the GRU today. We'll get a much
more extensive list of officials in the NKVD in Russia
during the war. We already know the approximate age of
our man. By analyzing the information he supplied, we
could find out which people in the various secret service
departments could have had access to that kind of
material during the war. We'll work by elimination and by
gradually narrowing the circle of people who suit our
criteria. You'll get all possible help from me: introduction
to foreign services who cooperate with us, contacts with
specialists on Russian problems, money for any purpose,
identity papers, men who can penetrate the society of
Russian émigrés. If you need to mount an operation of
any kind, I'll send you our best men. If you need Russian-
speaking agents to infiltrate Russian circles, I'll get them
for you. We must find Minerva and make him talk. I
can't tell you why, but I certainly can tell you that this is
the most important mission you have ever been assigned
to."

The four men got up to leave. "Two more things,"
Peled said. "Time is extremely important. I want you in
Europe in two weeks at the latest."

"And the second thing?" Profesor Heller asked, puffing
on his briar.

"The classification is top secret. I want the most rigor-
ous secrecy and compartmentalization. You must be very
careful. It's not the Arabs you're playing against. It's the
Russians. It might cost you your lives." Then he added,
not looking at them, "And the lives of many others."

8

November 22, 1972

At seventy-two General Lavrenti Alexeievich Blagonravov looked barely fifty-five. The crew cut of his gray-blond hair and the soft white skin of his big face gave him an almost boyish look. His tall, well-proportioned body was always erect, and his slender waist hadn't changed since his early youth. "Without the red star on your cap you'd look exactly like an aristocratic officer of the Czar's army," his friends would taunt him. He didn't resent it. Actually, if the October 1917 Revolution hadn't pulverized the old regime in Russia, he would certainly be an officer of the Czar's army. And he really was an aristocrat, an authentic blue-blooded nobleman. His father, Count Golovni, had been for years a close adviser to Alexander III and to Nikolai II. Owing to Czar Nikolai's absolute trust in him, he was sent in 1906 to Novorossiisk at the head of a Cossack army to establish order in the city and enforce royal authority in the rebellious region, still hostile to the throne after the bloodbath that had drowned the Revolution of 1905. Little Lavrenti grew up in his father's palace on the outskirts of Novorossiisk, but he spent most of his time with his warriors, the proud, wild Cossacks of the Don. He was fascinated by those lean, sunburned men with their ascetic, vaguely Asiatic faces, their crooked noses, black mustaches, and fiery eyes. He would admiringly caress the officers' long black robes, magnificently embroidered with silk and ornamented with clusters of huge live cartidges sewn to the cloth, over the chest. How masculine the Cossack leaders, the "atamans," looked with their leather belts, their polished high-heeled boots reaching the knees, their square leather kolpacks! At fifteen Lavrenti was offered his first Cossack uniform. And he most certainly deserved it, for he rode, shot, and cursed like a pure full-blooded Cossack. "Even your legs are becoming arched from too much riding," his father would say to him, and then add proudly, "I am raising a new Bielorussian ataman for the Cossack army of the Czar."

Count Golovni was wrong. He was raising a rebel in his own house. For there was only one man whom his son admired more than General Glebko, the ataman of the Cossacks: his old white-bearded teacher, Innocenti Blagonravov. Hours on end, day after day, the youngster would sit by his desk in the study and listen to his teacher's lectures. But Blagonravov didn't speak only of Pushkin and Dostoevski, of Peter the Great, Ivan the Terrible, and Boris Godunov; he didn't practice only French spelling and mathematical equations with the boy. Often his good, peaceful face would metamorphose into a passionate prophet's head, and he would speak of the poor and the oppressed, of the terrible suffering of the Russian people. He would enthrall the child with words like democracy, equality, revolution. He would bewitch him with the descriptions of a man, a legendary leader hiding far away, a man whose name was Ulyanov, but whom his friends and followers called Lenin.

The elderly Blagonravov was one of the first martyrs of the October Revolution. When Lenin's Red armies toppled the old regime in Petersburg, he made the mistake of loudly expressing his joy. The ataman Glebko and his men, in their rage, hacked the old man to pieces. The same night young Lavrenti escaped on his white mare and joined the Red Army. He didn't try to conceal his aristocratic background, but he adopted the name of Blagonravov. During the civil war he distinguished himself by his courage and devotion. He didn't shed a tear over the death of his father and the rest of his family. After the Revolution he remained an officer in the Red Army. He was tolerated, but his rise in rank and command was seriously hindered because of his origin. Other aristocrats were massacred by Stalin's order. He survived, but didn't reach the rank of captain for many years. His wartime comrades and subordinates were already colonels and generals. Lavrenti carried on. Old Blagonravov's teachings had been deeply sown in him, and he still believed fervently in the future of the Revolution. He was sure that he could be useful to his nation, even as a captain.

His slow breakthrough began at the end of the twenties, when secret relations were being established between the Russian Red Army and the German Wehrmacht. The Germans used Russian soil for maneuvers and development of arms, forbidden by the Versailles Treaty. The Russians studied in German war schools, and could finally quench their thirst for technical knowledge, for initiation to modern warfare. Blagonravov spoke German fluently, and he had always been good at mathematics, so he was sent to attend courses in German artillery schools, and stayed in Berlin for four years as a junior member of the Soviet military mission there. During this period he developed real friendship and camaraderie with many German officers. These were the early thirties, when the gifted Soviet warlord, Marshal Tukhachevski, created and strengthened the ties between the Russian and the German armies. It was in those years that Blagonravov's German friends began to ask him questions about Russia, the Russian Army, its war plans and potential. Blagonravov answered them all without hesitation. He often produced written reports and letters, and cordially handed them to his German contacts. Why shouldn't he? Their countries were allies, bound together to stand united against a hostile capitalist world.

Then came the great purges in Russia. During the years 1935-37 Tukhachevski and hundreds of the most talented Soviet officers were arrested, summarily tried, and savagely executed. In the Kremlin, Stalin had decided to reverse gears and eliminate the overriding German influence in the Red Army. But in doing so he also beheaded the Russian Army and dealt its leadership a terrible blow, from which it did not recover.

Blagonravov remained alive. It was precisely his aristocratic handicap that saved his life. He was fortunate to be only a major, a small wheel in the machine, and nobody bothered about him. He was recalled to Russia and appointed an artillery expert at headquarters, in Moscow. But he bitterly resented Stalin's bloody crime. He continued to meet and fraternize with German officers in the capital, in the official exercise of his duties. When his German friends asked him sensitive questions about the Red Army, he answered truthfully, keeping no secrets. But only in 1941, when Germany treacherously attacked the Soviet Union, did he understand that he had inadvertently become a German spy. In Moscow a German agent contacted him again. His first reaction was to refuse, but he was quickly reminded that he had no choice. His handwritten, signed reports were piled in the archives of the Abwehr. And the only way for him to save his life was to continue to cooperate with German espionage.

They were nice to him. His case officer asked him what code name he would like. Something of his childhood must have flashed before his eyes because he said, "Cossack of the Don."

When the war ended, he slowly began to realize that his agony was over. Nobody contacted him anymore, and none of the captured German spies disclosed anything about him. On the contrary, life started to go well for him. He was promoted to colonel and put in charge of the infant missiles and rockets branch of the Red Army artillery. His first act was to herd all the German rocket scientists he could find into camps and former research installations in Germany. He was aware that his country was poor in know-how. He knew that the Germans had built the redoubtable V-1 and V-2 rockets, and that in their safes and on their drawing boards they had detailed plans for huge deadly engines. Blagonravov tempted hundreds of scientists and thousands of engineers and technicians with promises of good food and warm lodgings in the starving, freezing Germany of 1945. He made them come back to their old research centers in the Russian zone and start working for his country. But it was not until the fall of 1946 that he carried out his secret plan. After thorough preparation that lasted more than a year, he moved, on the night of October 21, 1946. His special troops stormed into thousands of apartments; officers informed the stunned scientists and their families that they were being requisitioned by the Soviet Government and were leaving for Russia that very night. It was the largest kidnaping in German history. That same night, aboard ninety-two trains, about twenty thousand people were transported to the Soviet Union, where they were to remain from five to ten years. Blagonravov had figured out everything to the smallest detail. The scientists were divided into groups and sent to bases all over the Soviet Union: Moscow, Kuybyshev, Gorodomlia, Podberezia . . . On arriving every one of them was amazed to find his drawing board, blueprints, and instruments. The sequestered scientists were politely but firmly instructed to go back to work and start building a new generation of missiles for the Soviet Union.

It was, in a way, Blagonravov's revenge. The Germans had made him their slave during the war—now he made them slaves for him, for Russia. It was inhuman and barbaric, one of them told him. "Maybe," he said cynically, "but in history only the results count." And he got results. In October 1957 the first Russian satellite, "Sputnik," was launched into space. Thanks to Blagonravov, Russia won the space race. He was promoted to general and awarded the medal of the Order of Lenin. It had taken him forty years to overcome his aristocratic birth. To an American official delegation that visited the Soviet Union in 1962, Premier Nikita Khrushchev said proudly, slapping Blagonravov on the back, "We also have our Von Braun. You see Blagonravov? He is a count. He has the face of a mujik, but the blood, the blood, comrades, of an aristocrat. . . ."

That is how Blagonravov became one of the most important men in the Soviet Union. He took part in all the top-level government and Politburo meetings. His picture often appeared in *Pravda* and in *Red Star,* the official organ of the Red Army. He traveled extensively abroad, always surrounded by a pack of bodyguards and security agents. Wasn't he the man who knew more military secrets than any other Russian alive?

He was never again approached by a foreign secret service. Not once did he hear from his former case officer or run across the code name "Cossack of the Don." Sometimes he awoke at night, covered with sweat, but he soon calmed down, aware that the nightmare was over. He firmly believed that this dark episode in his life had been buried. He didn't consider himself a traitor. He loved his country, he believed in the Revolution and in communism. He hoped to end his long military career with a spectacular operation, which would bring him the highest decoration he dreamed of: Hero of the Soviet Union.

That is why he became the chief architect of project Aurora. It hadn't been his idea, but he had supported it enthusiastically. Often he let his mind wander over the fantastic victory that was coming for his country when, by a threat against the oil-producing states the Soviet Union would bring the West to its knees. And all that because of Blagonravov's missiles. For two years he had been covertly, patiently laying the infrastructure for installing his mighty weapons on Egyptian territory. He used any possible ruse, any opportunity, any new base offered by Presidents Nasser and Sadat to the Soviet Air Force in order to install his launching pads there, to assemble electronic devices, to smuggle rocket technicians. The Marsa raid had not slowed his activity; on the contrary, the Kremlin had given him a green light to speed up the process. He had built, with great precautions, two other control and guidance stations. Lately he had brought his first missiles into Egypt. He had smuggled them without the knowledge of the civilian government, and with the secret connivance of the Egyptian Chief of Staff, General Salem. In a year, maybe even less, the bases would be operational and missiles ready to strike.

Blagonravov couldn't guess that far away, in a small, modest office across the sea, a white-haired old man had started to spin a deadly web for only one purpose: to trap the Cossack of the Don.

On November 22, a little after midnight, Peled took leave of his guests. The party he had given for his "Russian team" was over. They had drunk many toasts to General Blagonravov, and even the Old Man had swallowed a small glass of brandy. Clumsily but sincerely he had thanked the team for their loyalty and excellent work. "You have focused my attention on Blagonravov," he concluded. "You did your best. I'll do my best not to disappoint you."

Now he was alone. He put in a phone call to the U.S. It was after six in Washington. He found Peter Wilkie at home.

"Jeremiah!" Wilkie's voice sounded pleased. "Well, what do you think of my boys? Did a splendid job for you, didn't they?"

"We are very grateful, Peter. I want to thank you."

"Well, maybe one day you'll tell me how you got that list."

"Maybe," Peled answered cautiously, then after a short pause he added, "Do you remember our little agreement? The joint project?"

"Sure."

"Well, it's your turn now, Peter."

PART THREE

The Bait

9

November 23, 1972 - February 9, 1973

Jenny Bacall could slam the phone on Peter Wilkie, but she didn't have much choice: she couldn't refuse him. His call was a combination of sheer blackmail and irresistible temptation, and for the second time in her life she experienced the alarming sensation of not having the situation under control.

Jenny was a statuesque blonde with a soft, sensual mouth and expressive, dreamy green eyes. For the past twelve years she had led a tumultuous life, and somehow the adventurous world she had known had made her, at the age of thirty, even more exciting and desirable. She would sometimes indulge in nostalgic reverie, reliving those adventures. And she would search in vain for the quiet, well-educated girl she had been until the age of eighteen. Then she would remember that frightful morning in Phoenix, Arizona, that had changed her whole life.

The event had made headlines at the time. It had started on a cool, glorious Sunday morning when she went with two girl friends to a picnic. She had taken the car belonging to her mother, a widow. The drive into the desert had been full of laughter, gossip, and teenagers' pranks. None of them had paid any attention to the repeated warnings on the local radio station about an escaped convict who had murdered a policeman on Route 47 and left his stripped body by the road. They were still giggling when a man in uniform stopped their car on the empty highway. Only when he wrenched open the door and jumped into the back of the Chevrolet, aiming the heavy service revolver at them, did they realize that something was wrong. Her two friends shrieked hysterically as the man

turned wildly on them and threatened to kill them if they
did not do his bidding. Jenny kept quiet and mastered the
paralyzing terror that gripped her stomach. She obeyed
his orders docilely and expertly passed through three police roadblocks, while the man crouched behind the front
seat, his gun pointed at one of the girls. Jenny even found
herself smiling at him in the rearview mirror while she
carefully weighed how she would act if the opportunity
presented itself. After driving for several miles she followed the man's orders and pulled to the side of the road.
Then at his dictation she scribbled a note to the police,
saying that she and her friends would be killed if the cops
did not immediately call off the search for Kreigh—that
was his name—and allow him to cross into Mexico. She
left the note on the windshield and with the other girls
marched toward the hills. He strode behind them while
she and her friends carried the blankets and a can of
water they had brought for the picnic. When night fell,
Kreigh tied their hands and legs. One of the girls fainted,
and the other screamed and shouted until he slapped her
across the face. Jenny just watched him silently as he tied
her up. She knew he intended to kill them. So calmly,
shrewdly, she devised a plan for survival. When he lay
down, quite close to them, she dragged herself to him and
shyly asked him to let her crawl under his blanket. "I'm
afraid to be alone in the dark," she whispered. "Please,
please, let me be with you." He untied her and took her
savagely. Two years in prison without a woman had made
him ravenous, and she did everything she knew to give
him pleasure. As dawn neared, he finally fell into an exhausted sleep. Quietly Jenny pulled the gun from under
his head, jumped to her feet, and coldly shot him twice,
aiming at his legs. Then she stood watch, smoking his
cigarettes, while her friends ran to get the police.

Only later did she understand what had happened to
her. She was shocked when she realized that she had actually enjoyed the whole episode: the thrill, the danger,
the suspenseful moments of ruthless calculating and planning, using her cunning and sex to gain the enemy's confi-
dence—and then the tightening of her whole body and

mind before she struck. And afterward the sweet, heavenly taste of success. She thought of a movie she had seen, about a correspondent during World War II who had gone to the front to find the answer to a question: why do men kill each other? The movie was cluttered with banal questions and answers, but she had remembered the end. After having fought heroically and saved (of course) the lives of several American soldiers, the correspondent was asked by the General, "Well, did you find out why men kill each other?"

He had replied. "Yes. For a simple reason. They just like it."

She had not enjoyed maiming, but she had loved the adventure. It was the first time she had deliberately used her voluptuous body, of whose power to excite she had been only half aware. She wanted more precarious adventures, so that she could feel the life pulsating through her veins and taste again those new emotions that welled up in the presence of terror and triumph.

She left college, and Phoenix. Inexperienced—but not helpless—she headed for the big game places. In the following years she drifted through Reno, Vegas, crossed the Mexican border, lived in a hippie colony in Nevada. She took up car racing and became an addict of fast driving. For a year she lived with a race driver. She left him for a professional gambler, went on a scuba-diving expedition off the shores of Guatemala, traveled with a boy alone through the jungles of South America, became the mistress of a wealthy bachelor, who took her on his yacht for a long cruise to the Galapagos and to India for a tiger hunt.

People who liked her pretended that she had a different kind of morality. But in a stormy scene, in a bar in Acapulco, a jealous woman told her that she was just prostituting herself. She wasn't offended. She simply didn't feel that way. As Jenny developed into a ravishing beauty, she always had her choice of men. She rejected those she did not like, she never got involved, and she never gave herself to any of them completely. Deep inside she was still nourishing the dream of someone very special, who would appear one day. Until then she would be quite indifferent to the men she met. Many of them proposed marriage to her, even though she didn't make a secret of her way of life. But she always refused, and was amazed to see how her rejection hurt them. Perhaps they were attracted to her because she was an alien creature—a kind of wild animal. Supple, intuitive, daring, and spontaneous, she was very different from the other jet-set girls they knew.

One day a young man she had met in a boat-racing crowd bought her coffee and made a strange suggestion. "You like adventure and danger," he had said. "O.K. Why not join us? We can offer you more thrilling adventures than you ever could dream of, and at the same time you could do something for your country." He had spoken with half a smile, as if he might be joking, but she felt he was carefully probing her real feelings.

" 'We'? Who is 'we'?" she had asked, and lit a cigarette.

"The United States Government. There are a lot of things that can't be done officially, you know."

She had a nimble mind. "Do you mean all this secret service stuff? Mata Hari and Company?"

"Well, I can't promise you'll become a Mata Hari"—he retreated cautiously—"but it could be quite exciting."

She eyed him thoughtfully. "You are serious, aren't you?"

"Yes," he replied. "We've been interested in you for quite a while. Think it over and let me know when you make up your mind."

"Why spend the taxpayers' money on another cup of coffee?" she said lightly. "I agree. I can always resign and go back to shooting tigers with my millionaires."

The man was taken aback by the quick answer. "I intended to make a smashing speech about freedom, patriotism, democracy, what you can do for America," he said almost disappointed.

"I wouldn't if I were you. If I join, it will be just for the fun of it. But I can promise you—you'll have no reason to complain."

They hadn't. She turned out to be a serious student in the training centers of the CIA. After more than a year of intensive preparation she was sent to her first assignment. Her charms being almost too obvious, she seemed fit for only one purpose. She flew to Spain, where she succeeded, without much trouble, in working her way into the bed of the Cuban ambassador. She took care of his nights for about a year, and there was nothing the ambassador knew about his country, and in particular about its ties with the Russians, that Jenny did not duly report to Washington. But she was too much for him. After a year the poor man died of a stroke, and Jenny found herself roaming through Africa as the friend of a Belgian mercenary colonel. In 1966 she was in Paris, pumping a senior French official in the Foreign Affairs Ministry. He readily gave her precious information about the secret activities of the Chinese diplomatic staff, which had turned its huge embassy in the avenue Montaigne into the headquarters of Chinese espionage in Europe. She had to leave in a hurry when a State Department official tried to sell back to the French the information she was getting from them. When her lover was dismissed from the quai d'Orsay and an exhaustive inquiry into his private life was ordered by an outraged de Gaulle, she was already far away. In 1967 she spent some months in Greece, trying to get inside information on the real political aspirations of the junta officers who had seized power in Athens. Washington, however, decided to recall her, fearing that if she blew her cover the CIA might be accused—quite unjustly, as everyone knew—of having played a role in the military coup. They kept her without an assignment for about a year. In 1968 she showed up in Beirut, and was conveniently picked up in a hotel lobby by a shady young millionaire named Selim, who was selling small arms at low prices to the Palestinian guerrillas. Her mission was to find out where he got the weapons. They were European- and American-made, but her superiors had a strong hunch that the Kremlin was behind the whole affair.

She spent several months in Beirut, and quite unexpectedly got involved in an amorous adventure with another man, something she had never done before. It was a passionate love affair, and she put her whole heart and soul into it, against all the rules of undercover work. One night, after a stormy row with Selim, she left, slamming the door behind her, and spent the night with her secret lover. That saved her life. The next morning, when she returned to Selim's apartment, she stumbled, horrified, on his mutilated body lying in a pool of blood. It was never established whether the guerrillas had discovered her true identity or whether they had quarreled with Selim about money. In any event, they had decided to get rid of him, and dealt with him in their usual way. Jenny was rushed through Customs and Immigration by the CIA resident agent in Beirut, and fifteen hours later was in Washington. But she was distraught. She had seen violent death, so close and so cruel, for the first time. And she had become terrifyingly aware that one couldn't always be on the winning side. In addition, her love affair had changed the easygoing attitude she had had about life and sex. She went to see Peter Wilkie and handed in her resignation. She suddenly needed a new life, quiet and unemotional, and longed for security and calm. "Maybe somebody will make an honest woman out of me," she said to Wilkie, looking at him wistfully, her green eyes hollow from so many sleepless nights.

Wilkie was very solicitous. He introduced her to Robert Bacall, a good-looking, considerate young major in the Air Force, who promptly fell in love with her. Jenny, tranquilized by his open, honest love and the feeling of security and worth it gave her, married him. She became a dutiful wife, and even enjoyed it, though she never forgot her love in Beirut. Bacall knew nothing about her past escapades, and she didn't tell him about them. When occasionally she thought about her life, she was certain that leaving the CIA had been the best decision she had ever made. She wouldn't go back for anything in the world.

That's what she thought until Peter Wilkie telephoned.

The first time he called her, she cut the connection. A couple of months later he called again and bluntly threatened to reveal her past to her husband if she refused to cooperate. "I'm sorry, Jenny, but we need you. You just can't refuse," he said. "Oh yes I can," she replied angrily. "I'm not going to start slaving for you again every time you threaten to reveal my past. Do as you like."

He abruptly changed his tactics and invited her for a drink. "For old times' sake, Jenny, just a drink," he persisted. She hesitated, but eventually gave in. She owed him something for Robert and her comfortable life. And anyway, she was confident that he couldn't break her resolve, so what did she risk? They met in an out-of-the-way cocktail lounge, and Peter greeted her with the same old charming smile. After their drinks had been served, he took a photograph from his breast pocket and handed it to her. As she looked at the handsome, smiling face, her heart started to beat wildly. A surge of passion and cherished memories overwhelmed her. She lowered her head and covered her wet eyes with trembling hands. Finally she looked up at Wilkie. "Where the hell did you find him?"

Joe. How many years had passed since that last night in Beirut? she asked herself. Three, four, an eternity? Remembrances of their love came back to her in a flood of sweetness and pain. She had met him while she was living with Selim, at a cocktail party at the French embassy. She was tense that evening, repelled by the slick, oily Selim. Not in the mood for exchanging small talk with diplomats, she had quietly moved to the magnificent palm garden overlooking the silvery bay of Beirut. It was a clear night, with a soft breeze and a sky full of stars. She had leaned on the marble parapet and simply enjoyed the beauty.

The smell of tobacco smoke had driven her attention to a shadow on her right. A man was standing under a small palm. She was sure he had been there before her. In the shadows she could not see his face, nor could he see her clearly. Perhaps that's why she felt so at ease. She had said something trite, like, "What a beautiful evening!" After a short silence he had answered in a pleasant voice with a strong French accent. He had talked about the nights in that part of the world, about the luminous oriental sky, its unique dome of bright stars. He sounded as if he had traveled a great deal, and shifted easily to vivid descriptions of South American starry nights. She told him of her adventures in the jungles of Guatemala and Brazil. They had talked on, losing all sense of time, two people discovering each other—for the moment happily forsaking all others.

Years later she decided that all of it had happened because she had been caught off guard that night. In public she had always kept a barrier around herself, protection against those hungry-eyed human wolves who were struck by her beauty and had only wanted to ravish her. This time the man hardly saw her, and she felt with pride that he enjoyed talking to her as a person, not because of her sensual beauty. For the first time in many years she had a wonderful feeling of freedom, forgetting just for once that she was a spy on a mission.

They had finally decided to go back to the party, and were puzzled by the sudden silence in the embassy. They found no one inside. All the guests had left, Selim included. She had looked at the stranger then in the brightly lit room. He was tall, handsome, and blond, a little over thirty, with gray eyes alight with humor, his eyes a contrast to the determined set of his jaw. "Well, I guess nobody missed us." He had laughed as he looked about the empty room. Then he had said, "I'm hungry. Are you?" She was. He took her to a restaurant in the city called Le Madrigal. They sat in a softly lit booth and gazed at each other with delight as they sipped champagne. He told her that he was Joe Gorsky, a Frenchman of Russian origin. He said that he was in the oil business. She didn't believe him; he just wasn't that kind of man. She felt that he was probably leading a secret life, maybe even the same kind of dangerous life as hers. But she didn't try to find out. As a matter of fact, she didn't even care after that moment when their eyes met, and locked, and they stopped laughing. She knew it was kitschy and even dangerous— but that was how it happened.

After dinner he drove her home. He drove slowly, and

they didn't speak. All this time he had not even held her hand. When he stopped the car in front of Selim's villa, she was suddenly afraid that she might not see him again. The very real danger in meeting him again she would not admit to herself. He got out of the car, went around to her side and opened the door, stared at her a moment, then shut it and went back to his seat. She hadn't moved. He kissed her tenderly on the cheek. Neither of them said a word. Then he started the car and drove swiftly to his apartment. She stayed with him all night, and when morning came they were certain they loved each other.

Selim had been very angry when she returned, but she told him coldly that she had spent the night with a man, would do it again, and that if he wanted to keep her he would have to live with that. Though he was miserable, he had finally accepted her ultimatum.

Jenny had never been so happy, though she tried hard to conceal the reason. She ignored Selim's jealous outbursts as well as the frantic and persistent warnings of her CIA boss in the city. And she refused to think about the future. Joe met her almost every day, and they were together often through the nights. She discovered a wonderful sensitivity to beauty and goodness in him, hidden behind a facade of toughness, and a reservoir of long-felt pain she hadn't suspected. She was sure now that she had guessed right: he was engaged in something secret, although he never made a slip in her presence. She was too well trained not to notice the sudden silences, the phone calls during the night, and the one-syllable answers. But she never asked questions; she was afraid she might lose him. Yet gradually she began to admit to herself that this enchanting existence they shared could not last.

The end came suddenly on that September morning when she discovered Selim's bloody, naked body and had to flee Lebanon. Her worried friends at the CIA didn't even allow her to meet Joe. They just promised to deliver to him the note she had scribbled and thrust in a plain white envelope.

"I love you," it read.

Now here was his picture, in Peter Wilkie's hand, in a

cocktail lounge in Georgetown. Anguish gripped her throat and brought tears to her eyes again. She had searched for him so long, put in so many calls to his Beirut apartment, written letters and cables, only to have them returned, stamped in Arabic and French: MOVED WITHOUT LEAVING A FORWARDING ADDRESS.

"You want to see him, don't you?" Wilkie asked. His lips were smiling, but his eyes were studying her face intently.

She knew she was at Peter Wilkie's mercy and hated him for it. "You know I do," she said in a low voice.

"You'll see him after you do something for us."

"You bastard!" she muttered.

His half-smile didn't fade. "It's all set, then. Remember Fred Hancock? He's head of DDI now." DDI was the abbreviation for Deputy Director—Intelligence, the information-gathering department of the CIA. "He'll call you in a couple of days."

She looked away.

Robert Bacall did not wonder why he was suddenly promoted to the rank of lieutenant colonel and appointed to the Israeli desk in the Air Force foreign section at the Pentagon. He was just happy and proud, and failed to notice Jenny's dispirited expression when he took her to dinner at the Jockey Club, to celebrate his promotion. Ten days later he was sent on a six-week tour of Israel and Jenny was called back to work.

"We need you as bait," Fred Hancock told her bluntly. "You'll go to all the international parties and pray that the Russians make contact. You know, of course, that you're not the only one. We have several other ladies and gentlemen on this job, but we can't really tell who's going to be the lucky winner."

For the next three weeks Jenny attended most of the diplomatic and other important social gatherings about Washington. Her friends in Langley Woods were busy getting her the invitations and supplying her with convenient, creditable escorts, who discreetly vanished after the official handshakes, letting her wander alone through the crowd. This night she was at a reception in the British embassy. Her knight-companion was a tall, hefty Texan who had been commercial attaché in some obscure mid-European industrial city. He had just left "for a drink" with a rather uneasy apology when she felt that someone was watching her. In a matter of seconds her trained eyes spotted a swashbuckling, black-haired young man with dark, lively eyes. Was that the Russian agent she was supposed to hook? She couldn't help feeling flattered. It was not just another handsome stud they were sending after her; this one was undoubtedly the best in their stable.

She pretended not to notice him while he was working his way through the crowd. Suddenly he was standing in front of her, a drink in each hand. "What would you prefer?" He had a frank, disarming smile. "I've got scotch and champagne."

She smiled back. "Champagne will do very well."

He handed her the glass. "Cheers!" he said. His rolling *r* betrayed his foreign origin.

"You aren't going to tell me that you have been wandering through that crowd looking for somebody you could talk into a drink," she said with a touch of sarcasm.

"Well, not exactly," he answered, unruffled. "You see, I saw you standing alone and I absolutely had to talk to you. So the best excuse I could think of was to grab two glasses and run before somebody else got to you first."

His candor was dangerously effective, Jenny admitted to herself, and he seemed to be quite at ease. Russian, or not, he was alluring, masculine, and confident, and could easily make a lot of conquests among the middle-aged, bored wives of diplomats and government officials in Washington society.

"And who are you?" she asked casually.

He bowed. "Well, I am supposed to be an implacable enemy of the free world." His eyes were filled with laughter. "I am Sergei Malinov, junior member of the Washington bureau of Tass, the Soviet news agency. I am full of ambition, I have graduated in Marxism-Leninism, but if I may tell you a secret, I am completely bewitched by the decadent West."

"You are Russian?" She looked at him with intensified interest. "How fascinating! I've never met a young Russian here in Washington. Most of them are middle-aged and rather square. They wear old-fashioned suits and have no sense of humor."

"I am the exception to the rule." Sergei declared with mock solemnity. "And what about you? Do you go often to this kind of party? I haven't met you before. Are you with the embassy, or the State Department?"

"No. My husband works for the Pentagon. But he is abroad quite often, and I like parties and people. My name is Jenny Bacall, and my husband is Colonel Robert Bacall."

He didn't react to the name, and seemed interested only in her. "I guess you don't have trouble finding someone to escort you to those parties when your husband is away."

"Not at all." She gave him a challenging look.

"And I understand that this is the case tonight?"

"Yes."

They talked for several minutes, until Jenny decided that it was time to look at her watch.

"Well," he said, "maybe we could have a drink later, I mean after the party?"

She shook her head. "I'm sorry, but tonight it's impossible."

He hesitated for a moment. "What about tomorrow? I'd like to see you again."

"I really can't say now, but perhaps another time." She smiled invitingly at him.

"Are you in the book?"

"Of course." She smiled at him again, then moved into the crowd. "Come on, friend," she said to her Texan, who was standing in a corner, staring, glassy-eyed, into a huge bourbon highball. "You've toiled long enough." He swallowed his drink in a single gulp, looked longingly at the row of unopened bottles standing on the bar, and followed her to the exit.

That same night she reported to Hancock. He sounded excited and pleased. "That's the contact we've waited for, Jenny! We know the guy. He certainly works for the KGB. Many Tass people do. It's one of their typical covers, like Aeroflot or the trade missions. You can go ahead."

The next afternoon she received a phone call from Sergei and agreed to meet him for a drink. Three days later, in his small apartment off Constitution Avenue, she surrendered to his charms.

"Darling," Sergei called, "could you come for a moment?"

She had awakened in his bed with the first light of dawn, after having slept restlessly for only a couple of hours. Their affair, two weeks old now, had already settled into an established routine: each night, drinks, dinner, then his apartment with its huge bed. Sergei was an expert lover, full of attention and gentleness; he knew how to satisfy a woman. Some years ago she might have even enjoyed this assignment. But all she felt now was disgust—with Sergei, with herself, with the things Wilkie, Hancock, and their friends forced her to do. She had started to dread those daily encounters with the Russian. Yet she was sure that he didn't suspect anything. She knew exactly how to behave—when to sigh, when to moan, when to claw at him in passionate embrace. She knew how to use all those small gestures—spontaneous caresses, soft words, dreamy looks—so characteristic of a woman in love. Her acting was perfect. Only in her sleep, when she was losing conscious control over herself, did an inner torment seize her, and she would awake with her nerves on edge, feeling tired, old, and filthy. Only her hope of seeing Joe again kept her going. He was all she cared for now. She never thought of Robert at all.

"Darling, come here!" Sergei called again.

"Coming." Jenny threw the pale green filmy robe she had brought there over her shoulders and tiptoed to the bathroom. He was shaving leisurely, admiring the reflection of his naked torso and powerful muscles in the mirror.

"Good morning!" he said cheerfully under his mask of white foam.

"Good morning."

"I wanted to talk. About us."

Jenny leaned on the door, studying his handsome profile.

"You told me that your husband is returning in a week. So I guess that we won't be able to go on meeting as we have."

"Oh, we'll find a way, I'm sure. *Quand on veut, on peut,*" she added.

Sergei was silent as he shaved the last inches of his dark, smooth skin. He had a preference for old-fashioned razors and used to sharpen his evil-looking long blades on a worn-out leather belt that hung by the mirror.

"Do you really love me, Jenny?" he asked in a different tone.

"You know I do," she said, and planted a light kiss on his shoulder.

"If you really do, you must do something for me," he said quietly.

"Of course," she answered. "Anything you say."

"Anything?" He looked at her intently.

She pretended to be taken aback. "What do you have in mind?"

"I think that you could help me with my work."

She played the naïve female to the very end. "How can I help you? I mean—"

"Well," he said slowly, "your husband works on subjects which are very interesting to me, you see?" He cast a quick look at her, and she nodded, a puzzled expression starting to settle over her face. He went on. "I would like so much to be able, once in a while, to see the documents that he brings home from work."

"But—"

He interrupted her. "Listen to me. I know he brings lots of papers home. Everybody does. Maybe you could give some of them to me over the weekend, or at night . . ."

His face brightened. "Look, I have an idea! Why don't I buy you a small camera. Then you can photograph them for me. It would take you no more than a couple of minutes each time, and you'd be doing me a great favor. What do you think? Isn't it—"

He stopped abruptly when he saw her expression. Her face had gone deadly pale. She clenched the lapels of her robe and wrapped them closer around her shoulders. Her eyes widened, and she looked at him with sudden understanding that quickly changed to hatred. "So that's it!" Her voice was trembling with contained rage. "You want me to spy on my husband for you! You filthy, treacherous, seducing son of a bitch! That's what you wanted from the start, isn't it? And I thought you loved me. You never did, did you?" She slowly backed toward the bathroom door. Sergei tried to take her in his arms.

"Don't touch me!" she cried furiously, and drew away from him. "Don't come near me! You just wait, Mister Russian Spy, just wait and see!" Panting, she ran to the bedroom, gathered her clothes and underwear, and wrapped herself in her fur coat. He ran after her and tried to stop her, looking ridiculous in his nakedness. "Please, Jenny, let me explain it to you."

"Go to hell!" she screamed. "I never want to see you again. Never!" She ran out of the apartment.

Only after she was in the elevator, going down, did she relax. It had been the best acting she had done for a long time, maybe because most of the words she had said expressed her real feelings. She wondered, smiling to herself, whether she would have sounded more convincing if she had thrown one of those beautiful china vases in the foyer at him. No, it would have made the whole scene too kitschy.

That evening, while she was alone at home, an unmarked brown envelope was slipped under her door. She opened it. Inside there were six photographs. She leafed through them without emotion. Actually, she was almost expecting them. The photographs showed her and Sergei naked in his bedroom, engaged in torrid lovemaking.

They had all been taken from the same angle, from a certain position where—if she remembered correctly—there was a huge oak-framed mirror. She looked at the pictures for a long time, thoughtfully, then went to the fireplace in the living room and burned them, one after another. She phoned Hancock. "I received some photographs tonight," she said calmly.

"Good," he replied. "Go on, as agreed."

She put down the receiver and then called Sergei. He was at home.

"It's me," she said in a small, miserable voice. "I got your present. Now what do you want?"

A week later Lieutenant Colonel Robert Bacall, sunburned and satisfied, was back from his trip to Israel. He had a joyful reunion with his lovely wife, but starting the next night and every night thereafter Jenny went stealthily into his study after he was asleep and photographed all the documents he had brought in his attaché case. Every day, at a different hour, she strolled to one of Washington's parks, to Arlington Cemetery, or to Capitol Hill; on rainy or snowy days she went either to one of the museums or skipped the outing. At each place she deposited the small roll of film in a hiding spot—a dead-letter box. Sometimes she found fresh rolls of film there. Once a week she dialed a number from a phone booth, always a different one, identified herself by a password, and gave her public phone number. Then she put the receiver back and waited. Two minutes later the phone rang and she listened to a neutral voice giving her fresh instructions: her new schedule for the week, new dead-letter collecting points, a new phone number, and a new date for her next call. She complied rigorously with her instructions.

She did not see Sergei again.

In Dzerzhinsky Square, in Moscow, people were very happy.

So was the Old Man, in Tel-Aviv, when Peter Wilkie phoned him from Washington. "Your turn now, Jeremiah," he said. "We have completed our part of the deal."

But Peter Wilkie had also made a deal with Jenny—and he had to keep it.

At the beginning of February, barely two weeks after the presidential inauguration, the Israeli Prime Minister, Mrs. Golda Meir, visited Washington, and the Israeli ambassador, General Yitzhak Rabin, gave a large party in her honor. Robert Bacall was, of course, invited to assist. Jenny's first impulse had been to stay at home, feigning a headache. She'd had one unpleasant experience at a diplomatic cocktail party, and she feared an embarrassing encounter at this one. But when she called Wilkie to ask his advice, he encouraged her to go. "I can promise you that Sergei Malinov won't be there. Please go, Jenny. You're living in a state of perpetual tension; some relaxation will do you good. And who knows? You might even meet some nice people, for a change."

She didn't understand the implication of his words, at least not until that moment in the embassy hall when she saw Joe in the middle of the crowd, a drink in his hand, wearing an Israeli Air Force uniform.

She froze—unable to move or utter a word. Joe saw her, too, and then her heart began to pound. They just stood looking at each other, his gaze caressing her face, taking in the large green eyes and the long, luxuriant, shining blond hair, as if there were no one else in the room. He moved forward, took her gently by the elbow, and walked her to a remote corner where they couldn't be overheard.

"I love you, too," he said, answering that note she had left for him so long ago.

They stood in the corner for a long time, talking, oblivious of the crowd. Joe's voice was soft. When he had met her in Beirut, he said, he was on a secret assignment, using a French cover. He couldn't reveal his true identity to her—it might have meant his life. He had been sent out of Israel on a mission. After he returned, he wasn't allowed to look for her or to contact her. But he had gotten her note and cherished it. "It wasn't an adventure, Jenny," he murmured. "It was a real love affair. It still is."

They were interrupted by Colonel Dagan, a stocky, jovial man in his forties, who was the Israeli air attaché in Washington. He was chatting with Robert.

"So here you are, Joe," he called loudly, then turned to Bacall. "I'd like to introduce you to my new assistant. Lieutenant Colonel Robert Bacall—Lieutenant Colonel Joe Gonen."

Joe nodded politely. "I am pleased to meet you, Colonel." Bacall shook his hand.

"And this is the beautiful Mrs. Bacall, of course." Dagan smiled gallantly.

There was a momentary flicker of surprise in Joe's eyes. Then he said evenly, "Yes, of course. We just met."

10

March 16 - May 12, 1973

On March 16, at 12:02 P.M., a TWA Boeing 707 took off from Athens. The plane was on flight 714, New York–Tel-Aviv, and after a refueling stopover in Athens started the last leg of its long flight. Barely five minutes after take-off the Athens control tower relayed an anxious message from the captain. "We are being hijacked!" he shouted into his mike. "We are changing direction." The plane circled for half an hour over the Mediterranean, approaching Yugoslav air space several times. At Zagreb Airport the control tower heard a woman's voice yelling into the plane's transmitter, "This is not TWA anymore. We now call the plane 'Gaza Strip.' This is 'Gaza Strip' transmitting. 'Gaza Strip' is in the hands of the Palestine Liberation Army, Al Fatah. We shall conquer all of Palestine again." She then sang the "Internationale" and several other revolutionary songs in a loud, joyful voice.

The plane crossed the Mediterranean and emerged low over Beirut. The local authorities refused to give it a landing clearance. It then flew over Israel. The Israelis didn't even answer its calls. Special Army units surrounded Lod Airport, while scores of vehicles were dispatched in rows on the runways, barring them at many points and forbidding any landing. The hijacked plane flew to Cairo, then tried Baghdad and Damascus. Everywhere it was refused permission to land. Finally, in the late afternoon, it penetrated Jordanian air space, flew east of the Jordan River, and landed in a cloud of dust, on a strip of barren, sun-drenched desert at Zarqa, about twenty-five miles east of the river. Soon after it stopped, the plane was surrounded by Palestinian guerrillas, who arrived in jeeps and trucks, rattling their submachine guns, their heads and faces covered by keffiyehs.

On the same day, at 12:39 P.M. a Swissair D.C. 8 took off from Kloten Airport at Zurich with 155 passengers, on flight 606 to New York. Over Paris the plane changed direction abruptly. The hijacking was announced by a woman speaking English and Arabic. She proclaimed that the plane had been taken by the Popular Front for the Liberation of Palestine, an extreme left-wing branch of the Al Fatah terrorist organization. The plane was solemnly renamed "Haifa One." It reached Zarqa, in Jordan, about half an hour after the TWA hijacked plane, landed, and came to a halt beside it.

At 2:50 P.M., three people—two black and one white—hijacked a 747 Pan Am jumbo jet that had just taken off from Schiphol Airport at Amsterdam. Further investigation revealed that the three hijackers had tried first to board an El Al plane, but had aroused the suspicions of the security officers of the Israeli airline and were turned down. Only then did they board the Pan Am flight. They could not land at Zarqa, because the landing strip was too short for a jumbo jet. Threatening to blow up the plane in mid-air, they succeeded in forcing the Egyptian authorities to allow them to set down at Cairo International Airport. The passengers were hurriedly evacuated, and a few minutes later the jumbo jet was blown up in an ear-shattering explosion.

At the very moment the Pan Am plane was captured over Amsterdam, a dramatic struggle was occurring—according to Israeli sources—in a 707 El Al Boeing that had taken off from Schiphol. It was on flight 218, New York to Tel-Aviv, with stopovers in Amsterdam and Athens. The Israeli plane had had quite a long and unexplained delay in Schiphol. Although it had left New York about half an hour before the hijacked TWA plane, it didn't take off from Schiphol before 2:07 P.M. Soon after it became airborne, a young blond male passenger who had just boarded the plane suddenly jumped to his feet. Yelling savagely, he drew a gun and a hand grenade, and ran toward the cockpit shouting, "Fatah! Fatah! Fatah!"

His companion, a black-haired girl, produced two more hand grenades that had been hidden in her bra and ran after him.

But here the resemblance to the other hijackings stopped. According to strict regulations for cases of attempted hijacking, the captain automatically locked the cockpit door. An Israeli security guard, conveniently disguised in the first class section, suddenly emerged and shot the hijacker dead. Another man, who had been sitting beside the girl (he later refused to disclose his name, saying that he was an American and didn't want any trouble), hurled himself at her, immobilized her hands, overpowered her, and knocked her to the ground. With the help of some air stewards, and using neckties, he tied her arms and legs together. While the flight continued, the pilot violently rocked and tossed the plane, in order to put the terrorists off balance.

At three fifteen the plane executed an emergency landing at London's Heathrow Airport and taxied to a remote parking area. "You were lucky that you flew El Al," the captain happily told the passengers, who responded with loud cheers and began singing Israeli folksongs, under the direction of a pretty stewardess. The captured girl and the body of the dead hijacker were handed to the British police. The girl turned out to be the notorious terrorist Leila Khaled, who had participated in the hijacking of a TWA plane flying from Rome to Tel-Aviv the year before.

Leila Khaled's capture triggered the last act of the Palestinian hijack offensive. On the next day Arab terrorists took over a BOAC VC 10 en route from Bahrein to Beirut, and landed it successfully in Zarqa, bringing the number of hijacked planes concentrated in this desert spot to three. The BOAC plane was "Safed One." Fatah headquarters in Beirut announced that the passengers of the BOAC plane would not be set free before Leila Khaled was permitted to leave Britain.

But these were not their only conditions. They tried to negotiate the exchange of the passengers of the three captured airliners for the release of hundreds of terrorists held in prison in Israel. Israel flatly refused. The Western powers started to exert a growing pressure on the Jordanian Government for the immediate release of the passengers. Jordanian Army units moved toward Zarqa. They had to stop at about two hundred yards from the planes, which were surrounded now by an exhilarated mob of guerrillas, who had hoisted Palestinian flags and stamped the passengers' passports with a seal of the "Revolutionary Airfield of the Palestine Liberation Movement." They threatened that if the Army came nearer they would blow up the planes and their passengers. They said that they had planted hundreds of dynamite sticks in the airliners. The terrorists also encircled the planes with machine guns, mortars, and bazookas. In an inner circle stood jeeps carrying 50 mm recoilless guns.

For three days there was hard bargaining in the desert, while the sequestered passengers survived only because of meager quantities of food and drink that the Red Cross was allowed to supply them. Finally a compromise was reached. Leila Khaled was freed; other Arab terrorists, held for murder, hijacking, and sabotage in European countries, were released and flown to Beirut. The terrorists liberated the passengers group by group, and they were taken, exhausted and terrified, to Amman. When the Zarqa area was cleared of people, the guerrillas blew up the three hijacked planes with all the luggage and freight that was aboard.

That is how March 16, 1973, became known as "hijack day."

The only Israeli who suffered as a result of the hijacking was a young diplomat, posted in Washington, who hadn't even come close to the planes. He was second secretary in the embassy, and it just happened that on this very day it was his turn to fly to New York and deliver a diplomatic pouch to the personal care of the El Al captain on flight 218. It was not "Category A" classified material, which was transported only by diplomatic courier in a special pouch, chained and locked to his wrist. These were "B" and "C" documents, and the custody of the El Al people was adequate.

Unfortunately, because of a last-minute conference in Washington, the young Israeli missed his plane and took a later flight. When he reached Kennedy Airport, the El Al Boeing had just taken off. Aware that the pouch was expected that same night in Tel-Aviv, the secretary did what he and his colleagues had done often before, although it was against regulations: he sent the pouch as air freight on the TWA plane, the same one that was hijacked and blown to bits in the Jordanian desert.

When these facts were established, the young man was immediately fired and recalled to Israel. It was rather a routine disciplinary measure. Actually, the Foreign Office senior staff was not particularly worried by the loss of the pouch. First, there was nothing of real value in it; second, the information coming from Amman indicated beyond any doubt that all the luggage and the air freight in the TWA liner had been blown up by the guerrillas. The security officer of the Ministry of Foreign Affairs was certain that the pouch never fell into the hands of the enemy.

He was wrong. Before blowing up the 707, the Fatah chief of operations, Abu Ayad, and his men thoroughly examined the air freight on the plane. A month later the heavy pouch, its seal broken, arrived in Moscow via the Soviet embassy in Beirut. Hebrew-reading specialists of the Middle East department of the KGB systematically scanned its contents and carefully read each scrap of paper. They discarded the printed brochures, the duplicated technical reports, the minutes of the Senate and the House deliberations, as well as the files of cuttings from newspapers and magazines. But among the few items that retained their attention they found something of value. It was a private, handwritten letter that had been sent by the Israeli air attaché in Washington, Colonel Jacob Dagan, to an old buddy of his in Tel-Aviv, formerly of the Air Force. The letter dealt with routine matters for the most part. But there was one paragraph that captured the sharp eyes of the KGB specialists: "I am very worried about our old friend, Joe Gonen. You know he's with me now. I think the guy has lost his self-control. Maybe it's the cumulative effect of his inability to fly anymore. Anyway, he chases girls, drinks too much, and spends his weekends and his salary at the roulette tables in Vegas or Reno. He might run into trouble. I don't want to report him before I try seriously to reason with him, but I'm quite pessimistic."

Dagan was right. Something was very wrong with Joe, and the first one to notice it was Jenny.

About two weeks after they met in the embassy, they spent a weekend together in a secluded motel in Virginia. Robert Bacall had left two days earlier for a tour of the aircraft industries on the west coast, and she hurried to telephone Joe. He was eager to meet her, but insisted on precautions of secrecy that seemed excessive even to her. However, once they were alone, she forgot her concern. For her their first night was a perfect fulfillment of the dreams of so many restless months. It was a kind of explosion of the love, passion, and tenderness that had accumulated in them since they were torn from each other in Beirut. Joe was very much in love with her. She could sense it in the way he looked at her, touched her, talked to her. She cried that night, and told him it was just because she was happy. She didn't tell him about the sacrifice she had made in order to see him again. She didn't tell him about Sergei, nor about her double-agent assignment for the CIA. Joe assumed that they had met by coincidence, and she left it that way. She didn't want anything to interfere with the ecstasy that engulfed her.

But during the next day and night Jenny noticed the old familiar signs. Again she felt—as in Beirut earlier—that she had only a part of him. Her lover grew restless, lapsed into long silences, and his frowning forehead, his nervous gaze, betrayed deep anxiety and tension. She said nothing, and tried to behave as naturally as she could, but a little before dawn Joe drew her close to him, as if he wanted to reassure her—or maybe to reassure himself.

"Jenny"—he spoke with difficulty—"Jenny, for a while we won't be able to see each other."

She stiffened and pulled away from him. "What—" she began, but he put his hand over her mouth.

"Please, don't say anything. I love you. You are all I have—and I don't even have you. But please, trust me. We can't see each other now. Not even in secret. Don't ask me why."

Jenny didn't ask. With trembling fingers she tried to light a cigarette, and after she had vainly used half the matches in the box, she crushed it angrily in the ashtray on the bedside table. She got up and dressed. Joe didn't try to stop her. She sped along the rain-wet deserted highway in the half-light of early morning, heedless of the blinding tears that streamed down her face. She had never felt so hurt and so disappointed.

She didn't see him for months after that, but she heard his name over and over again. Rumors began to spread over Washington about Joe Gonen—his fast life, his heavy drinking, his immoral behavior. Nobody mentioned her—their affair remained secret. But she suffered each time Robert innocently repeated the stories people were telling about the swinging times of the handsome playboy from the Israeli embassy.

Once again Jenny felt she was going to have a breakdown. To know that the man she loved was so close yet refused to see her, to listen to those stories of his amorous exploits—it was an agony of humiliation and despair. One night, certain she couldn't live with this terrible knowledge and longing another twenty-four hours, she phoned Joe. He was distant and reserved, though he agreed to see her. He gave her detailed instructions about how and where to meet, to be sure they wouldn't be followed. He chose a hotel room in downtown Washington, where Jenny registered under an assumed name. When she opened the door to let him in, she hardly recognized him. He looked nervous and depressed; he was half drunk.

She ached to put her arms around him and comfort him, but suddenly and inexplicably she was overcome with anger and jealousy. She began to rail at him, repeating the stories she had heard.

He looked at her strangely. "Other women? Oh, yes, that's what people are saying." Then he touched her face tenderly with the tips of his fingers and murmured wearily, "There is no other woman but you, Jenny. All those rumors are not true. But you must never deny them."

"I don't understand," she cried. "If the stories are not true, why the hell is everybody talking?"

He sighed. "Let it be, Jenny. Please trust me. There's nothing to it."

She felt exasperation and defeat. "Then why don't you—why doesn't anybody say anything? Why can't I see you? What's it all about, Joe? What's happening to us?" Her voice was plaintive.

He took her in his arms and kissed her softly on the lips. There was pain in his eyes. "Jenny darling, when all this is over—"

She drew away. "What has to be over, Joe?"

His face was expressionless. "Nothing," he said.

11

May 13, 1973

In Moscow, General Lev Ivanovich Yulin, Director of the Eighth Department, Middle East, summoned his aides for an urgent meeting in the "little conference room" on the fourth floor of the KGB Center.

There were six people in the room, which was bathed in artificial light. The blinds were drawn, and heavy black curtains covered the windows. A big screen hung on the wall facing the conference table. At the opposite side of the room, a slide projector was mounted on an aluminum support. Its motor was humming softly. The technician, a stocky middle-aged matron, waited patiently to start. The people around the table were conversing in low tones.

The door opened and Yuri Andropov, Chairman of the KGB, entered, followed by his secretary, Nikitin. After them came General Yulin and elderly Colonel Timosheev, who had been Yulin's deputy for many years. Andropov and Yulin took their places at the table. "You may start, Comrade Timosheev," Yulin said. Timosheev approached the screen and picked up a long white stick that had been leaning on the wall. He nodded at the technician. "We are ready," he said.

The room plunged in darkness; a bright yellow rectangle appeared on the screen. A metallic click came from the slide projector and a black and white picture filled the screen. It showed a smiling blond youngster in an Israeli Air Force uniform, officer's cap, paratrooper's and pilot's insignia pinned on his chest, the silver paratrooper's wings on the right side, the blue cloth pilot wings on the left. On his epaulets were the bars of a second lieutenant. Timosheev commented, "Joseph Gonen. This picture was taken on the day he graduated from flying school, August 11, 1960. He was twenty years old. The photograph was published three years later in the *Bamahané* soldiers' weekly, where Gonen had been interviewed about the aerobatics he had performed over Tel-Aviv in a Fouga-Magister jet on Independence Day. According to routine security, his family name was not given in the article and he was referred to as simply 'Joe.' Next, please."

The apparatus snapped. A color picture blossomed on the screen. Gonen, bareheaded, was alighting from a Mirage III-C jet fighter, dressed in green overalls and heavy leather boots. On his hip he carried a gun in a holster.

"Nineteen sixty-six," Timosheev said. "Gonen was a Mirage pilot. We don't know his combat rank at the time, but we suppose he was a captain. This picture and the following photo were taken from an eight-minute propaganda movie called *Theirs Is the Sky*. It was produced and distributed by the Israeli Air Force to encourage young men to enlist in flying school. The movie officially represented Israel at the Festival of Military Films in Versailles, France. Next, please."

The next picture, from the film, showed Gonen, wearing a flying helmet, at the command of his Mirage. On another one he was seen walking with friends toward a blood-red setting sun in a perfect sky; a blurred green line on the horizon suggested a faraway forest.

"We had no trouble identifying him," Timosheev continued. "Gonen was twenty-six and a good pilot. Next."

Snap. The new picture was somewhat blurred, black and white. It showed a close-up of Gonen lying on a pillow, his hair disheveled, with a blanket drawn under his chin. His eyes were closed, his cheeks unshaven and sunken. "The picture was taken on June 7, 1967. We cut it from a larger one, and only by magnifying it could we distinguish Gonen's features. Will you show the full picture, comrade?" On the screen Gonen's head was replaced by the view of a stretcher being lowered from the open door of a helicopter. A man in white and several bareheaded soldiers in crumpled khaki uniforms were holding the stretcher. Gonen's face on the pillow was small and barely recognizable.

"The story about him," Timosheev said, "was published in the Israeli Air Force monthly, in the special issue celebrating the victory of the Six-Day War. He was a squadron commander, and had distinguished himself in the first air strikes on Egyptian territory. He was shot down over the Nile delta, and was eventually rescued by a helicopter that brought him back to Israel with a badly broken leg. Still referred to as Joe. Next, please."

A new, rather smudgy picture appeared. It seemed to have been taken covertly, from the interior of a car. It showed a very crowded street in an oriental town. Most of the men wore European clothes, but some were dressed in long white robes and Arab keffiyehs. A circle drawn with chinagraph on the slide surrounded two faces: those of a small, mustached, curly-haired Arab and a blond European, who looked as if he were talking to him. The European was wearing dark glasses. "This is a very curious picture," Timosheev said. "Look." The projector clicked in rapid succession, each time throwing a closer, more magnified impression of the blond man on the screen. Timosheev approached the screen. "You see, we cannot be positive, but this face here bears a very close resemblance to Gonen. This photograph was secretly taken by a team of ours in Beirut, in 1968. You certainly remember the operation that failed there at the end of the summer."

"Operation Firebird?" Andropov asked, surprised.

"Exactly. As you will recall, our people tried to convince a Lebanese pilot to defect with his Mirage and fly it to Baku for the sum of two million dollars. But somebody betrayed our man in Beirut. Twenty-four hours before the operation secret agents of the Lebanese Deuxième Bureau, guns in hand, burst into the apartment of our man, Vladimir Vasilyev. They attacked and wounded Vasilyev and another of our agents, Aleksandr Komiakov. Both were expelled from Lebanon. This was the end of project Firebird. Now, sometime earlier, while the operation was still under way, we had put the Lebanese pilot who was to bring us the Mirage under routine surveillance. We tailed most of the people he met while he was negotiating with us. The small Arab, here"—Timosheev pointed at the screen—"was one of them. We still don't know who he was. We didn't suspect him at the time. But when we followed him and photographed the people he met, we also got that one." He touched the face of the European with the tip of his stick. "As astounding as it might seem, it could be Joe Gonen, which suggests two conclusions. First, that after he was wounded and incapacitated as a pilot, he began to take part in undercover operations in Arab countries. Second, that he might have been the man behind the scene who thwarted our operation and is responsible for the failure of project Firebird. If it was really he in Beirut that summer, meeting somebody who met the pilot, then the Israelis might have actually directed all the Lebanese moves. Anyway, this is an indication that Gonen might be quite an important agent in the secret service."

"Just a moment," Andropov interrupted. "First, I'd like to know when you discovered that picture of Gonen."

"Oh, I think it was only last year. We always run comparative checks on pictures in our archives, as you know. It wasn't before we established a picture file of Gonen that we ran a routine comparative check with all the Mideast pictures described in our computerized catalogue as showing unknown men with similar physical features."

"My second question is," Andropov continued challengingly, "can you give me a logical reason why an Israeli pilot, wounded in the Six-Day War, should pop up a year later in Beirut to conduct secret operations for the Lebanese against the Soviet Union?"

"Well, there is a logical explanation, Comrade Chairman," Timosheev said with some hesitation. "Gonen couldn't fly. He was therefore given a new function in the Air Force. I think that he joined the Air Force intelligence by the end of 1967. Now if we consider that a fair assumption, he might have learned from Israeli agents in Beirut about our operation. It's obvious why the Israelis were determined to prevent the Mirage from falling into our hands. The Israeli secret services often use officers and civilians from other categories for undercover operations abroad. Since Gonen was already in intelligence, since he, himself, had been a Mirage pilot, familiar with the technical aspects of the project and with the mentality of a pilot, they might have sent him to Beirut to sabotage our plan."

"Yes. Possible," Andropov admitted. "Proceed."

"Next," said Timosheev.

The next picture showed Gonen in the uniform of a lieutenant colonel, a glass in his hand, surrounded by several men in light tropical suits. All of them were smiling into the camera. "This is the Fourth of July, nineteen hundred seventy-one, reception at the American embassy in Tel-Aviv," Timosheev explained. Gonen was invited in his official capacity as head of Air Force intelligence."

"This is very important," the Chairman of the KGB said. "Are you sure of the date? The year?"

"Yes."

"It means that at the time of the Marsa raid Gonen was already head of air intelligence. So he should know everything connected with Marsa. If the Israelis have devised any countermeasures, he most certainly should know about them."

"Exactly. I'd say even more, Comrade Chairman. I think that he was appointed assistant to the air attaché in Washington precisely because of his thorough knowledge of the Marsa affair. Maybe it is in Washington because of a joint enterprise Israel might undertake with the Americans."

Andropov lapsed into thoughtful silence. "Yes," he grunted finally, "but how do you explain this story about heavy drinking, girls, gambling?"

"He was very badly affected by his inability to fly, Yuri Vladimirovich," Timosheev explained. "During the last five years he underwent a series of operations that might have resuscitated some inert muscles and nerves in his right leg. All those years he lived with this hope, which became a kind of obsession with him. He grew irascible and short-tempered. Six months ago he was informed by his doctors that he would never fly again—and that was a final diagnosis. It was a terrible blow to him. He had lost the real meaning of his life. You know those pilots, comrade, flying for them is an addiction."

"What is your source of all those psychological analyses?" Andropov's voice was sarcastic.

"An inside source in the British embassy in Tel-Aviv, comrade. It's a girl who types the reports of the British air attaché. It has been confirmed by inside Pentagon sources in Washington."

"What do you think, Lev Ivanovich?" Andropov addressed General Yulin, who had been silent the entire time.

"I don't know." Yulin's tone was reserved. "It seems too much of a coincidence to me. Just by coincidence an Israeli diplomatic pouch turns up on the hijacked TWA plane, just by coincidence there is a letter in it concerning Gonen, just by sheer luck Gonen is the man we most anxiously want, and just by chance Gonen is a heavy drinker, gambler, and sex maniac. I don't believe in sheer luck and coincidences. I don't like them, either."

"So what do you suggest?" Andropov was becoming impatient.

"I'd rather check that story again thoroughly," Yulin answered evenly. "I'm not sure we should start an operation at this stage."

The KGB Chariman seemed to ignore the answer. "Do you have anything else, Timosheev?" His voice sounded disturbed and angry.

"Yes, Comrade Chairman. A last picture." Gonen appeared on the screen in civilian clothes, his tie knot loose, his face drawn and tired. He was bent over a large roulette table, in the middle of a group of people.

"This was taken in Vegas last Sunday," Timosheev said. "After the interception of the letter about Gonen we decided to check it. The letter is genuine, comrade. All the reports from our men in Washington confirm that Gonen is on the decline. He drinks, and he spends large sums of money in the gambling spots."

"Good," Andropov said. "Turn on the lights."

The people around the table blinked uneasily in the new brightness of the room. Andropov looked at Yulin. The General sat motionless in his place, avoiding his gaze. Everybody in the room suddenly realized that for the first time in years Andropov was going to overrule the foxy old master spy publicly.

The KGB Chairman shrugged. "Very well, then. Lev Ivanovich and you, Timosheev, will you please come to my office. We shall take care of Tovarishch Joe Gonen. And if, as you say, Timosheev, he was responsible for the fiasco in Beirut, we shall make him pay for it."

12

May 13 - June 7, 1973

They say Las Vegas is like the midnight flower, that miracle of the wilderness. Only after the red desert sun disappears behind the barren mountains of Nevada does the flower come to life, open its rich, glistening leaves, and blossom in a breath-taking harmony of vivid colors. At night the shops and offices close, ordinary people vanish, and the deep, regular heartbeat of the city shifts to a frenzied pulsation, pumping greed, fantasy, and irrational hopes into hordes of invaders from all over the world, seeking fortune and pleasure. For several hours the eternal desert loses its hold over the cluster of steel and glass and concrete structures, so small and defenseless against its hugeness, and a new bright-colored world emerges, metamorphosing illusion into reality.

At night Las Vegas becomes a festival of the senses. Those who visit there plunge into a whirlpool of sounds—the perpetual clicking of the slot machines, the silvery patter of a shower of coins, the hopeful shouts of gamblers from the roulette and crap tables, the rhythmic notes of music wafting from the night clubs and theaters, the coquettish, promising laughter of women. The candid gaze of the newcomer avidly tries to grasp the ever changing kaleidoscope of lights and sights around him: the famous entertainers' names on the glittering billboards, the millions of electrical bulbs forming other signs, lights, moving figures, rivers of gold and silver, the crowds of sunburned men and elegant women clustered around the large green-clothed tables in the dim atmosphere of the casinos, the transparent, starry desert night forming a canopy over the blazing city. The senses are teased by the exquisite fragrance of French perfumes, the rich odor of expensive cigars, the sharp taste of liquor, and the delicate flavors of the gourmet dishes in the lavish restaurants. But most of all one longs for the touch. The touch of money, of immense fortunes seeming so close, hiding in a spinning wheel or in a pair of dice.

Such were Gonen's thoughts as he stood in the magnificent entrance of the Roman Palace and lit a long black cheroot. He liked the dry climate of the desert and the cool feeling on his skin when it came in contact with the thirsty air. He cast a last glance at the magnificent succession of water fountains and pools, beautifully illuminated from the inside, then turned back and walked into the enormous casino lobby. It was after 3 A.M., but it was Saturday, and people were still crowded around the tables. He went past the batteries of slot machines, cast an admiring glance at a couple of long-legged show girls who hurried, smiling at him, in the opposite direction, and finally reached the brightly lit counters of the cashiers and accounts department. He leaned on one of the marble counters and suddenly felt fatigued. His head leaden with whiskey, he had skipped dinner because of a roulette game, and hadn't slept more than a couple of hours since he had arrived on Friday.

"When do you intend to pay your debt, sir?" asked the accounts manager, jolting him out of his lethargy. He was polite, but his voice had a distinct edge and he wasn't smiling.

"Send it to the embassy in Washington," Gonen answered, and deftly picked a glass of bourbon from the tray of a passing waitress.

"I'm very sorry, sir, but for two months now, we've been sending your bills and notices of your gambling debts to your embassy and we haven't received any payment yet."

Gonen wiped his perspiring forehead and reached uncertainly for the glass he had put on the counter. "You know these things take time. And I did sign my bill, didn't I? Don't tell me you do not trust the signature of a colonel and a diplomat." He paused. "I'd like to see the manager, now."

The man bowed slightly, but his frosty demeanor didn't change. He turned around and disappeared into the inner office. Gonen exhaled the acrid smoke of his cheroot and then drained the glass. A couple of minutes later the accounts manager was back. "It won't be necessary to talk to the manager, sir. We'll accept your signature."

"Good," Gonen said curtly, and glared at the man, who returned a blank gaze and pushed a printed form on the counter. He signed it without looking.

"So it's two thousand dollars, sir?"

"Yes. In fifty-dollar chips."

"You may sit at any table you like, sir. A security officer will bring you the chips."

"Very well." Gonen walked away. He beckoned a mini-skirted waitress, took another generously filled glass, and wandered aimlessly among the tables. Finally he chose an empty roulette table off the center of the casino. The bored croupier, who was sitting idly, gave him a nod of recognition, got up, and sent the wheel spinning. Gonen sat down at the table, put out his cheroot in an ornate ashtray, and picked a French cigarette from the courtesy tray. A thickset security man, wearing a uniform and a holstered gun, bent over him. "Colonel Gonen? Two thousand dollars in fifty-dollar chips, sir. Will you please sign the receipt?"

He signed, and put four chips on 13, 15, 17, and 19. He didn't even look at the wheel when he heard the ivory ball falling into a compartment, and didn't wince when the croupier announced indifferently, "Thirty-two, red." He immediately placed four other chips on the same numbers.

At the far end of the casino, close to the brightly lit arcade that led to the swimming pool, two men watched him. Both were in their late forties, medium-built, expensively dressed. But there the resemblance ended. One was bald, with a reddish complexion. He wore horn-rimmed glasses and smoked a big cigar. He looked efficient and dull.

The other man was suntanned with a sharpness in his blue eyes and abundant dark hair that turned silver at the temples. He wore a mod-cut gray suit over a white silk shirt with a pattern of small, light gray lozenges. A dark red foulard scarf was impeccably tied around his neck. He looked like an adventurer.

"Go now," the bald man said to him.

Gonen didn't even glance at the stranger who took a seat at the far end of the table. He was looking at his numbers, his glass empty again, while the stack of chips in front of him was steadily diminishing. He heard the man ask, "What's the limit at this table?"

"Two hundred and fifty dollars on a number, sir." The croupier pointed at a discreet sign that hung above the table.

"O.K. Two-fifty on thirty-six, red; another two-fifty on thirty, red."

Silently two men moved from the inner enclosure formed by the roulette tables and took positions behind the gambler, carefully observing his behavior as well as that of the croupier. A bet of five hundred dollars was not unusual, but one couldn't rule out the possibility of a secret deal between the croupier and a gambler.

Gonen slowly turned to his right and appraised the new player. The man gave him a friendly nod. He had a frank smile. "How's luck tonight?" he asked.

Gonen shrugged and pointed at his stack of chips. "Not very cooperative."

"You should bet on my numbers," the man said. "I've got a foolproof system. It has to work."

But it didn't. Half an hour later Gonen's chips had vanished and the other man hadn't been any luckier. Gonen reckoned that the stranger had lost about five thousand dollars. Regretfully he pushed back his chair. The other man got up too. "Well"—he smiled—"tomorrow is another day. Come on, let's have a drink."

"Why not?" Gonen replied. He accepted the expensive Havana cigar and the firm handshake the man offered him. "Jackson is the name," he said. "Lew Jackson."

"I am Colonel Joe Gonen, of the Israeli Air Force, now with the embassy in Washington."

"Israel?" Jackson seemed genuinely pleased. "I admire your country, Colonel. And your Air Force, of course. I was a combat pilot too. Fought in Korea, Vietnam, Laos. Wounded twice, downed once."

"Really?" Gonen's face was alight with interest. "What were you flying?"

"Well, in Korea we had the Sabre, later, the Starfighter, the Skyhawk . . ."

The two men walked toward the Roman Galley bar. Gonen asked him what he did for a living. Jackson said something vague about buying and selling. Gonen didn't pursue it.

The bald man observed the whole scene from his post in the slot machine section. His expression didn't change, but he was very satisfied.

It was after five in the morning when Jackson and Gonen parted. At noon they met for brunch and a swim. They had a lot in common. Both were strong, confident, and attractive men. At the pool they became the center of interest for several pretty girls, who had visions of excitement and money. Actually, Gonen's financial situation could hardly have been worse, but when he declined Jackson's suggestion to gamble again, his new friend slapped him on the back and said, "Come on. You'll gamble with me. I'm loaded this weekend, and you can help me spend the dough. Easy come, easy go."

They gambled for several hours and again lost heavily. Jackson's cheerful mood did not change. That same night they went out with two of the girls they had met at the pool.

On Monday morning, before Gonen headed for the airport, Jackson asked him casually, "Will you be coming next weekend?"

"I really don't know, Lew," he answered uneasily. "I'm completely washed out."

"Don't let that bother you," Jackson said. "I know some people here in Vegas. I can vouch for you. They'll advance you money if you just promise to give them part of the profits when you win."

"Come on, now." Gonen looked at him warily. "I wasn't born yesterday. What's the gimmick?"

"Nothing you wouldn't like," Jackson replied earnestly. "Come here next weekend. Be my guest. I have something that might interest you. We'll talk about it, and if you want to you'll meet some of those people. It's entirely up to you. If you like it—fine. If not—we would just have spent another fun weekend here. O.K.? No strings attached, no hard feelings."

"I'll come," Gonen said thoughtfully.

Lew Jackson was a first-class operator. By the end of that second weekend at Vegas he had Gonen softened enough for his last move. After forty-eight hours of drinking, gambling, eating in the best restaurants, and sleeping with a gorgeous redhead in the suite Jackson had booked for him, Gonen seemed ready to do anything to continue this kind of existence. Jackson had sized him up right: a man like that would never bend under pressure or threats. He had to be manipulated in a way that would allow him to keep his pride and—at least outwardly—his self-respect. Jackson had thought of the perfect solution.

The two quiet, serious-looking men who came to see Gonen on Sunday afternoon introduced themselves as NATO intelligence officers. They spoke at length about the Russian threat to the free world, especially today, when the magic word *détente* had lulled the West into dangerous serenity. Even certain influential circles in NATO had been misled by the peace offensive of the Soviet Union. As a matter of fact, the Russians' real intention was to use the relaxed attitude of the West to undermine and weaken it. In this new situation NATO had to do everything possible to prevent the Soviet moves.

"We are extremely worried about the Soviet buildup in the Middle East," said the visitor who had introduced himself as Major George Mackenzie, from Canada. "We know the same applies to your country. Our objectives are identical. We'd like to suggest that you cooperate with us and help us with information about Soviet involvement in the Arab countries. We would appreciate it if you could also tell us about the countermeasures Israel intends to apply in case of crisis in the area."

"We have, as you may know, an important budget allotted for that purpose," said the second visitor, a huge, blond Swede, Major Songström. "We can put a part of our funds at your disposal."

"Why don't you try to get your information by direct contact with the Israeli secret services?" Gonen asked cautiously.

"Because we know we wouldn't get a thing. Secret services, by their very nature, are suspicious and parsimonious in any exchange of intelligence, even when it is for the benefit of their own country."

Gonen smiled wryly in agreement. "May I see your credentials?"

"Of course," Mackenzie replied. They both produced their passports and their personal NATO ID cards.

"O.K.," Gonen said. "We have a common purpose. I'll cooperate with you."

While he was shaking their hands, he wondered if they assumed he knew that NATO had no intelligence service at all.

Three weeks later, in the headquarters of the Eighth Department, the intercom on General Yulin's desk buzzed and the young, eager voice of the Chairman's secretary, Volodya Nikitin, said, "Chairman Andropov would like to see you, comrade."

Andropov was standing by the window in his office, looking thoughtfully at the low gray sky. It was late spring, but the weather in Moscow was unusually cold and a monotonous, annoying drizzle continued to fall without interruption.

Yulin knocked at the door and entered. "Come in, come in, Lev Ivanovich." Andropov rubbed his hands and spread them open over the radiator, which stood beside the window. "I've ordered some tea. Sit down, please."

The KGB Chairman seemed in a particularly good mood today.

Yulin waited patiently.

"I've just come back from a meeting of the Politburo," Andropov said. "I reported about the progress of our Israeli project, and everybody was very satisfied." He cast a speculative glance at the little General. "But not you, Lev Ivanovich."

Yulin looked back at him stubbornly. "No, I am not satisfied." He sighed and added, "Not yet, anyway."

Andropov's good mood changed abruptly. "I don't understand you. What's happened to you? Why are you so suspicious? We got this colonel. He is talking, and talking well. A report every week. Facts, figures, estimates. Did you check his information?"

"Yes," Yulin said. "Everything looks authentic. My Air Force experts say the information is the best they could hope for."

"So what's bothering you? Don't you trust him?"

The door opened, and a thin middle-aged woman brought two glasses of dark, sweet Russian tea. "Thank you, Vera," Andropov said absently, and took the glass with both hands, the Russian way.

Yulin thrust his head forward doggedly and pressed his clenched fists to the table.

"I just don't like it, Yuri Vladimirovich." He spoke slowly and tried to control his voice, but there was a note of suppressed anger in it. "Three or four months ago we did not know anything about the Israeli Air Force. Now, all of a sudden, we have two informers. A man and a woman. The best. She supplies us with all the Pentagon papers about their Air Force; he produces regular reports based on firsthand knowledge. I told you I didn't like this diplomatic pouch story. I don't like this Las Vegas gambling stunt. I studied Gonen's file very thoroughly. It just doesn't become him. I can't see him drinking and gambling. I can't understand why he wasn't recalled yet. His scandalous behavior is well known. The Israelis recall diplomats for lesser breaches. And there was this meeting with Gehlen. I can't get that out of my mind. The Israelis must be up to something after the Marsa raid and the Gehlen contact."

"But these are only suspicions you have, nothing tangible," Andropov said heatedly.

"Yes, but why am I the only one who has suspicions?" Yulin exploded. "You were known to be as suspicious as I was. Why don't you want to check it more thoroughly? Why are you so sure everything is fine?"

Andropov's face reddened. "I don't like those insinuations, Yulin. I am satisfied with the situation. Our people are not a bunch of fools. We have checked and rechecked everything. We'll go on with the operation, as decided."

Yulin got up. "May I go now?"

"Yes," Andropov said forcefully. His face was a mask of anger.

Yulin rushed into his office, muttering furiously under his breath. He sent for his Chief of Operations, Lavrenti Karpin, a young, efficient Ukrainian who had risen in the Eighth Department and carried out various assignments abroad. Karpin tiptoed apprehensively into the office since the secretaries had already briefed him on the General's ferocious mood. He found Yulin pacing nervously back and forth in the office, talking to himself. He stopped and saw Karpin.

"Lavrenti! I want you to start several operations immediately. Top secret. I mean you are not to inform any other department. Report only to me, in person. Understand?"

"Yes, Comrade General," Karpin replied, puzzled.

"Good. I want you to mobilize all your informers among the Palestinian guerrillas. I want them to find out exactly how 'hijack day' was planned and carried out. I want to know which planes were to be hijacked originally and if there were any changes of plan. I want to know who knew about the projects and if there could have been a leak of any kind. I want to know if there is the slightest chance that the Israelis might have infiltrated the Fatah organization and on what level. I want to find out, at any cost, if it was just a coincidence that the El Al plane was the only one not to be hijacked, and that this damn diplomatic pouch was so conveniently delayed to be sent precisely by the TWA airliner. You do whatever is necessary. Do you understand?"

"Yes, Comrade General," said Karpin gravely, earnestly scribbling on his note pad.

"And one more thing, Karpin, I need a swallow in America. One of the best, someone who is sexually skilled and expert in obtaining information."

"That will be no problem. We have several operating there now. There is a French girl, Annie Blaine, working in the UN Secretariat. We also have two American air stewardesses. There are some other women, too, but the first three move around quite a lot and we can use any of them."

Yulin didn't wait for him to finish his answer.

"I want one of them to work her way into Gonen's bed. I don't care how. But I want it quick, and I want her to stay with him for a while—a month, two months, on weekends and holidays. See if you can send her to Vegas. He always stays there at the Roman Palace. She must try any trick in the book to make him talk. I want her to report everything he does, everything he says, every phone call, every letter, every note. I want to know everything about that man."

"Yes, Comrade General." Karpin paused a moment, then said softly, "You can rely on me, Lev Ivanovich. I'll take care of everything."

"Good," Yulin replied, and dismissed him.

Karpin took care of everything. Detailed reports from communist agents in Al Fatah flowed into the Eighth Department in Moscow. Simultaneously the charming Annie Blaine was picked up by Gonen on a flight to Vegas and thereafter regularly shared his weekends in Nevada. She reported everything, as instructed.

But on both operations Yulin drew a blank.

PART FOUR

The Duel

13

June 7, 1973

The break Lev Ivanovich Yulin was so desperately searching for came from a completely unexpected direction. He had almost abandoned hope when Valery Bykovski, head of the obscure Special Service One (the information service), First Chief Directorate, asked to see him. Bykovski was a shy man, with a scholar's head: long hair, large forehead, thick glasses over short-sighted eyes with a lost, faraway look. He entered Yulin's office almost surreptitiously and moved to the edge of a chair, where he assumed something vaguely resembling a sitting position. He was wearing a black suit that was worn out at the cuffs, and his fingers twitched nervously on the cover of a thin file.

"I don't know how to start, Comrade Yulin," he said in a deep voice that belied his appearance. "It's only a suspicion, really, but I thought that if I told you about it you could reassure me."

"Of course, Bykovski." Yulin encouraged him with a smile. He was familiar with his colleague's shortcomings, but he also remembered that many years ago Bykovski had had one of the most brilliant minds in the service.

"You see, we found out something very curious about certain events that took place last November." Bykovski glanced, embarrassed, at his file. "On November 13, in Montevideo, Uruguay, a man was mysteriously murdered. His name was Hermann Bauer, German origin, citizen of São Paulo, Brazil. A thorough check of his fingerprints by Interpol and investigation of his family gave us positive proof that he was really Heinrich Roehm, a former intelligence officer in the German Army who had disappeared in 1945 with a list of pro-German agents in Russia."

The head of the KGB's Middle East department groaned. He bent over his table and looked intently at Bykovski. "Yes, yes, proceed."

"Well, we found out that on the next day, November 14, an envelope deposited, probably by an ex-Nazi, in a Swiss bank was remitted to a person who gave the code word and the code number to the manager of the secret accounts and deposits department."

"What?" Yulin jumped to his feet. His mind worked feverishly, connecting the pieces of information in a series of inductions and gradually producing a pattern that made his blood run cold. "Are you sure of what you are saying?" he bellowed.

That made Bykovski shrink into his chair. "I told you it was only a suspicion, Lev Ivanovich," he said in a rather apologetic tone. "We still cannot definitely connect the two events. Bauer—or Roehm—was killed in Montevideo on November 13. The package was remitted to an unknown man in Bern on the next day."

Yulin leaned forward on his elbows and covered his face with his hands. He felt a tremor run through his body. His instincts were frantically conveying an alarm. He bit his lips and tried to regain control of himself. But when he spoke, his voice lashed at poor Bykovski with cold anger.

"It is June now, comrade. You are speaking about November. Seven months ago. What happened? Why didn't I hear about this before?"

Bykovski spread his hands helplessly, palms up. "Comrade Yulin, we had no idea that Bauer and Roehm were the same person. Nobody disclosed that. Interpol established the true identity of the murdered man only about a month later. At that point our people started to investigate because of Roehm's Nazi record. It took them a long time to find out that the Israelis had killed him. We still didn't think that was exceptional. Israel still hunts Nazi criminals at large, you know. But I was surprised that nobody, even anonymously, informed the news agencies about the death of a Nazi criminal. Before there was always a so-called 'Avengers Organization' that took care of that."

"All right, so they didn't," Yulin said impatiently.

Bykovski went on, "The second piece of information, about the package, came through a different service, much later, and was buried in the files of a different section for a while. You see, the financial subdivision of the Fifth Department has a kind of part-time informer in the Banques Helvétiques Unifiées in Bern. He tells them occasionally about unusual events. He reported that an envelope deposited at the end of the war, probably by a Nazi on the run, had been handed to an old man who gave the code word. Nobody in our services could link the two pieces of information."

"So how come you found out?" Yulin pressed him.

"You know that our main task is to assemble and distribute within the Center all the routine information obtained by the various European branches of the First Chief Directorate. We keep chronological lists of every month's events, which are brought up to date once in a while. Only this morning, when I read through the list of the last eight months' events, did I find the entries indicating that the deposit of an ex-Nazi was retrieved from a bank in Switzerland less than twenty-four hours after the death of an ex-Nazi in Uruguay."

Yulin spoke slowly. "Only this morning, you say."

"Yes," Bykovski admitted unhappily. "You see, I really didn't understand that . . ."

But Yulin understood the real meaning of the sequence of events: the discovery by the Israelis that something was happening in Egypt, remotely controlled by the Soviet Union; the hurried trip of the Israeli chief of the Mossad to Gehlen's residence; the murder by the Israelis of Heinrich Roehm, former aide to Gehlen, case officer of a ring of Nazi espionage in Soviet Russia during the war, and the man KGB was trying to find since 1945; the mysterious appearance of the stranger who took the envelope from the bank.

"It was an envelope, not a package, right?" he asked, playing nervously with his pencil.

Bykovski looked at him. "That's what they said. An envelope."

"And I know what's in that envelope," Yulin shouted, enraged. "A list of names. The bastards are trying to get inside us, to find exactly what's going to happen."

Oblivious of the terrified Bykovski, he darted through his outer office. "Karpin!" he roared. "Karpin!" His fist crashed on the desk of a startled secretary. "Find Karpin and bring him to my office. Immediately!"

The panic-stricken girl ran to fetch the Chief of Operations.

By the time Karpin came running into his office, Yulin was his old, precise, dangerously efficient self. "You are leaving tomorrow morning, on the first flight of Aeroflot to Geneva." He pounded his fist on the table as if to emphasize the urgency of the mission. "You'll establish your headquarters there. Take anybody you want with you. You can have all the men of the operational section. Take them off any other assignment if you need them." He told Karpin succinctly about the murder of Roehm and his secret list, which was certainly in Israeli hands.

"You must find out what the Israelis are doing with that list. You must find the names of the person or persons who got it. We have to know what they intend to do with it and what names are on it. The names, Karpin, this is the most vital piece of information we need now!"

Karpin had a quick mind. "Do you think that their people in Europe might know anything about the list?"

"Not their regular residents, of course. You must watch for any unusual Israeli activity in Western Europe, maybe even in some East European countries. But start with Bern. We have a lead there. Maybe you could learn more about the people who got the envelope. Capture Israeli agents, anywhere in Europe. Make them talk. Use any means you like. Kill if you need to. Somewhere, somebody must know something. The Mossad is a small service. Among a limited number of people any irregular trip, any arrival or departure of an operational team, is known.

Get this information. As for the means, you'll be covered by me. I give you full authority."

"But, Comrade General," Karpin objected, "that's not our domain. Not our department and not our section. This kind of operation belongs in the European section or the Mokroie Dela," he added, emphasizing the latter in an oblique reference to its bloody political murders and kidnapings.

"Stop that nonsense!" Yulin exploded. "The European section and the Mokroie Dela won't move their little fingers." He walked around his desk and stood facing Karpin, his powerful gaze straight into his aide's eyes. "The future of this country may depend on it. We must find out, no matter what it takes—do you understand?—no matter what it takes, who the traitors are among us!" Yulin sank into a chair heavily, as if all his energy had drained away. "Go now," he said quietly.

14

July 2, 1973

The Old Man buzzed his secretary, a brisk, red-haired woman of forty-five who had been his faithful assistant since Jeremiah Peled's days as an obscure section director. "Dalia, is the car ready?"

"Yes. Yossi is waiting downstairs."

"Good. Tell him I'll be down in five minutes. You can send the car with the bodyguards right away. And tell them once again to move around, to show themselves, to make their presence as obvious as possible."

He pressed the intercom switch and once again looked at the documents neatly arranged in front of him. One was a yellow oblong sheet of paper, diagonally crossed with two thin red lines, which automatically classified it top secret. It carried the decoded text of a telegram sent by the "Main station" of the Mossad in Switzerland. Except for its operational centers out of the borders of Israel, the Mossad had local stations in most of the West European countries. Their primary task was to gather routine information and assist Mossad teams on *ad hoc* missions. The station in Switzerland was in Zurich, but the report in front of him, dated June 28, concerned Bern:

> On June 23 a tall blond European male carrying an *Austrian passport rented a chauffeur-driven Rolls Royce from the "Compagnie Gontrand, voitures avec chauffeur," 137, Davos Street. While filling out the routine documents at the office he asked about a friend of his, a German banker of about sixty-five, who might have rented a Rolls from the same com-*

*pany during the first two weeks of November. It
seems that he got some fairly detailed answers from
the secretary on duty. He used the simple tactic of
giving a certain name. The secretary checked
through the November file. When she didn't find the
name, the man expressed surprise and asked to look
through the list. The girl gave it to him in good faith,
and he checked names, addresses, and passport numbers. He finally apologized, pretending he had made
a mistake. Our man on the spot overheard a part of
the conversation and contacted us. According to our
instructions, he kept a close watch on the office, and
when the Austrian returned the car on June 26, he
managed to get two shots of him with a B-32 miniature concealed camera we had supplied him. Photographs forwarded to you by special delivery.*

Jeremiah Peled looked at the pictures. They were a
poor, amateur job. One was completely smudged, but the
second one, although blurred, showed the Austrian's face
distinctly: wide cheekbones, delicate nose, small porcine
eyes, thin lips.

Once again he compared the snapshot with the photograph that was stapled to a large yellow cardboard file.
The faces were identical except for the fact that on
Peled's photograph the man looked younger and his hair
was black. There were several documents in the file, but
he wasn't interested in them. His attention was focused on
two lines typewritten on top of the file cover: "Nikishov,
Nikolai Vassilievich, alias Rudy Shoenke, alias Gert
Knutt, alias Bruno Heiffer. KGB operational agent, Ex-
ecutive Action Department (Department V—Mokroie
Dela), First Chief Directorate, 1967–1972; Eighth Directorate (Middle East), operational section, since September
1972."

Peled put the documents in his current tray, got up,
and went quickly through the outer office. The elevator
took him directly to the underground garage, where his
driver, Yossi, a young ex-paratrooper, waited for him at
the wheel of his off-white Volvo sedan.

Peled put on his sunglasses and sat beside the driver.
"To Old Jaffa, Yossi," he said. "Café Aladin."

Café Aladin was an old Arab house with a dome-
shaped oriental roof. The house itself was small. There
was barely room inside for a circular bar, two round
wooden tables, and several benches, sunk into small rug-
padded niches in the wall. But the unique asset of the
Aladin was its magnificent terrace, which gave the impression that it was floating over the emerald green waves
of the Mediterranean. It offered a magnificent view of
Jaffa Bay. On the left one could see the picturesque old
city of Jaffa: the round-domed, whitewashed mosques, the
sleek, needle-shaped minarets, the serene French and Italian churches, the ancient walls and meticulously restored
ruins of the ageless city. On the right side, beyond the
crescent formed by the bay, loomed modern Tel-Aviv:
tall buildings, a lavish hotel row along the sandy beach,
large seaside drives bustling with traffic.

It was early, eight thirty, on a sunny July morning. In
an hour the tropical sun would hit the city and a wave of
heat and humidity would settle upon it. But at this hour
the air was crisp and limpid and a pleasant wind was
gently rustling in the palm thickets. The white tables on
the Aladin terrace were surrounded by wrought-iron
chairs padded with cushions. Drawn under the shadow of
gay red and green umbrellas, they were ideally located for
a relaxed morning chat over a cup of thick Turkish
coffee.

Eight people had seated themselves at two square
tables on the northern part of the terrace, which was the
coolest at this time of day. Most of them were men in
their forties, of various builds and appearances. Some
looked quite well off from the way they were dressed;
others wore modest summer clothing. But they shared
something: they were all associated with the Israeli secret
services, former Mossad, Shin Bet, and Aman agents. After
fifteen to twenty years in the services they had retired and
turned to more peaceful occupations—business, insurance, official government jobs.

This meeting, after years of "civil" activity, created the atmosphere of an old school reunion. The former spies were happily slapping one another on the back and exchanging wisecracks; alone on the terrace, they could even indulge in recalling feats from the past.

Peled's appearance on the threshold brought the gaiety to an abrupt end. He was smiling and friendly, and they greeted him by his first name, as usual. They didn't depend on him anymore, and he was no longer their boss. Nevertheless, the natural authority he exercised brought them back to the same respectful behavior that had been a part of their way of life for years.

"I called you here now in spite of the fact that I have been preparing this reunion for many months," he began. "You might ask yourselves why in a public place? The answer is precisely because it is a public place. I pray to God that our meeting is remarked and reported, and that somebody succeeds in identifying me and several of you. I want Moscow to know about this meeting."

"Is that the reason you sent four bodyguards in a car fifteen minutes ago?" asked Jacob Barnea, former deputy chief of the Shin Bet and a close friend of the Old Man. "They were running around with their walkie-talkies, flashing their guns, and we started to think that something was wrong with the service."

"Nothing is wrong with the service," Peled said, "but you are right about the bodyguards. They behaved exactly as they were instructed. Now I'll tell you why."

He lowered his voice and chose his words carefully, avoiding any disclosure of irrelevant information.

"Some months ago we obtained a certain list bearing the names of several Russians who were foreign spies. Among those names we found one that is very important to us. We have to establish contact with this man in the near future on a vital matter. I won't tell you when, where, or how this contact will be made.

"I expected that sooner or later the Russians would find out that the list is in our possession and would do everything possible to learn the names. Three days ago I received definite information that this was so. The Russians know that we have the list, and they have tried to find out, through an intelligence operation in Switzerland, the identity of the man who obtained that list. I have nothing to fear there, we have covered all our tracks, and the Russian investigation will soon reach a dead end. On the other hand, the Soviet secret services will be—or already are—on the alert, watching for any attempt on our part to establish contact with the spy or spies inside Russia. Now I want to start a diversion that will enable me to establish contact with the man I need while KGB attention is focused elsewhere."

"And that is where we come into the picture," Barnea said.

"Precisely. I need you as a smoke screen."

"What do you want us to do?" asked a thin, wiry man who was sitting at the far end of the table. "I'm afraid we're not in the same shape as before."

Peled smiled. "It doesn't matter. What I really need is your name and your face."

"What do you mean?"

Peled glanced around the tables. "I don't know whether you noticed that the common denominator among you, except the fact of being former agents, is that all of you are well known to the KGB. You, Jacob, were deputy chief of the Shin Bet at the time when we arrested Soviet agents Beer, Sitta, and Collier. You, David, and you, Shmuel, actually carried out the arrests. Bernard and Abraham, of the Mossad, worked against the KGB in Poland and Czechoslovakia at the time of the huge arms deal between Egypt and the Soviet bloc. Amos was expelled from Finland after the Soviet embassy lodged an official complaint against him. Michael had enraged them when he thwarted their attempt to start an underground anti-Western movement in Cyprus. And all of you remember the troubles of Mandy, here, with his Russian colleague in the UN."

"So we are quite famous, it seems," Barnea said casually.

"I am sure that the Russians have your pictures in their files, as well as your detailed biographies."

"So?" Michael asked eagerly.

"So I am going to send all of you to the Soviet Union and other communist countries. Some of you begin leaving tomorrow."

"What?" Jacob was astounded.

"You heard me," Peled said calmly. "I'm sending you behind the Iron Curtain."

"Under what cover?" It was Michael again.

"No cover," Peled said softly. "Your real names, your real occupations. For months I've been planning adequate pretexts for all your trips. Jacob is leaving for the world citrus growers' convention that opens in Moscow on July fifteenth."

Peled turned to his former deputy. "It's exactly in your line of business, Jacob. Michael is flying to Helsinki, for a visit to the Salora television factories. That's what you import, right? During your stay there you'll take a two-day tourist trip across the bay to Leningrad. The American tractor company you work for, Bernard, will send you to Moscow also, to conclude an import deal."

Bernard smiled knowingly. "So you're working hand in hand with the CIA, Jeremiah."

The Old Man shrugged. "One can expect a certain amount of goodwill from the CIA in this matter," he said noncommittally. Then he went on, "David and Shmuel, you are close friends, so you'll take your wives on vacation to Europe next week. In Paris you'll join a tourist group organized by Agence Franco-Russe and you'll fly to Moscow, Kiev, Volgograd, Odessa, and Sochi."

He looked at his papers. "Yes, Amos. You'll fly to West Berlin. You'll represent the government in this seminar on housing. While there, you'll spend one day in East Berlin. Mandy is going to Rumania, for a new deal of meat imports. Abraham is flying to Turkey, and will enter Bulgaria by car, where he'll be seeing his aunts and uncles he left behind twenty-five years ago. That's it. Did I forget anybody?"

"Oh, come on, Jeremiah!" Barnea protested. "You

must be out of your mind. They won't let anybody in. They won't ever let me enter Moscow. I was never *persona grata* in Russia, especially after they severed their diplomatic relations with us."

Some of the other former agents voiced their agreement.

"Don't you worry, Jacky," said the Old Man. "I'll bet my life that they'll let you in. You and all the others here. Don't you see? They know I have the list, they know I intend to use it. I'm sure they have half of the KGB waiting and hoping that somebody establishes contact. Now, all of you: when you reach the Soviet Union, or the other communist countries, you'll have to work hard. Go out in the streets as much as you can. Stop people on the corners, sit by lonely people on benches in the park, talk to them, ask them questions. Telephone unknown people you pick at random in the phone book and apologize. Say it was a mistake. Try to contact as many Russians as possible, and take care to be seen or heard talking with them."

"I'm going to say something very cowardly," Bernard interrupted. "It's quite a risk."

"Nonsense." Peled waved him aside. "The KGB won't touch you. It's *their* people they are after. They'll start to tail and interrogate everybody you talked to. With the eight of you operating in Russia and the Soviet bloc for a couple of weeks, eight former secret service agents who are on file in the KGB Center, I'll have the Russians completely confused. The Americans might also help us and send some people along for the same purpose. It will be a fantastic smoke screen. The only contact I need will be made very smoothly and quietly."

There was silence.

"Do you understand me?" Peled asked. They all nodded. He went on, "Business matters, salaries, and all the rest will be taken care of. Remember what I told each of you when you left the services. You never really quit. Of course, you can refuse and I won't hold a grudge against you. But as I know you"—he smiled broadly—"I have a hunch that nobody will walk out of here."

Nobody did.

Back in his office the Old Man buzzed his deputy. "Mike, any news from the team we sent to Europe to look for a new lead on Minerva?"

Mike Avivi's voice came over the intercom: "I got their weekly report yesterday."

"Well?"

"Sorry, Jeremiah. The report is negative. Not a single hint."

Peled sighed. "Cable them to go on searching. They must find something. I want this man."

15

August 3 - September 26, 1973

There was nothing unusual about the Kubbeh Palace in Cairo that night. Most of the staff—clerks, employees, secretaries, department heads—had left the presidential palace at 5 P.M. At six the huge gates opened for the presidential limousine, escorted by four motorcycle police and two cars of secret service bodyguards. The curtains of the limousine windows were drawn, and the crowd in the busy Cairo streets couldn't get a glimpse of Anwar el-Sadat. The small motorcade headed toward the fashionable residential suburb of Heliopolis, barely twenty miles from the center of the city, where Sadat's family had their summer residence.

The presidential car went to Heliopolis, but the President wasn't in it. While the noisy crowd was cheering his empty car, Sadat was in his palace, showing some top-secret visitors into his private office. First came the Minister of War, Ismail Ali. He was followed by the Chief of Staff of the Egyptian Army, General Salem, and his Chief of Operations, General Gamasy. Some minutes later a military car brought three foreign visitors, who had arrived in Egypt incognito: General Hafez Assad, the President of Syria; his Minister of War, Mustafa Tlas; and his Chief of Staff, General Shihabi. They had just arrived from Damascus aboard a military plane and landed at the Cairo-West military air base.

The group conferred for many hours. The exquisite ornamental wall clock in President Sadat's office had long since chimed midnight when he shook the hands of his distinguished foreign guests and escorted them to their car. The Syrian leaders were driven back to the airport and took off immediately for Damascus. In Kubbeh, Sadat gave some last instructions to his aides.

"Do you have any suggestion for the code name of the operation, sir?" General Salem asked.

"Yes," Sadat said thoughtfully. "I'll call it 'operation Badr.'" Salem and the others were pleased, for in the Battle of Badr, Mohammed, the prophet of Islam, had won his first military victory, in 624, a victory that was described by the Koran as an expression of divine goodwill.

During the following days banner headlines in most of Cairo's newspapers heralded the forthcoming great maneuvers, scheduled to start on September 1 and to last for about six weeks. The first auxiliary units of the Egyptian Second and Third armies started to move into position along the Suez Canal. The Egyptian press also pointed out that the General Staff was considering a mass pilgrimage of several Army divisions to Mecca during the Moslem religious holidays in November.

Meanwhile, in carefully guarded secrecy, a few hand-picked senior officers in the Ministry of War were planning the initial stage of operation Badr.

At the KGB Center in Moscow, Yulin was summoned by his chief, Yuri Andropov. Since their quarrel over Gonen's credibility their relationship had been cold and distant. The Chairman of the KGB would address Yulin in a formal way, without any trace of the old camaraderie that they had shared for years. Often he would turn directly to Yulin's deputy, Colonel Timosheev. But for major decisions or advice he still needed Yulin's brain. The little General, on the other hand, stubbornly stuck to his views. With a burning conviction he continued to carry on his secret private quest for the explosive list of Major Roehm.

Actually, the summons by Andropov this September morning worried Yulin. He feared that the KGB Chairman might have overheard something about his unauthorized operation in Western Europe and intended to make him stop all activity. He might even ask him for his resignation, Yulin thought gloomily.

But Andropov's first question was enough to reassure him. "I urgently need some information about the Israeli Air Force, Lev Ivanovich. What have you found out about their contingency plans to hit our bases in Egypt?"

"Nothing," Yulin replied. "Neither the American woman nor the Israeli pilot has mentioned anything about that. Their reports read as if Marsa never happened."

Andropov lit a cigarette with a quick, nervous gesture. "Our schedule has become pretty tight lately. We might have to move very fast. I must know, in the shortest possible time, what they intend to do in case of a war with Egypt."

"Maybe we'll have to tighten the screws on our sources," Yulin said calmly.

"Right. We must do that." Andropov frowned. "Yet pressure wouldn't get anything from the American woman. She gives us what her husband brings home. She can't ask him anything. The Israeli pilot is our man. He still reports regularly?"

"Once a week, on the dot," Yulin answered, sarcasm permeating his voice. "Your experts are very satisfied."

"But I am not satisfied," Andropov retorted. "That entire operation had one purpose: to find out what they intended to do after they discovered Marsa. We have nothing on that yet. And time is running short."

"I told you I didn't trust Gonen," Yulin said, but Andropov wouldn't be drawn into their old argument.

"Tell me, this Gonen, does he suspect that he is working for us?" he asked.

"Apparently not," Yulin replied carefully. "Our men say that he believes he reports to NATO."

"And what do you believe?" Andropov eyed him warily.

Yulin shrugged and didn't answer.

"We have no time, Lev Ivanovich." Andropov got up, walked to the window, and opened it. It had rained this summer morning in Moscow, and the fresh smell of clean air penetrated the room. "We have no time," he repeated, slamming the desk with both hands. "We must make Gonen talk. We must squeeze every possible bit of information out of him. Is that clear?"

"My people reported that he intends to go home on leave in a week or two," Yulin offered.

"That's good!" Andropov's face brightened. "We'll ask him to spend a weekend with our people when he is on his way to Israel. Some quiet place in Europe will do. Close to the sea. Maybe Italy, or the French Riviera. Three or four days will be enough. Just a polite questioning. Always use the NATO cover. Have a fishing boat ready, in case of emergency."

Yulin was agreeable. "Very well. I'll take care of it." He couldn't help admiring Andropov's phenomenal capacity to devise a good operational plan on the spur of the moment. He felt a little of the old warmth and respect for his boss. And he said in a somewhat different tone, "Another thing, Yuri Vladimirovich. I'm very worried about that list the Israelis obtained from the Germans. I'm afraid they may have somebody among us."

Andropov looked at him condescendingly. "Come now, Yulin. It has become an obsession with you." He tried to sound soothing and reassuring, but Yulin had the curious impression that the Chairman was trying to conceal his true feelings. "Do you believe that a list that was discovered—if discovered it was—thirty years after the war could be of any importance? I don't. Why, it could even be a provocation. They could name anybody at all, even me." He chuckled extravagantly at the absurdity of the whole idea, then turned and left the room, saying something about an important meeting of the Politburo. Behind him Yulin stared at the door, perplexed.

Gonen was absently munching a poorly cooked T-bone in a popular steakhouse outside Washington when somebody put his tray in front of him.

"May I?"

Gonen nodded. He didn't even raise his eyes. He knew that the man asking to share his table in the crowded restaurant was George Mackenzie, his NATO case officer.

Mackenzie would never meet him in a small, secluded cocktail lounge, in a tiny coffee shop, or on a park bench. "The safest places," he'd said, "are the crowded ones. Everybody is pushing everybody, and nobody pays attention to you. You just get lost in the crowd." Gonen hadn't argued.

They talked casually for several minutes. To any unsuspecting observer their conversation seemed to be just a routine exchange of pleasantries between two strangers who happened to share the same table. After a while Mackenzie came to the heart of the matter.

"On your way home to Israel, during your leave, we'd like you to drop in for a couple of days to see some of our friends in Europe."

"What for?" Gonen asked, his guard up.

"They would just like a more thorough conversation with you, a kind of exchange of views on the situation in the Middle East."

"Why can't they come here?"

"Because they just can't." There was an edge to Mackenzie's voice now. "They want to meet you in a peaceful and relaxed atmosphere. We have a nice, quiet place on the French Riviera. You'll arrange your ticket back to Israel with a stopover in Nice, and we'll take care of you there. You can always explain that you wanted to spend a weekend in Cannes or Saint-Tropez."

"I don't like that," Gonen said tartly. "I won't do it."

"Oh yes you will," Mackenzie retorted.

For the first time Gonen looked straight into the Canadian's eyes. "What the hell makes you so sure?"

"Cut the crap, Joe," Mackenzie said flatly. "You know damn well you have no choice."

"Really?"

"Yes, really. By now you have gone too far. Or do you want me to remind you that I have your handwritten reports, your receipts for cash payments over a period of nearly five months, and what else—"

"There was nothing in our agreement about going to one of your bases in Europe," Gonen said heatedly.

"Maybe you didn't read the small print." Mackenzie chuckled sarcastically.

"You son of a bitch!" Gonen pushed his tray away and abruptly left the restaurant.

That same night, in a small motel in Silver Spring, he was with Jenny. He had called her in the afternoon and begged to see her. The very sound of his voice hurt her. "I can't go through all that again, Joe," she said sadly. But he pleaded, and she heard an unmistakable note of despair in his voice. Still, she had come fearing a painful confrontation.

He opened the door, and his heart stopped at the sight of her, the long, thick golden hair, the green eyes that rebuked him now, and the sensuous contours of her body that he remembered so well. He wanted to seize her and vent all his loneliness and passion; instead he smiled tenderly, took her gently by the hand, and sat her down beside him on the bed.

He looked pale and careworn, and his voice was shaky as he held her hand hard and said, "Jenny, this horror we've been through will be over, maybe very soon. I still love you." He sounded vulnerable, and she felt a twinge of pain in her heart. "Will you leave everything and come with me? Share my life, all of it, no parting, ever?"

She gazed at him for several moments, and noticed with dismay the new gray hairs at his temples, but she kept her voice even. "Do you mean marriage?"

"Of course." His anxiety was plain. "I do mean it, darling," he added softly.

She closed her eyes and looked down at their clasped hands. "It's too much for me," she said slowly. "I can't just say yes after everything that's happened."

"I know. It must have been terrible for you. It was rotten for me, too. But I can explain it, and I will. I need you, Jenny." His voice sounded desperate now. "I want you to leave Robert, your friends, everything. Just be with me always. I'll make you happy, you know I will."

She couldn't resist him. He leaned toward her, and their lips met. The familiar consuming flame flared within them. A surge of joy went through her and she moved to him willingly.

Much later, in the dark, she gave voice to a niggling worry. "For someone who wants to live with me, Joe, you know very little about me . . ." She said it tentatively, holding her breath as she waited for him to speak.

"Is there anything terrible?" he asked, half in jest. He was relaxed and gloriously happy. Nothing at this moment could spoil that.

She hesitated, then said firmly, "No, of course not."

When it was time for him to leave, he put his arms around her and kissed her softly on the lips. "I love you, Jenny. Remember that. When I get back from Israel, everything will be all right." He looked deep into her eyes. "I promise."

She gazed at him searchingly without saying a word.

On September 26, 1973, at 2:15 P.M., Gonen disembarked from an Air Force Caravelle jet at the sunny airport of Nice-Côte d'Azur. It was a domestic flight; he had made the connection in Paris, where he had stayed overnight. He collected his luggage and went through the spacious, elegant hall of the terminal. A small man in a gray double-breasted suit approached him near the information desk. "Monsieur Gonen? I've been sent to take care of you. Welcome to Nice. This way, please."

The man took his suitcase and led him outside. Behind the row of cabs a black Citroën DS was waiting. There were two men inside. The driver, wearing a chauffeur's black cap, opened the door for them, and Gonen and his companion entered the car.

On the first floor of the terminal a small silver-haired man wearing sunglasses watched the scene from his seat in the glass-paneled restaurant. When they drove off, he nodded with satisfaction, took off his glasses, and raised his goblet of red wine. "To success, Timosheev," he said contentedly.

"To success, Comrade Yulin." Timosheev smiled, then drained his glass and looked at his watch. "We have another hour until our flight. Everything seems to be under control."

One floor above them, on the visitors' terrace, another man witnessed Gonen's departure in the black Citroën. It was Jeremiah Peled. His satisfaction was very like General Yulin's, except that he had no glass in his hand. "So they got him," he said to his deputy, Avivi, who was standing behind him. "Exactly according to plan. Let's start the next stage now."

16

September 27 - October 3, 1973

The escape took place on the night of September 27. According to the Israeli press, seventeen terrorists of the Fatah organization serving long prison terms succeeded in breaking out of Ramleh prison, where about eight hundred Arab inmates were held. It had started with a riot during a movie in the early evening. Hundreds of prisoners had rushed out of the projection room and set fire to benches, tables, mattresses, and blankets. The riot had doubtless been staged by the Fatah leaders in the prison in order to create a diversion. While the guards were struggling against the excited mob, about twenty inmates reached the outer wall of the prison. Seventeen of them succeeded in climbing over it with the help of ropes and ladders that had been supplied by people who waited outside. At that moment the escape was intercepted by armed guards, who captured the last three prisoners before they went over the wall.

The police and the Army were immediately alerted. No prints of tires were found near the wall, so it was clear that the fugitives had made at least the first part of their escape on foot. Ambushes and roadblocks were set up, and the border patrols were doubled. Special units were dispatched to the big Arab cities under Israeli occupation, on the assumption that the terrorists would try to disappear in the crowds there. Gaza, Nablus, Hebron, Jenin, Jericho, and East Jerusalem were combed. The Shin Bet mobilized its Arab informers. Within forty-eight hours the police arrested ten of the fugitives. Two more were captured off the Sinai shore a week later, while they tried to escape to Egypt in a fishing boat. But five of the prisoners were more fortunate. They reached Northern Galilee on the very night of the escape, and by dawn had successfully crossed the border into Lebanon. By noon they were proudly recounting their adventures in front of the cameras and microphones of Lebanese TV and radio.

Shortly after the press conference two of the escaped prisoners were taken to a small muddy hut in a refugee camp outside Beirut. Members of the Fatah organization, wearing commando fatigues, rubber-soled boots, and red kaffiyehs, escorted them through a cheering crowd of Palestine refugees, flourishing their Kalachnikov submachine guns and continuously shooting in the air, to express their exultation. But in the hut the atmosphere was different. The crowd was kept away by Fatah guards. The two escapees were invited to sit on a bench. In the windowless room there was just a wooden table and some chairs. On the table a kerosene lamp was burning. When their eyes became accustomed to the darkness, the fugitives noticed the immobile silhouette of a man standing in the shadows, watching them. He said softly, "Welcome, Hassan. Welcome, Ali. We thought you were dead."

They didn't see the face, but they recognized the voice. It belonged to Abu Ayad, the Fatah chief of operations, known as the right hand of Yasir Arafat.

He moved noiselessly and sat behind the table, keeping his face in the dark. "We thought you were dead," he said again. "I saw your photographs and names in the Israeli newspapers more than seven months ago. What happened?"

Hassan Kailani and Ali Baker exchanged glances. "You tell him," Ali, the younger of the two, said.

Hassan began hesitantly. "Abu Ayad, you remember our mission, seven months ago?" he asked timidly.

"Yes, I do."

"We had to take part in hijacking the planes on 'hijack day.' But our mission was the most risky. We had to penetrate into Israel through the Lebanese border and board an El Al plane in Tel-Aviv, using forged Turkish passports. We were instructed to take over the plane. We were equipped with belts made of plastic explosives, which we had to wear under our clothes. The moment the plane was airborne, we were to expose the belts and say that we would blow ourselves up with the plane if the pilot didn't obey our orders."

"Yes, I remember all that perfectly," Abu Ayad said coldly. "Maybe you forgot that I devised the whole system. Using plastic explosives in belts, under your clothing, was the only way to escape detection by their electronic devices."

"I know that," Hassan said. "But we were caught."

"When?"

"We crossed the border two weeks before the hijacking. That same night we were captured near the kibbutz Rosh Hanikra. We had no arms, as you remember, and with the plastic explosives on our bodies we were like live bombs. We ran into an Army ambush, close to the border. They started shooting. We surrendered."

"And the pictures in the papers?"

Hassan smiled faintly. "They published a picture of other fedayin who had been killed on the border. You can't recognize two corpses. They also published our pictures and names, but that was to mislead you."

"Why?"

"They wanted to know what we were up to. They told us that everybody thought we were dead, so they could interrogate us at will and kill us if we didn't tell the truth. They questioned us for days and nights without stopping."

"And what happened?"

Embarrassed, Hassan looked at his friend. Ali's shoulders had shrunk and his head was lowered. "What happened?" the commander barked.

Hassan sighed. "Forgive him, Abu Ayad, be merciful. He is a young boy, he didn't want to die."

"You mean he talked? Ali, is that true? You told them?"

The boy nodded slowly, without raising his eyes.

"What did you tell them?" the Fatah commander shouted.

Ali didn't answer. He held his head in his hands. Muffled, uncontrollable sobs shook his body.

"He told them everything," Hassan said in a tired voice. "Everything about the hijacking, about our mission, and about the other hijackings, too."

"The other hijackings?" Abu Ayad leaned forward. The lamp-light fell on the amazed expression of his lean, dark face.

"Yes. Since Ali had worked with you on the planning, he knew everything: which planes were going to be taken, which companies, which flights, where, when, who was assigned on each job."

Abu Ayad jumped to his feet. "My God!" he shouted. "You mean to say that the Israelis knew everything about the hijack projects in advance? They knew we were after El Al, TWA, Pan Am, Swissair? And the exact dates and hours?"

"Yes," Hassan replied.

Abu Ayad clawed at his face with rage. "My God!" he said again. "They knew it—and they didn't do anything! They just protected their own plane. And they sent a diplomatic pouch with a plane that they knew was going to be hijacked and brought to Zarqa!"

He rushed to go out of the hut, then stopped at the threshold. "Say your prayers, Ali," he said in a voice heavy with hatred. "You traitor. We'll kill you like a dog."

Two hours later a phone rang in the Soviet embassy in Beirut.

"I have something to report," said a voice in English with a strong Arab accent.

In Moscow, General Yulin looked, mesmerized, at the cable that had just been brought to him. He read it once, then read it again. "So they knew," he said slowly. "Do you get it, Timosheev? They knew everything!"

His deputy stared at him, bewildered.

"And I was right from the beginning." Yulin ran trembling fingers through his sparse silver hair. There was no triumph in his voice. "I felt it. Everything was a plant, Timosheev! Everything. They planted that letter about Gonen in the pouch, and they planted the pouch aboard

that plane. They wanted us to get Gonen. They pushed
him into our hands. And we fell for it like idiots!"

Timosheev was grateful that Yulin didn't directly ac-
cuse him of the blunder.

"What do you intend to do, Lev Ivanovich?"

"You will see." Yulin regained his composure quickly.
He buzzed the intercom. "I am returning to France. Immediately. Have a special plane ready." He muttered under his breath, "Now we'll get some results!"

The "nice, quiet place" of Gonen's friends on the
French Riviera was actually a magnificent villa in Cava-
laire-sur-Mer, about nine miles southwest of Saint-Tropez.
The two-story white residence was surrounded by thickets
of exotic trees, spreading their luxurious foliage under the
benign rays of the September sun. Fresh, pleasant
fragrances emanated from patches of rose bushes and
lavender planted on both sides of the villa entrance.
Gravel-covered paths led through lawns toward a small
bay. There was a private beach covered with soft sand
and protected from Mediterranean gales by the miniature
harbor nature had built around it. Two motorboats were
moored by a small wooden pier, which belonged to the
estate.

The house was well protected. High walls, topped with
broken glass, surrounded the estate on all sides. The
heavy iron doors that gave access to the inner drive were
kept locked, as were the two smaller gates on the paths
leading to the beach and the pier. It was a de luxe prison,
but a prison all the same.

Gonen had just finished his leisurely breakfast in the
tropical garden and walked slowly toward the house between two hedges of myrtle bushes. The last two days had
been almost amusing, with those poor Russians trying so
hard to act like polite and worldly English, Belgian, and
Canadian intelligence officers. He didn't know why they
still stuck to that fake NATO cover. They questioned him
affably about Israeli combat contingency plans, and he
parried their questions quite easily. Yet he knew very well
that this was just the beginning. Sooner or later, in an

hour, in a day, they would remove their masks, and then the most dangerous part of his mission would begin.

But right now, walking in the sun, he felt relaxed; more than that, he felt very tired. He had the sudden sensation that all the years of excitement and stress he had lived through were becoming a dead weight on his shoulders. He was still young—thirty-three—but he had been struggling and fighting, alone, all his life. He had never known his parents. He had been a two-year-old child in wartime Paris when his father and mother were arrested by the Gestapo and sent to the gas chambers. He had been saved by the Catholic concierge of their house, who had kept him hidden until the war was over. In 1947, when he was still a little boy, an uncle had taken him in an attempt to immigrate to Palestine, which was then a mandate held by the British. Their ship was intercepted by the Royal Navy, and little Joe was sent to a detention camp in Cyprus. And then came the new state of Israel, the kibbutz in the Negev, the War of Independence, and the death of his uncle. He was alone again, a youngster in a frontier kibbutz, leading a life of constant danger, where terrorist ambushes, mines exploding under the tractor wheels, sniping from across the border were daily routine. He was fourteen when he used a machine gun for the first time, during a guerrilla attack on the kibbutz. He was sixteen when his best friend was killed in an ambush laid by terrorists on the road to Beersheba. At eighteen he enlisted in the Army. It was only natural that as a member of a kibbutz, belonging to the pioneering elite that saw itself to a large extent responsible for the very survival of the state, he would go into the flying academy. He was driven by a strong ambition to succeed—and he did. When he became a pilot, he felt a sense of accomplishment for the first time in his life. But it didn't last long. His war wound in 1967, and its results, affected him deeply.

Maybe it was his passion for adventure, which he wouldn't admit even to himself, his unconscious quest for challenge, or even his instinctive patriotism that pushed him into the path of danger again. As head of the Air Force intelligence he carried out several perilous missions in Europe, in the Arab countries, in Africa. But the one he remembered best was that assignment to Lebanon, under a French cover, when he had succeeded by deft maneuvering in blowing up the ambitious Soviet plan to steal a Mirage III. Yet during that same mission he had lost his self-discipline and fallen headlong in love. Later he tried to blame himself for his love affair, which was the worst blunder a spy could make in enemy territory. But his involvement with Jenny had made him discover himself and learn that under the tough exterior of a fighter he was a vulnerable and romantic human being. By coming into his life Jenny had triggered the eruption of a potential of love and tenderness he had never suspected. Only after he knew her did he understand what it was to love and be loved. Only when she disappeared did he realize how lonely he had been all his life.

Yet the most painful and trying period in his life started after he had met her again in Washington: having to lie to her, to fool her, to cheat her in so many ways in order to carry out his mission and to build an image of a corrupted, pleasure-seeking swinger for the KGB. He had had enough of this kind of existence. This current mission was going to be his last. Once he was through, he would settle down. He was sure that Jenny would leave everything and come to live a normal life with him, without having to fight and constantly face challenges. The thought of her buoyed him. The terrible burden lifted from him, and for a little while he escaped the harsh prospect before him and let himself dwell on the pliant warmth of Jenny.

Then he emerged from his reverie. First, he told himself, he had to carry out his assignment. He stopped, lit a Swiss cheroot, and looked around him. The sun was hanging in a perfect blue sky. In the blissful quiet he could hear the humming of busy morning insects. The green fields and forest, the calm blue sea, everything seemed so peaceful. Could this really be the setting for a deadly dangerous mission on which his country's very existence might depend?

The blow on the back of his head caught him completely by surprise. Before he knew what was happening, he was knocked down by a hail of savage punches and kicks. He tried vainly to roll over, to raise his hands and protect his head from the fierce blows. There were four, all of them professionals, and they beat him with cunning cruelty. Through a sort of red curtain he saw their bulky, powerful bodies, their big hammering hands that hit viciously, everywhere; he heard their quick short breaths. They didn't exchange a word among themselves. Choking, bleeding, gasping for air, he writhed helplessly on the gravel. The last thing he saw before he passed out was the indifferent expression on their faces.

That was also the first thing that he saw later, when he came to his senses in a small, poorly lit cell in the basement of the villa. They were waiting for him, all four of them. When they noticed that he was starting to open his eyes, they got up slowly and came to him again. And again they beat him, coldly, systematically, in total silence. He didn't know whether he cried out. He probably did; the pain was unbearable. Suddenly one of the men pulled his head back by the hair and the others hit his face until it was nothing but raw bleeding flesh. He fainted again.

The second time he woke up, there was no one in the cell. He couldn't touch his swollen, bleeding face. Dried blood had formed a crust in his left eye; the other was puffed, and he could hardly see out of it. He moved his hands over his body. When he touched his right side, he felt an excruciating stab of pain. At least one of his ribs had been broken. His throat was on fire. He looked around for some water, but there was none. He was afraid to call and ask for some, lest the four come again. He lay, panting, on the cold floor. Sometime later—an hour, two hours?—the four men appeared again.

The last satanic beating made him completely lose his sense of time. His watch hadn't been broken, but when he saw the dial show ten he didn't know whether it was ten in the evening or in the morning of the next day. Suddenly he heard footsteps in the corridor. The door to his cell opened and a man came in. With agonizing effort Gonen opened his blood-covered eyelids and looked at him. He was small, dressed in an old-fashioned black suit, blue shirt, and blue tie. His wrinkled face was inscrutable.

The man stood over him. "I am General Yulin," he said in a monotone. "I am with the Soviet counterespionage. And you, Colonel Gonen, you are an Israeli spy."

Even if he had wanted to, Gonen couldn't protest. His lips were swollen, and he felt that the effort needed to open his mouth to speak was beyond him.

"We know everything," Yulin went on. "We know that you were deliberately pushed into our hands, that the letter about you was a plant, and that your secret services planted that letter in the TWA plane because they knew it was going to be hijacked. We know that you put on an act for us by drinking, gambling, and getting into debt. You intentionally worked your way into our hands. We know now that your services wanted you to supply us with false information."

Gonen began to shiver from cold and weakness.

"Why did you do it?" Yulin asked. "I warn you, we are not playing games anymore. I think that's been proved in the last twenty-four hours. That was just a start. You have a simple choice. Either you tell or we'll kill you."

The pain racked Joe Gonen's body. He closed his bloodshot eyes. "O.K.," he whispered in a croaking voice. "I'll talk now."

"That's right," the General said matter-of-factly. "We'll let you recover a little, and then we'll talk."

Eight hours later, having eaten, drunk and slept, Gonen was carried by two other unknown men to a neighboring cell and thrown on a bed. In the cell there were two chairs; one was permanently occupied by an armed guard. A bare electric bulb bathed the cell in crude light. The door opened, and Yulin came in again. Drenched in sweat from the effort, Gonen propped himself up on his elbow.

"Shall we start?" Yulin asked, and sat down. His voice was almost gentle now.

Gonen looked at the guard, a medium-built man with short-cropped hair and small blue eyes. The Russian stared fixedly at the opposite wall.

"We know quite a lot about you," Yulin continued in the same conversational tone, not waiting for an answer. "We know that before you came to Washington you were chief of Air Force intelligence."

"Yes," Gonen admitted.

"Tell me exactly what happened and why you went to Washington."

Gonen spoke slowly, very quietly. "Since the beginning of that year some dangerous leaks were detected in our Air Force. Vital, top-secret information about our potential, airfields, armament, and early warning system had reached the enemy, especially Egypt and Syria."

"How did you know that?"

"We have agents planted in the Egyptian and Syrian armies. In January they started to report that a sudden flow of intelligence about the Israeli Air Force had reached both countries."

"Did they also tell you the nature of this intelligence?"

"Yes. They had read some of the reports. We became extremely concerned. It was top-secret stuff."

"So?"

"We tried to locate the leaks and failed. We didn't succeed in discovering any suspect in a sufficiently important position who could have supplied the information to the Arab countries."

"Yes," said Yulin, "go on."

"After a while we concluded that the information was coming from the KGB."

"What made you think so?" Yulin asked sharply, his eyes narrowing.

"It was pure logic. The information was being fed simultaneously to the secret services of two countries who are in a state of confrontation with us. Both those countries have close relations with the U.S.S.R. Jordan, the third party to the conflict, and Lebanon—both pro-Western states—didn't get the information."

"It could have been that Egypt was supplying the information to Syria, or vice versa," Yulin suggested.

"No. Both countries were getting identical reports. It had to be you."

"Go on."

"I will, but may I have some tea? I can hardly hold my head up."

"Of course," Yulin said courteously. He spoke in Russian to the guard, who left the cell quickly. Then he turned back to Gonen. "Tomorrow, when you feel better, we can continue talking in the garden."

Gonen smiled bitterly. "The Shin Bet and air security started to check the assumptions that a pro-Soviet spy ring was in operation, or that even a lone operator could be on the job. We didn't find anything. We knew that after you closed your embassy in 1967, following the Six-Day War, and after your scientific mission in Jerusalem was also recalled, your activities in Israel were sensibly reduced."

The guard came back, carrying a huge mug filled to the brim with steaming tea. Gonen took it with unsteady hands. A trickle of the liquid ran down the side of his mouth and chin and dripped on the soiled collar of his shirt. He didn't bother to wipe it.

The General waited patiently for him to continue.

"We decided then to mount a counteroperation," Gonen said.

"Who is 'we'? Peled? The Commission? Be precise, please."

"Peled. He planned that one of us, someone of high rank in the Air Force, would work his way into your hands, for a double purpose. First, to feed you carefully chosen true and false information, to counter the effect of the reports of your spy, whoever he was. Peled intended to make you doubt the credibility of your agent by supplying you with different information from a more credible source."

"And second?" Yulin pressed him. He never left loose threads in a conversation.

"The second purpose was to try to deduce, from the nature of your questions, exactly what you did know and what you didn't. Later, by checking thoroughly who had access to the material you got, and by the gradual elimination of suspects, we expected to discover your source."

"Why were you chosen for the job?"

"For several reasons. First, I was former head of air intelligence, and I had a lot of experience in this kind of work."

"Yes, like Beirut, for example," Yulin interposed with a sardonic smile.

Gonen was obviously startled.

"You didn't suspect we knew that?" Yulin asked. "We also knew other things, Colonel. But don't let me interrupt you. You were saying that you were chosen for the job because of your experience."

"Yes, I was also in a very convenient position. I had just arrived in Washington, a few months earlier, as an assistant air attaché. You operate very intensively in America, so it was easy for me to be picked up there by you."

"But all this bullshit you fed us about your drinking and gambling was just bait, right?"

Gonen nodded. "Of course. We wanted to make you contact me. So I started this kind of life, the attaché wrote a letter, it was planted in the TWA plane—which we knew was going to be hijacked and for the first time brought to a terrorist-controlled field at Zarqa. We assumed that before blowing up the plane the terrorists would check the luggage, which was what happened. We further assumed that if they found something of value they would hand it over to the Russians. And indeed, once you got it, you fell for it. In Vegas you contacted me, and I started reporting."

"And if it had not worked out that way and the diplomatic pouch had really been blown up on the TWA plane?"

"Oh, that." Gonen smiled faintly. "Peled had devised

half a dozen gimmicks to force me on you. You would have gotten another letter, or something else. Don't worry, you would have found me in the end."

"Yes, I don't doubt it," the General conceded thoughtfully. "And why did you agree to come here?"

"I thought you wanted a more thorough debriefing. I was ready for that. I didn't know that you had smelled a rat."

Yulin changed the subject. "So you say that all the information, all those weekly reports we were getting from you, were false?"

"No. I told you it was a mélange of true and false information."

"Very well. We have all your reports here." Yulin looked at his watch. "You'll eat now and go to sleep. In five hours we'll wake you and you'll go over all those reports with one of my men. You'll tell him exactly what was false and what was true."

Gonen didn't react.

"By the way," Yulin said when he got up to leave, "did your people succeed in locating the source of the leak?"

For the first time Gonen hesitated. But he didn't—and couldn't—grasp the terrible significance of the question. "I think so, yes. My superiors decided that the leak was outside of the country, and that you were getting your information from a source friendly to Israel, which had access to classified reports concerning our Air Force. We thought you got it from an American agent in the present U.S. Administration."

Yulin didn't comment, but left the cell briskly. He mounted the stairs to the ground floor of the villa, crossed the spacious hall, and entered a small room with a writing desk, a telephone, and a narrow bed. He reached for the telephone. "Call Poliakov," he said.

The man Gonen had known as George Mackenzie came into the room.

"The Israelis suspect that we have a source in America who keeps us informed about their Air Force," Yulin told him. "That means we have to take care of Jenny Bacall.

The Israelis have come too close. If she talks, she might endanger our people in the U.S."

"Take care? How do you mean, General?"

Yulin's expression didn't change, neither did his cool, detatched voice.

"Kill her," he said.

17

October 1 - October 4, 1973

No hint about the death sentence pronounced on Jenny Bacall reached the prisoner in the villa in Cavalaire. He was interrogated day and night by various teams. Following each period of questioning he ate, then slept for several hours, after which he was awakened and questioned again. He was sure his food and drink were drugged, because he felt sleepy most of the time. But his memory was good. His power of resistance seemed to be destroyed, and they didn't torture him anymore. Yulin used a classic, extremely effective method of getting his compliance: first, break the prisoner, bring him to the verge of death; then be kind and gentle, let him feel grateful. The mixture of terror and gratitude was a sure prescription for success.

When the General came to see him for the second time, Gonen was slowly recovering. He had climbed the staircase to the ground floor, helped by one of the Russians, and had limped, leaning on his shoulder, to an easy chair they had set for him in the sun. One guard brought him breakfast—coffee, toast, and cheese. He estimated that there were fifteen to twenty people in the villa, which gave him an idea of the tremendous importance somebody in Moscow attached to his interrogation.

Yulin brought an upright chair for himself and sat close to him. He had taken off his jacket, and in a short-sleeved white shirt he looked frail and harmless. That is, when he wasn't looking straight into the eyes of his prisoner, for in those small blue-gray eyes burned a frightening will power.

"Today we shall talk about a different matter," he began, and leaned forward. His voice was low, as if he didn't want to be overheard by the three guards who were sitting about twenty feet away, their silencer-equipped revolvers ready on their laps. "What do you know about the Marsa raid?" he asked.

Gonen didn't answer immediately. "What raid?"

Yulin's face flushed with anger. "Don't try to gain time. I know the game too well. I asked what do you know about the Marsa raid?"

"I know it was an operation organized by the Air Force to steal a radar station in Egypt, in January, 1972."

"You know more than that. You took part in that raid. You were head of air intelligence at the time."

Gonen was shaken. "Who told you I was there?"

"We know it," Yulin snapped. "And don't forget that I'm interrogating you, not the other way around."

"Yes, I was there." There was no use pretending.

"I believe you personally inspected every piece of machinery and every document that you captured."

"Yes."

"So you know the character of the installation."

"I do."

"Describe it."

Gonen breathed deeply. "Marsa was a purely Russian base. The equipment we found on the spot was an installation for the control and guidance of intermediate-range ballistic missiles."

"Did you find out what the targets of the missiles were?"

"Yes. We found some documents indicating that the missiles were aimed at the principal oil-producing countries in the Middle East. At the time we captured Marsa, the missiles had not been installed. We estimated that it would take you at least two or three years to complete the buildup."

"You speak about documents. What documents did you see?"

"I am sorry, General. I don't read Russian, and the matter wasn't in my domain anyway. All I can tell you is that I remember, very vaguely, seeing the translations of one or two top-secret documents."

"What kind of documents were they? Try to remember."

Gonen shrugged. "I can't, I don't remember." He hesitated. "All I saw was some report about your general project. It dealt with your threat to the oil-producing Arab countries. I remember that it was linked in some way with a military revolt in Egypt, called 'The Blue Night.' Could that be exact?"

Yulin's expression was enigmatic. "Go on," he said.

"There was a document about the missile installations, with a lot of code words and numbers." Gonen's tone was uncertain. "Some of the code words struck me as peculiar: 'Young comsomol, Red guard, Cossack of the Don, Crimean Tartars . . .' It was marked 'top secret.' "

"Was it signed?" the General asked eagerly.

"I think so, yes," Gonen answered slowly, and then closed his eyes. Then he said, "Belagov or Blaranov. Could it be? It was a general."

"Maybe Blagonravov?" Yulin was suddenly excited.

He thought a moment. "Blagonravov? Yes, that might be the name. General Blagonravov."

General Blagonravov, in light summer uniform, alighted from his desert-yellow Russian jeep. It was late afternoon, and a cool, refreshing wind was blowing from the east on the Soviet air base at Kabrit, in Egypt, close to the Suez Canal. Blagonravov looked appraisingly at the huge new hangar that had been built at the far end of the north-south runway. He knew that from the air it appeared to be identical to six other hangars that had been skillfully dispersed over the camp. It seemed perfectly normal that one of the maintenance hangars would be placed close to the runways. A large area in front of the hangar had been recently covered with asphalt. Blagonravov walked over it. At an equal distance from the hangar's gigantic iron gates—about three hundred yards—five white crosses had been painted on the tarmac, forming a sort of large crescent. The distances between the crosses were also equal—about one hundred and fifty yards. A big sign, NO ENTRY, in Russian and Arabic, was painted over the hangar, but it was not strictly enforced. About fifty Russian soldiers, naked from the waist up, were feverishly running in and out of the hangar. They carried crates and boxes into several trucks that waited beside the gates, engines running.

A small, wiry major jumped to attention in front of Blagonravov. "At your orders, Comrade General."

"At ease," Blagonravov said calmly, and with deliberate gestures filled his pipe with tobacco and lit it attentively. He blew at the spent match and put it back in the matchbox he carried in a zippered compartment of his tobacco pouch. "What is our situation, Major Koritin?"

"Everything is ready, Comrade General. We are in full combat readiness."

Two Soviet-made MIG-21 fighters, painted with Egyptian colors, landed in close succession on the east-west runway. Koritin followed them with his eyes.

"Ours?" Blagonravov asked.

"Yes, Comrade General. Routine evening patrol. For two weeks no Egyptian soldiers or pilots have been admitted to the base."

"And before? Didn't they ask questions about the hangar?"

"They never came near the hangar. We took care of that."

"And the underground command post?"

"Neither. Security regulations were followed to the letter."

"Good." Blagonravov looked at his watch. "Well, I just received confirmation from the bases at Matruh, Luxor, and Aswan that they also have completed preparations. I think it's time to check all that."

"Yes, Comrade," Koritin replied, but his hesitant manner indicated that he didn't understand what the General had in mind.

"What I mean is a surprise emergency combat drill, carried out in all the bases simultaneously. I want to check timing. Come with me."

With wide strides he marched to his jeep, Koritin hurrying behind him. On the right front seat of the jeep, beside the driver, a soldier was listening to a communication set.

"Get me the command post," Blagonravov ordered. He darted a cursory glance at the soldiers who had finished loading the trucks and were now putting on their shirts and exhaustedly climbing into the automobiles.

"Command post, Comrade General," the young soldier said, and handed Blagonravov a telephone receiver.

"Novikov? . . . Blagonravov here. Listen to me. In three minutes—surprise emergency drill. Combat readiness of all Aurora components in all our bases. You alert Kabrit by sirens, according to standing instructions. Call the other bases immediately on the scrambler phone and order them to perform the same drill simultaneously. Have them report progress and timing. . . . What code is in use today?"

"Yellow code, Comrade General." The voice came with a metallic echo.

"I'll join you immediately after execution, to check timing. Synchronize watches. I have exactly five seventeen."

"Five seventeen, Comrade. . . . Yes, Comrade. . . . Three minutes. Emergency drill. All bases. Scrambler phone. Sirens."

"Right. Execution."

"We have nothing to do now but wait," Blagonravov said, and climbed into the back seat of his jeep. He immediately stood up again and pointed, shouting, "Hey, what's that?"

A lone figure on a motorcycle appeared at the far end of the runway. The man wore a helmet and was bent over his machine as it rushed toward them at break-neck speed.

"Get that idiot off the runway!" Blagonravov yelled. "He'll ruin everything!" He waved frantically to the rider to clear the runway, but in vain. The roaring machine headed straight for them. It came to a brake-screeching stop barely three yards from the jeep. A soldier wearing sergeant's stripes jumped from the bike, propped it on its support, and ran to the jeep.

"What the hell—" Blagonravov started heatedly, but the sergeant snapped to attention and produced a sealed blue envelope. "Comrade General, urgent cable. Top priority."

Blagonravov, a little confused, took the envelope and started to open it. "Yes," he said, "thank you. Move your machine aside, there behind the jeep."

At that instant the alarm sirens all over the base burst into an ear-piercing wail. "Now we'll see some action." Blagonravov chuckled and absently put the cable in his pocket. "Check timing, Koritin," he ordered. "It's exactly five twenty now."

A low whine came from the hangar, and the giant steel doors slowly started to move in opposite directions, creating a large, ever widening gap.

"That's the emergency crew inside; two people. Fifty-five seconds," Koritin said. "Good work."

Blagonravov stared into the dark interior of the hangar, beyond the moving doors, but couldn't see anything. Koritin caught his glance. "You can't see, Comrade General. Because of security regulations the operational part of the hangar is concealed by a metal partition. It will start moving only after the outward gates are opened."

"Yes, of course," Blagonravov agreed. The large steel gates opened now. Another low sound, of a different kind, came from inside. The far wall of the hangar seemed to be moving in the darkness.

"That's it." Koritin pointed. "Interior partition."

Dark monstrous shapes could be seen at the far end of the hangar, covered with cloth. "Tarpaulin inside covers," Koritin recited happily. "They will be automatically lifted by separate winches, installed over each unit." Indeed, the big pieces of cloth spread over the equipment were slowly shrinking and being carried up by barely visible cables. The light-colored pieces of cloth, swaying in the blackness, looked like a giant grotesque ghost dancing.

Five jeeps and one station wagon darted along the runway, went around the hangar, and could be heard stopping behind. After several seconds running footsteps were heard on the concrete floor of the hangar.

"The crews," Blagonravov said, and looked at his watch again. "Ten minutes. Not so good."

"Message from command post, Comrade General," said the soldier manning the transceiver. "Colonel Novikov reports that the command post is in full combat readiness. The guidance and control station at Ras Banas is warming up the equipment. The station at Sidi Barrani reports technical malfunctioning."

Blagonravov nodded. Inside the first dry coughing of a starter was heard, then a second, a third; the rest drowned in the roar of heavy engines.

"Two minutes' regular warming up," Koritin said. "Then they'll start coming out."

"Radar ready, communications ready, television monitors ready, communications check positive," the radio operator chanted.

On the runway more and more cars were coming, two stopping at the regulation distance of fifteen hundred yards, others rushing to the hangars, some unloading equipment and soldiers at various points. Several half-tracks climbed on the low hills on both sides of the base. Koritin announced, "Emergency crews for the anti-aircraft guns."

Blagonravov looked at his watch. "That's very bad, Koritin. Fourteen minutes. It means that until now the base was without protection."

"These are only emergency crews, Comrade General." Koritin was disconcerted. "The regular crews man other positions and are ready to function around the clock."

"Skeleton crews," Blagonravov said with contempt. "They couldn't stop a fly."

Inside the hangar the engines roared. "They're coming, General," Koritin shouted excitedly. "Fifteen minutes."

In the dark hangar blinding lights suddenly blazed. The earth trembled slightly, or so it seemed. And then slowly, clumsily, the first monster appeared in the sunlight, an enormous truck moving on sixteen giant wheels, pulling a heavy trailer behind it. Over the automobile, its sharp warhead boldly pointing forward, loomed the huge cylindrical body of an SS-14 missile. The heavy truck gently turned to the right, slowed down, and came to a stop, standing with its front wheels on the transverse bar of the first white cross. One after another, like prehistoric monsters emerging from their lair, four other missiles mounted on trucks appeared in the entrance of the hangar. Each one was pulled to a white cross. In less than two minutes the five trailers were in place.

"Operational position now," Blagonravov murmured to himself. He looked with satisfaction at the steel monsters. "We have to note in the drill report that we didn't take into account the fifty-five minutes needed for arming and mounting of the nuclear warheads," he said quietly to Koritin, who hurriedly scribbled a note on his pad.

A new, different kind of rattle emanated from the engines of the missile-bearing trucks. Slowly the erectors—the built-in hydraulic cranes—started to raise the missiles into a vertical position. It was a sight both beautiful and terrifying at the same time. Like five fingers of a giant hand the needle-shaped heavy missiles rose and stood still, pointing at the sky.

"Magnificent!" Blagonravov exclaimed. "Just magnificent. How long?"

"Eighteen minutes and a half," Koritin reported.

"To the command post now, quick!" he said to the driver. The small jeep whirled around and moved beside the steel monsters like a tiny, helpless bug running between the feet of big animals. The jeep darted southward along the runway, and after about two thousand yards turned right on a narrow lateral asphalt strip that led to a large concrete and steel bunker. Only a short part of the structure was protruding over earth level. Most of it was underground. General Blagonravov nimbly jumped from the jeep and ran past the armed guard, down the staircase. He swept past a second guard and pushed a button by a heavy steel door that bore the inscription in Russian: WAR ROOM—ENTRY FORBIDDEN WITHOUT SPECIAL AUTHORIZATION.

Somebody checked him from the inside through a

peephole in the door. He entered a large room, bustling with activity. In the middle of the room, brightly lit by clusters of neon lamps hanging from the low ceiling, stood a large table on which stood an enormous relief map of the Middle East. Trajectories leading from Kabrit, Matruh, Luxor, and Aswan to Libya, Saudi Arabia, and the oil states in the Persian Gulf were marked with broken blue and red lines on the map. Various circles, triangles, and lozenges represented radar coverage, ground-to-air missile protection, ranges of planes and missiles from various bases. Small, shining glass dots at the important points of the map showed it could be operated electrically. And indeed, at that very moment Luxor, Aswan, Kabrit, Rãs Bãnas, and Matruh started to pulsate in green and red lights. Sidi Barrani remained dead.

"Sidi Barrani still malfunctioning?" Blagonravov turned angrily to Colonel Novikov, who was bent over a paper map and reporting some bearings. He wore a set of earphones and didn't hear the question.

Sergeants and officers were scurrying around. Along two walls of the war room stood a pair of long, narrow worktables. On the wall in front of them hung several field telephones. The tables were covered with maps and documents. Outlets for the earphone plugs were conveniently installed by each chair. Over the tables were two rows of television monitors. They were all functioning, but only five, at the right far end, transmitted a picture— that of the five missiles standing on alert at Kabrit. At the far end of the room a small computer was humming. Several series of green numbers and equations were running on its small television-like screens. Two engineers were manipulating the switches and writing down some of the numbers on note pads.

Novikov took off his earphones, got up, and came to Blagonravov. He was a young man with sharp eyes. "I think everything is ready, General," he said, raising his voice to be heard. "Matruh just reported combat readiness. All in all, twenty-seven minutes. Sidi Barrani still has some trouble, and in Aswan two of the trailers didn't move. They're taking them apart now. They have twelve missiles there."

"What about television monitoring?" Blagonravov indicated the dead screens.

"I didn't want to activate our TV transmitters," Novikov said apologetically. "This is only a drill, and I didn't want to jeopardize the whole project. The Egyptians might intercept the transmissions. It's too risky. We're getting all the necessary information by phone."

"All right," Blagonravov said, and sighed, releasing all the tension that had built up in him. "Considering the conditions, it's very good, Comrade Novikov. About half an hour to prepare for operation is quite a reasonable time. If the order is given, we can fire right away, can't we?"

"We could have even earlier, General. In Kabrit, here, and in Luxor, missiles have been on the launching pads for four minutes now."

"Very well. You can sound relief. Summon the men later to the large dining room and tell them I am proud of them. Good job, Novikov."

The colonel's young face blushed with pleasure. He snapped to attention. "Serving the Soviet Union, Comrade."

Blagonravov smiled, amused. "Come on, come on, stop that. We're adults here, not military students."

He turned toward the exit and fumbled in his pocket for his pipe. His fingers found the envelope he had received before the drill started. From it he took a thin blue piece of paper and looked at it. Then he stopped, thunderstruck. His face became ashen. He swayed and collapsed into a chair.

The cable had been dispatched to him from his Moscow office in red code—an unusual precaution. It was classified TOP SECRET—FOR YOUR EYES ONLY. The priority was also unusual: TOP EMERGENCY. He figured that the telegram had been sent with his name to his office. His assistants had added just one line before coding it again and transmitting it to Egypt: GENERAL BLAGONRA-

VOV FOLLOWING TEXT URGENT TOP-PRIORITY CABLE RECEIVED OCTOBER 3 1235.

The cable itself read:

ISRAELI TOP RELIABLE SOURCE REPORTS CAPTURE AT MARSA RAID JANUARY 1972 TOP-SECRET DOCUMENT PROBABLY SIGNED BY YOUR HAND. DOCUMENT CARRIED VALUABLE INFORMATION AURORA AND SEVERAL CODE WORDS QUOTE: YOUNG COMSOMOL—RED GUARD—COSSACK OF THE DON—CRIMEAN TARTARS UNQUOTE. ALL OUR INQUIRIES AT LOWER ECHELONS YOUR SERVICES ABOUT THAT DOCUMENT BROUGHT NEGATIVE RESULTS. YOUR URGENT COOPERATION NECESSARY TO ESTABLISH NATURE AND IMPORTANCE CAPTURED DOCUMENT. ISRAELI SOURCE NOW IN OUR HANDS COOPERATES WILLINGLY. PLEASE CABLE ANSWER TO TOP PRIORITY. SIGNED YULIN DIRECTOR EIGHTH DEPARTMENT FIRST CHIEF DIRECTORATE KGB.

A coded address for the answer followed.

Blagonravov slowly got up from the chair and walked out. He noticed the puzzled looks of the soldiers and officers in the war room who had witnessed his sudden weakness, but that wasn't important. They would certainly attribute it to his old age or to his excitement connected with the drill. He climbed the steps and walked away from the bunker and from his waiting jeep. The burning red African sun was starting to set in the west. The dry desert sand crunched under his feet. He tried to think, to overcome the terrible fear that had suddenly paralyzed his brain when his eyes had focused on the code name "Cossack of the Don." He shivered in his summer uniform. Slowly, painfully, he succeeded in gaining control over his emotions and put some order in his thoughts. Of course, there had never been any document he had signed. There had never been any code names like the Crimean Tartars or the Young Comsomol. They were just a part of the setup, of some cunning, devilish plan to convey to him the message, "Cossack of the Don, we know about you. We need you. We want you to report for duty." It all boiled down to that. They had him, after almost thirty years. He didn't know how, but the Israelis had succeeded in unearthing the truth about him. And they had found a way, by using Yulin himself, to order him to appear.

He thought for a second—just for a second—of the heavy Tokarev service revolver he kept in his drawer. But he dismissed the thought immediately. It was too early—or too late—for that. He had to play the game until the very end. Maybe there was still hope. From the cable it was clear that Yulin didn't know what it was all about. The Israeli source was the only one who knew. So there was only one thing he could do.

He beckoned his radio operator. "Rush to communications and cable this message to that address," he said. "Red code. Top priority."

He scribbled on the envelope: "Arriving immediately to question source. Inform urgently care of military attaché, Cairo, where the source is." He signed, "Blagonravov."

Half an hour later he took off on a special plane for Cairo. He intended to call the office of the military attaché from the airport. He would have his answer by then.

At dawn on October 4 his chartered plane—he wanted to avoid flying in a Soviet military aircraft—landed at the international airport of Nice-Côte d'Azur. He came down from the Mystère 20 wearing civilian clothes. Two people waited for him. They accompanied him to a car parked outside.

In Tel-Aviv a phone call awakened Peled. It was his deputy, Avivi. "We just got a call from the night shift man at Nice Airport," he reported. "Your Cossack just arrived. He looked very much in a hurry."

The Old Man smiled contentedly.

18

October 4, 1973

Jeremiah Peled returned the telephone receiver to its cradle, threw aside the thin woolen blanket, and got up from his bed, wearing only the shorts of his summer pajamas. He loved the warm, dry October nights and welcomed the new grayness of dawn that colored the open window. A cool, gentle wind blew in the morning air, scented with the delicate perfume of orange leaves.

When he had dressed and eaten a meager breakfast, he walked out through the gracious french doors. The beautiful garden was still shrouded by the early morning mist, which bestowed upon it an illusion of enchantment and unreality. This place was his secret joy. This voluptuous composition of green lawns, thickets of five-year-old trees, rose bushes and bright colored flower beds was his design and the work of his own hands. He wandered among the orange trees, carefully picking a broken twig, a fallen leaf, letting the cool freshness of the new day caress his warm skin.

A sweet feeling of fulfillment, so long doubted, started to rise within him as he continued to walk beside his beloved flowers and changed to exultation. After all, his plan, so meticulously prepared and executed, had borne its first fruits. He had succeeded in introducing Gonen into one of the nerve centers of Soviet power. To establish his credibility in the eyes of General Yulin he had blown his cover at the right moment. Joe had taken over according to their plan and must have convincingly simulated a total breakdown. By an ingeniously planned "confession" he must have then established the crucial contact with General Blagonravov, the "Cossack of the Don." The hurried appearance of the General at Nice International Airport en route to Cavalaire proved that Joe had flawlessly carried out his part so far. In a few hours, maybe at this very moment, Blagonravov was going to meet him and talk, for he had no other choice. He would be blackmailed into disclosing all the details of the Egyptian project—and Gonen would convey them to Israel.

Of course, the KGB knew about the list that had belonged to Heinrich Roehm. Of course, the KGB expected a contact. But it would never guess how that contact between the agent of the Mossad and Gehlen's dormant spy was actually made. Instead the Soviet secret services were busy running hither and yon, exactly as he had planned.

Swarms of KGB operators were earnestly checking every inch in the elephant trails the smoke-screen commando of former Mossad agents was leaving through the Soviet bloc. The Old Man chuckled when he recalled the report sent by Jacob Barnea, the first of his men to return from Moscow. He had driven his KGB shadow to despair by roaming through the Soviet capital, making telephone calls at random, talking to people in the streets, in parks, in sidewalk cafés. Similar reports were coming from the men Peled had sent to Kiev, Odessa, Leningrad, Sofia, and Berlin. In a few days the last of them was due back in Israel. As he had anticipated, the Russians hadn't bothered them, concentrating exclusively on the people they had contacted.

The only operation that hadn't yielded any results yet was the attempt to discover the identity of Minerva. Since last November four of his best men—Dori, Brandt, David Ron, and Professor Joseph Heller—had been engaged in a febrile search, all over Europe, for a clue that could lead them to Gehlen's man in Moscow. They had interviewed scores of specialists, scholars, Sovietologists, historians, world-famous authorities on Russia and on World War II. They had spent months in research and documentation centers in Germany, England, France, Austria, and Switzerland. They had spoken to former Abwehr officers, to Russian defectors, to the leaders of numerous Russian émigré associations. But up to this moment it had all been fruitless. Minerva remained a mystery.

Well, Peled sighed, while lovingly examining the glistening new leaf of a baby palm tree, you can't have it all, Old Man. Minerva might be dead, retired, or so ingeniously camouflaged that we couldn't unmask him in fifty years. And anyway, once we got Blagonravov, Minerva's identity didn't really matter. One source of Blagonravov's caliber was enough.

He made a mental note to recall the Minerva team from Europe. His current operation, patiently mounted and executed, piece by piece, over two years, would be over in twenty-four hours. At the final curtain he would rather have all his men home. He would find some kind words to say to the Minerva men. They certainly did all they could. They didn't obtain any results, but then they didn't commit any blunders, either. That was real undercover work: you try hard, you build watertight covers, you plan daring operations, you extend your sensors boldly, you raise your antennae, you risk the lives of your closest friends. Most times you fail, but sometime, somewhere, somebody breaks through, and there lies success. On this pleasant, serene morning Peled felt at peace with himself. The final success of the operation was almost in the palm of his hand. Without any apparent reason he kept repeating to himself that old cliché, "Everything is proceeding according to plan."

He was wrong.

At this very moment his sophisticated, cunning operation was being blown to bits.

A week earlier Lavrenti Karpin had been ordered to Paris.

Since last June the Chief of Operations of the Eighth Department (Middle East), KGB, had been striving to carry out the most frustrating operation of his career: to pick up the trail of the Israeli agents connected with the Roehm list. Until now it had been one failure after another. In Bern the traces of the old gentleman who had recovered the list from the Swiss bank led to a cul-de-sac.

Informers of the Soviet secret services in Paris, Bonn, and Rome didn't know anything about a secret Israeli operation. Close shadowing of Israelis who were definitely connected with the Mossad yielded no positive results. Karpin had the impression that the Israelis were observing strict compartmentalization rules and their resident agents in Europe didn't know a thing.

About a month ago he thought he had gotten a break. The Frankfurt station had reported that a so-called American journalist visited the headquarters of the Narodny-Trudovoy Soyouz (People's Labor League), a Russian émigré association. Because of the violent anti-Soviet activity of the NTS it was closely watched by KGB agents. The journalist, they reported, had asked many questions about the leaders of the movement left behind in the Soviet Union and operating underground. He hadn't been satisfied with the answers he received and had left the office quite disappointed. An immediate check established that he had never stayed in the hotel he mentioned. But he didn't show again, and all trace of him disappeared.

A week later another hope had glimmered and then faded. On the night of September 9 unknown persons had tried to break into the offices of the Organization of Ukrainian Nationalists, in Munich. OUN was an anticommunist group of Ukrainian separatists who dreamed of establishing an independent Ukrainian state. Ukrainian independence was not a new idea. During World War II thousands of Ukrainians had collaborated enthusiastically with the invading German armies. Many of them had joined the division of traitors, commanded by General Vlassov, who fought on the Nazi side against the Red Army. After the war a great number of Ukrainians holding important positions in the government had been unmasked as German spies, summarily tried, and executed by the NKVD. Nevertheless, a powerful undergound organization, led by Stefan Bandera, successfully fought against the communists until 1947. When the underground was crushed, most of its leaders, including Bandera, succeeded in fleeing to the West. They had undoubtedly been aided by highly placed accomplices. In the late fifties the KGB once again became very worried about the subversive activities of the revived Ukrainian underground in the Soviet Union, which was controlled from Munich. A specially trained assassin of Department V, Bogdan Stashinsky, was sent to Germany to take care of the heads of the OUN. Using an infernal weapon, a noiseless, hydrogen-cyanide gun, he murdered OUN ideologist Lev Rebet on October 12, 1957, on the stairway of his office building. On October 15, 1959, he killed the head of the organization, Stefan Bandera. Since then the Moscow center kept a close watch on Ukrainian activity. The KGB even succeeded in planting its agents in the various branches of OUN in Western Europe.

It was the KGB's resident agent in Paris who urgently requested that Lavrenti Karpin come to France the previous week. They had met, following strict conspiracy rules, in the bustling Hotel Meridien, on the avenue Gouvion Saint-Cyr, where the resident retained a two-room suite under an assumed name.

When he was alone with Karpin, the resident told him, "I want you to meet somebody." He opened the door to the adjoining room and admitted a thin, shabby, miserable-looking man, who seemed nervous and frightened. He was quite aged, bald, and wore wire-rimmed round spectacles on his emaciated face. "This is Ilya Zelenev," the resident said. "He is one of our men here. He is Ukrainian. I want him to tell you a story."

Zelenev had furtive eyes and a low, shy voice. "I have been in Paris since 1958," he said. "Formerly I worked as an undercover agent for the Kiev section of the Nationality direction of the Fifth Directorate. In 1958, I was sent here by the Eighth Directorate to penetrate the Ukrainian émigré organization. I managed to work my way to the top of the OUN. Since 1964, I have been working as publishing director of the bimonthly magazine *L'Ukraine Libre*. This is the organ of the OUN in France. Its offices are conveniently housed in the same apartment where the OUN has its Paris headquarters. The address is 37, rue de Grenelle. I have free access to all the OUN documents, and I know all its secrets."

He coughed nervously and continued, "Yesterday, when I was alone in the office with Nikolai Volodin, the chairman of the Ukrainian anti-communists, we were visited by two men. I can give you their description if it's needed. One of them spoke fluent French, the other didn't say a word. They showed us their credentials." He glanced rapidly at a crumpled piece of paper he had produced from his breast pocket. "They were Georges d'Arbois and Michel Azeau, both from the Service de Documentation Extérieure et de Contre Espionnage. That, you know, is their secret service. D'Arbois spoke very bluntly and asked for information about people we had still in Russia—in the Ukraine or in Moscow. He said that we were mere guests in this country, and we were allowed to stay and carry on our activities thanks to the hospitality of the French Government. The French Government now needed, in return, the names and addresses of our top people who were still living in the Soviet Union. Volodin, our chairman, refused, of course. D'Arbois said then that if we didn't comply they'd close the paper, disband the OUN, and expel us from France. I tried to gain time. I said that most of our papers were not here, but in our headquarters, in Munich. I explained that on leaving Russia, Bandera had taken with him many important documents about our network there, but everything was kept in our secret archives in Munich, and to get copies we would need a few days. D'Arbois said then that they would come back tomorrow."

"So?" Karpin looked at the resident, baffled. "This doesn't prove anything. Nothing to do with me, anyway."

"Oh, yes, it does," said the Russian. He waved Zelenev to the other room, and after he had closed the door behind him continued eagerly, "I have good contacts in the French secret services. We have a man quite high up in the SDECE." He smiled proudly. "He informed me that no Georges d'Arbois or Michel Azeau ever worked for them, and that French intelligence had never tried to ob-

tain any information about the secret leaders of the
Ukrainian underground in the Soviet Union."

"Yes, I see now," Karpin conceded. He walked to the
window, pulled the transparent curtain aside, and
thoughtfully looked at the huge Concorde-Lafayette Hotel
on the other side of the narrow avenue. "So it must be
our Jewish friends again. They are frantically looking for
information about some Ukrainian underground leaders
who might still be in the Soviet Union. They tried to get
information from the NTS in Frankfurt; then they tried to
break into OUN headquarters in Munich. They failed. So
they try the Paris end now."

"But why Ukrainians?" the resident asked.

Karpin knew he could speak freely to this man. "The
Israelis might have learned that some Ukrainian leaders
had spied for Germany during the war." Then he suddenly smiled. "Never mind," he said briskly. "What we
need now is a nice, friendly talk with those two fellows.
Will you call Zelenev back?"

The sad-looking little man was admitted into the room
again. Karpin gazed at him intently. "Could you manage
to keep your chairman, what's his name—"

"Volodin," Zelenev replied quickly.

"Volodin, yes. Could you keep him away from the office when the two SDECE men come again?"

Zelenev thought for several moments. "Yes," he said finally. "I could convince him to stay home, pretending to
have a cold. I'll tell him that if he doesn't show we could
gain another few days from the French."

"Good." Karpin was pleased. "You'll be alone in the
office, then."

Zelenev nodded.

"When did you say they were coming back?"

"Tomorrow evening," Zelenev answered. "At six."

"Tomorrow at six," Karpin repeated. "Very well. We'll
be there."

It wasn't five yet, but the dark clouds hanging over
Paris had plunged the city into a premature night. Sudden
gusts of wind were splattering heavy raindrops on the

gray walls of the rue de Grenelle. The narrow sidewalks were slippery, and the pedestrians, their heads lowered, were hurrying along, irritated by this first encounter with the typical Parisian autumn.

At the intersection of the rue de Grenelle and rue Saint-Guillaume the brightly lit corner café Chez Basile was bustling with life and cheerfulness, in contrast to the gloomy wet darkness outside. The rue Saint-Guillaume had become famous all over the world as a synonym for "Sciences-Po," the Faculty of Political Sciences of the University of Paris, housed in two inconspicuous buildings facing each other. For fifty years Sciences-Po had produced some of the most brilliant French and foreign political leaders, journalists, and diplomats. On October 1 studies had resumed. Crowds of young students, chatting and laughing, were streaming into Chez Basile for a quick "demi" of draught beer or a strong Italian espresso before their next class.

No one paid any attention to a man of about forty-five who came in through the Saint-Guillaume entrance, ordered a *ballon* of beaujolais, and took his glass to the far end of the counter, in front of the large windows overlooking the rue de Grenelle. He unfolded a fresh copy of the latest edition of *Le Monde* and concentrated on the front-page articles, apparently oblivious to the noise and laughter around him. Actually, he didn't pay any attention to the newspaper. He was carefully observing the entrance of 37, rue de Grenelle, across the narrow street. The man was David Ron, one of the Minerva team of the Mossad. His assignment tonight was routine: to cover the entrance of the building, where two of his colleagues, Brandt and Heller, posing as French intelligence agents, had an appointment at six.

Half an hour later another Minerva member, Raphael Dori, entered the café. He was sweating profusely and scowling. For forty-five minutes he had circled around in his rented Renault 16, looking for a parking place. It had been very frustrating. The rue de Grenelle and the rue Saint-Guillaume were both one-way streets, jammed with students' cars parked on the sidewalks and at pedestrian crossings. Dori couldn't afford to park illegally, although he intended to remain in the car. In no case could he take the risk of being questioned by a policeman, or of getting a traffic ticket, which would record the presence of his car. Eventually he found a space in the rue Saint-Guillaume, very close to Chez Basile. Now as he entered the café he looked around, brushed past Ron, who glanced at him indifferently, and went back to his car. He sat inside, in the darkness, waiting patiently. Everything seemed normal.

Neither Ron nor Dori noticed the two cars, a blue Peugeot 404 and a powerful gray Mercedes 300, parked farther down on the rue de Grenelle. In each of the cars there were three men, all of them members of Lavrenti Karpin's operational team. Ron and Dori also couldn't know that since the early afternoon Karpin and three more of his men had secretly entered the offices of the anti-communist Ukrainian organization. The building at 37, rue de Grenelle was a low structure of three floors, all of them used for offices. The OUN office, on the second floor, had its windows on the back, overlooking a small yard. In the late afternoon most of the other offices were deserted. By six there was no one in the building. At precisely 6 P.M., Brandt and Heller walked inside.

David Ron watched his two friends until they disappeared into the dark entrance. They climbed the worn wooden steps of the old French house in silence. Reaching the second floor, Heller turned to the left. A cheap brass sign, in French and Russian, was fixed on the big oak door. It read, ORGANIZATION OF UKRAINIAN NATIONALISTS, and under it, in smaller type, UKRAINE LIBRE—RÉDACTION GÉNÉRALE. Heller knocked on the door. It was almost immediately opened. Zelenev, one of the men they had met here the day before yesterday, bowed ceremoniously. "Please come in, messieurs," he said in heavily accented French, and moved aside to let them enter. His mouth was twitching nervously. They walked in through the poorly lit corridor into a large, shabbily furnished office. Heller entered first, and turned toward the man who was sitting behind the old oak desk in the middle of the room.

And then, all of a sudden, he realized that something was wrong. The man behind the desk wasn't the same one they had met here two days ago. A thousand tiny bells of alarm screamed in his head even before he saw the heavy Mauser in the man's hand pointed at him, even before the edge of his eye caught the swift movement at the door on his right and another man appeared. "Attention!" he yelled in Hebrew, simultaneously turning on his heels and flinging himself toward the dark corridor and safety. But he knew instinctively that it was too late, that it wouldn't work, and oh God, he wasn't even armed. Somebody leaped on him and hit him on the back of the neck, his legs buckled, and he collapsed. Before he lost consciousness, he heard Brandt's footsteps running toward the exit door, and then the familiar plop of the silenced gun and the heavy thump of a body on the wooden floor, and everything went black.

He regained consciousness when someone emptied a bucket of cold water on his head. The moment he opened his eyes two heavy men dragged him to a chair and tied him expertly. He looked around him. On the floor, in a puddle of blood, lay Brandt, breathing irregularly. Blood was still oozing from a wound in his abdomen. Bloody tracks on the bare wooden floor indicated that he had been dragged here from the place where he had fallen, probably by the exit door.

In leisurely fashion Karpin got up from behind the desk, went around it, and faced Heller. A wild flame burned in his black eyes. "I have no time for games," he said in clipped English. "I don't have time for tortures and interrogations, either. We know who you are. You and your friend are Israeli agents. You are here looking for information that could help you find some traitors in the Soviet Union who spied for the Nazis during the war. Their names are on a list that is in your boss's hands. We want to know the names."

Heller gazed at him stonily. He hadn't been prepared

for such a calamity. Frantic thoughts flashed through his mind, but he was unable to put them together rationally.

The Russian spoke again. "You have a choice. Your friend, here, is dying. If he doesn't get immediate medical treatment and a blood transfusion, he will be dead in half an hour. If he doesn't die, we shall kill him—and we shall kill you, too. We have no time."

From his pocket he produced an ordinary leather-bound cigarette case. He lifted its lid and opened it. The case was full of cigarettes, the tips of which protruded visibly. He carefully picked a cigarette and pulled it. All the other cigarettes in the case started to come out with it. Suddenly Heller realized that the cigarettes were only camouflage. Barely half an inch long, the tips were glued to a thin metal plate and served as an innocent-looking cover for something that was concealed within the case.

From it Karpin now took out a strange-looking device. It was a rectangular-shaped box, made of gray steel, and fitted into the palm of his hand. He approached Heller and turned the box before his eyes, so he could see it from all sides. Two curiously shaped springs were fastened to the top. On one of the sides two round black openings, roughly the size of a gun muzzle, had been drilled. Two yellow metal pieces protruded from the opposite end.

"This is an electric pistol," Karpin said conversationally. "It fires poisoned bullets, like these." He produced two long glass capsules that contained a colorless liquid. "They are filled with prussic acid, more commonly known as cyanide. The acid is in the form of gas." He put a capsule into one of the twin muzzles. Heller heard the click of the spring snapping into place. "The gun is loaded now," he continued. "When I press these springs, the hammer is released." He pointed helpfully at the shining yellow cylinders. "The hammer breaks the capsule and projects the prussic acid into the victim's face—like that!"

With a swift violent move his hand darted forward, sticking the infernal device into Heller's face. He smiled with satisfaction as the tiny beads of sweat appeared on Heller's forehead. "They say death is quite unpleasant."

He withdrew his hand and looked thoughtfully at the strange pistol. "We have been using it for years, and with success." Then he smiled. "You certainly know about Rebet and Bandera, the Ukrainian traitors who were executed some years ago. We killed them both with this kind of gun. Tonight we might add you to the list."

Heller's face turned chalk-white. "You see," the Russian went on, almost friendly now, "this gun has two great advantages: first, it is noiseless; and second, it doesn't leave any traces. After you die and the cyanide gas evaporates, no doctor would guess that you were poisoned. Your body shows all the symptoms of a heart attack. Simple and effective."

Heller passed his tongue over his dry lips.

"The only trouble is that the man who uses the gun might also get hurt by the gas. But, fortunately, this can be remedied by antidotes." He was moving briskly around his prisoner, like a scientist in his lab, happy to display his latest achievements before a distinguished visitor. From an inner pocket he took out a small white vial and carefully shook a pill into the palm of his hand. "Before shooting I have to swallow one of these pills. It neutralizes the effect of the gas for about three hours." He shoved the pill into his mouth, jerked his head upward, and swallowed. "After shooting I have to swallow another pill. Then I'm safe."

Heller, tied to his chair, followed like one hypnotized the movements of the man in front of him.

Abruptly Karpin roared, "So you see now what awaits you? Death! Death for you and for your partner. Now!"

With catlike suppleness he slid to his knees and bent over the unconscious, bleeding Dan Brandt. "Move aside, all of you!" he ordered his men. The KGB agents hurriedly retreated to the corners of the office. Karpin pointed his poison gun at Brandt's face, but his eyes were riveted on Heller.

"That's your choice," he said in a harsh voice. "If you refuse to talk, I am going to kill him. Then you. If you talk, I'll let you go, both of you. You can still save his life."

Heller bit his lips. A tiny trickle of blood appeared at the spot where his teeth had torn into his flesh.

"Will you talk?" the Russian roared again. "I will kill him now! I will not wait!"

Heller was trembling violently. "Don't!" he whispered faintly. His voice, his whole demeanor, admitted defeat. "Don't kill him. I'll talk. I'll tell you all I know."

He did. Nothing could have stopped him. In a broken voice, shaking with fear and shame, he told the Russians about the list, about General Blagonravov, about the mysterious Minerva, about their unsuccessful search for additional information concerning him in the émigré centers of Europe. Lavrenti Karpin looked at him in savage triumph, while one of his assistants was diligently scribbling the stunning revelations on his note pad. Heller spoke rapidly. In five minutes he had told everything. Then he glanced furtively at Karpin. He had an anguished, desperate expression. "That's all I know. Will you let us go now? He is dying."

A sly smile spread over Karpin's face. Heller felt his blood run cold. "You didn't really believe you could just walk out of here, did you?" the Russian replied mockingly.

Terror-stricken, Heller watched Karpin thrust the gun in the face of his wounded friend and release the spring trigger.

He distinctly heard the glass capsule break and smelled the faint odor of bitter almonds. He saw Brandt's body jerking on the ground, shaken by spasms. Then Karpin was on his feet, feeding another glass capsule into the noiseless gun. Heller felt sweat break out all over him and his bowels became distended. "No, don't!" he cried. Then he looked into the muzzle of the gun and heard the click, and the poisonous gas burst into his face and nose and filled his lungs with death.

Karpin turned to his men, who were standing along the walls. One of them, a young blond giant, was crouching in a corner, vomiting. Karpin looked at him with disgust. He swallowed another pill from his vial.

"They're dead," he said. His voice was normal. "We'll

clean the place. Pack them in something and get ready to leave." He looked at his watch. "We'll remove the bodies later, when the street is empty. We can't do it yet. It's only eight o'clock."

At a quarter past eight David Ron put two one-franc coins on the counter of the now deserted Chez Basile and left through the rue Saint-Guillaume entrance. The Renault 16 was parked in front of the glass and nickel door. He knocked on the driver's window. "It's past eight now," he said. "Something must be wrong. I'm going in. Have the car ready, just in case." Dori nodded and switched the engine on.

Ron crossed the rue Saint-Guillaume, turned the corner into the rue de Grenelle, walked about a hundred yards in the opposite direction of number 37, then crossed the street and came back quietly, keeping mostly in the shadows. He slipped unnoticed—or so he thought—into the entrance of number 35, crossed the dark entrance hall, and emerged into the backyard. He had reconnoitered the place some days ago and remembered it well. He jumped lightly over a low stone fence. Now he was in the backyard of number 37. He moved into the deserted stairway and took the steps two at a time to the second floor, quiet as a shadow in his rubber-soled shoes. He approached the door of the OUN offices cautiously and stood there for a long while, listening intently. What he heard made every muscle in his body tense. He hadn't much time to plan. He knocked on the door. "Open quick!" he shouted in Russian, trying to impart urgency and fear to his voice, and praying silently that nobody would ask him for a password. He drew his gun from his shoulder holster and moved aside, disappearing from the field of fire of anybody standing in the doorway. He heard slow, cautious steps, then the door opened. He knew it was a matter of seconds. He tried to guess exactly the position of the man at the door, the way he was holding his gun. The Russian had to open the door with his right hand, and if the man wasn't left-handed he would be slightly handicapped for a moment. And that was the moment. Ron hurled himself into the open doorway. At the very moment of impact he brought down both his arms with crushing force on the firing hand of the Russian who had opened the door, then viciously kicked him in the groin. When the man jackknifed and gasped in pain, he tore the gun from his numb hand and pushed him in. He knew there were others inside, he knew they would be waiting for him now, and realized that his life and those of his partners could be saved only through his speed. He pushed the panting Russian in, through the dark corridor, pointing the gun at his face. The KGB agent staggered backward silently until they reached the open door of the office. Ron savagely shoved him in, swiftly moved behind him, and crouched in the doorway, covering the group of men who stood in the center of the room with his gun. He shouted in Russian, "Don't move! One movement and . . ."

His voice died in his throat when he saw his friends lying dead on the floor. Then he saw a face that made him yell with rage: "Karpin!"

That was all he said. From behind the massive desk two shots were fired at him. A bullet hit him in the right shoulder, and a wave of pain shook his body. Automatically he emptied the whole magazine of his gun at the people facing him, fell back, slammed the office door, then ran, out and down the stairs, still waving his now useless pistol. From above he heard the thump of running footsteps. They were coming after him. He didn't have time to slow his frenzied descent when he saw some indistinct figures lurking in the stairwell by the house entrance. His empty gun must have saved him, because the men moved aside hastily. Breathing heavily, choking for air, he darted across the rue de Grenelle and burst like a gunshot into Chez Basile. Behind him he heard shouts, and a lonely shot echoed in his ears. He pushed his way frantically through the few customers still in the café, knocking down a terrified waiter carrying a tray laden with glasses, and emerged from the second entrance into the rue Saint-Guillaume. They were shooting from all over now, but their aim was ineffective in the dark street. It took them barely thirty seconds to realize that he had run through the café to the next street. But that was exactly what Dori needed to let him get into the Renault and gun the car to full speed toward the crowded boulevard Saint-Germain, barely two hundred yards away. The Russians also had their cars waiting, engines running, people ready behind the wheels, but they were parked farther down the one-way rue de Grenelle. By the time they succeeded in maneuvering backward and squeezing into the rue Saint-Guillaume, the Renault was definitely lost.

"Straight to the airport," muttered Ron while Dori deftly piloted the car through the heavy traffic on the boulevard Raspail and drove around the huge statue of the green rock lion in the center of place Denfert-Rochereau. "Every minute we spend in Paris is a minute too much."

He told Dori briefly what had happened in the office. Dori listened intently, helpless fury showing in his face. "What do you want to do?"

Ron groaned with pain. "Orly Airport. Abandon the car. Dispose of the guns. Jump in the first plane that goes out of the country, no matter where." He looked at the rapidly expanding bloodstain on his jacket. "I'll put on your leather coat; they won't see the blood. I'll survive."

Dori cast a worried glance at him. "Maybe we should stop and dress your wound?"

"Not now," Ron mumbled stubbornly. "Maybe if we have time, in the toilets at the departure lounge. You've till got those morphine tablets?"

"Yes."

"Good. They'll make me sleep during the flight. Before we board, you send a cable to Peled. Our special code. Just one sentence: 'Karpin killed Heller and Brandt, apparently made them talk.'"

"How do you know he made them talk and how do you know it was Karpin?" Dori asked without taking his eyes from the road. They were on the Autoroute du Sud now, and he pressed hard on the accelerator.

"I know Karpin. One of his first assignments, when he started to work for the Eighth Department, was Israel. He was sent as agricultural attaché to the Russian embassy in Tel-Aviv. I tailed him for months, didn't you know? I discovered that he was Beer's case officer, and I testified on that in court. He was expelled from Israel on my evidence. I'd recognize his face in a million."

He clenched his teeth with pain. "And I know his bloody character. He wouldn't have killed Heller and Brandt if they hadn't talked. He is too clever for that."

"Maybe we shouldn't have fled," Dori speculated. "We could have tried to stop them, to prevent them from relaying the information they got."

"You must be crazy," Ron snapped. "I was useless with my arm wounded. You were alone. And they had people swarming all over the place. What do you think, they would have waited for you to kill them one by one?"

Dori didn't answer.

They threw the guns through the car windows in a nearby field, abandoned the Renault in the parking lot at Orly, and successfully boarded a flight for Geneva.

Later that night a prowl car of the Gendarmerie Nationale reported an automobile accident near Fontainebleau. A Simca 1100 had apparently slipped on the wet highway while taking a turn, broken through the guard rail, and hurtled down the slope. The gas tank had exploded, and the car caught fire immediately. By the time the rescue squad reached the scene, there was nothing to rescue. Only charred carcasses remained of the two men trapped inside the car. Nobody could recognize that they had been Professor Joseph Heller and the Mossad agent Dan Brandt. The car had been stolen that same evening near the Porte d'Orléans, in Paris. The police didn't link the accident with the mysterious shooting, earlier that evening, in the rue de Grenelle. That case remained unsolved and the detectives of the quai des Orfèvres tended to attribute it to underworld strife.

That same night, within half an hour of each other, two cables were dispatched from Paris. Both were in code and sent to cover addresses. One went to Lev Ivanovich Yulin. The second to Jeremiah Peled.

In Jerusalem the Prime Minister of Israel was urgently called to her office in the parliament building, in the midst of a debate on immigration from the Soviet Union. A haggard, pale Jeremiah Peled was waiting for her. He told her what had happened in Paris.

The Prime Minister covered her face with her hands. "It's terrible," she murmured. "Two people killed."

"That isn't all," the Old Man said gloomily. "Before they killed them, they made them talk, which means that Blagonravov's life isn't worth a cent now. And once they get Blagonravov, they'll get Joe Gonen. They'll kill him. My best man."

The Prime Minister sat motionless for a long while. "You mean that the whole operation was a failure." She looked gravely at the chief of the Mossad.

"I assume full responsibility," Peled said slowly.

PART FIVE

The Kill

19

October 4, morning -
October 5, 1973, dawn

Gonen awoke to the sound of rapid footsteps down the stone stairway and through the narrow corridor that led to his cell. He looked at his watch: it was six o'clock in the morning. But he knew only because he'd kept track of the hours. No daylight penetrated to his underground prison, and the bare electric bulb over his cot burned day and night. The steps stopped in front of his door. He heard some muffled sentences in Russian, then a key turned in the rusty lock. The heavy iron door pivoted on its hinges. A man stood in the doorway: tall, gray-haired, clad in a light blue suit. His stiff upright posture betrayed the military, but Gonen didn't need to guess who he was. He knew the face—every line, every inch of the aristocratic features. He had spent hours studying the man's photograph and devoted long, trying moments in a nerve-racking effort to bring about this very moment: to find himself face to face with him.

The man turned around and in a low voice said some words in Russian. The guard, looking back over his shoulder into the cell, slowly walked away. The visitor stepped in and closed the door behind him. Painfully Gonen got to his feet.

For some seconds he and Lavrenti Blagonravov gazed at each other wordlessly. He was ecstatic. He had succeeded! Blagonravov was here, alone, in his cell! It had been a long, hard road since that night in Marsa.

He suddenly became aware that his vistor was frightened. His face was pale, and his restless eyes cast worried glances around the cell. Finally he spoke.

"What do you want?" he said in English.

Gonen gave it to him straight. "You know the meaning of 'Cossack of the Don.' You know that I slipped that code name into my deposition in order to make you come here. Now listen: my country has in its possession a document that could lead you straight to the gallows. It is a list of names of former German spies in Moscow. The list was made by a man you may have known. His name was Heinrich Roehm. During the war he was your case officer. We have the original of Roehm's list. Your name and your code name are on it. We can have you condemned to death."

Blagonravov managed to supress his panic. Only his voice became tremulous.

"What do you want?" he said again.

"I was sent to make a deal with you," Gonen answered. "I can promise you that nobody will ever hear of the Cossack of the Don. In return I want you to tell me, now, the full details of the projected attack against Israel: the timing, the operational plans, the units, and the strategy that will be used. I also want full details about your missile installations throughout Egypt, and I want to know the targets of your IRBM's. I think your missiles are in Egypt already, and according to our estimates, they are operational. And one more thing: I want you to get me out of here. Find a pretext: take me for questioning, for cross-interrogation, organize my escape any way you want."

Blagonravov's handsome features were contorted with hatred. "How can I be certain that you won't go on blackmailing me over and over again?"

Gonen smiled coldly. "You can't. But you don't have much choice, do you?"

The General's shoulders sagged. "No," he said slowly, "I don't have much choice."

He told his story quickly, as if he were anxious to get it over with, to make this shameful betrayal as brief as possible. "Syria and Egypt have been planning to attack you simultaneously, in order to recover their territories lost in the Six-Day War. Syria is going to attack in the Golan, Egypt intends to cross the Suez Canal. Jordan has refused to join the coalition. The Egyptian and the Syrian offensives will be synchronized. Our military experts have been instructing the Egyptian Army for three years now in expediting a waterway crossing. The model used for training is the famous crossing of the Dnieper, which has become a classic subject in our War Academy. I can't tell you what the ultimate aims of the Syrians and the Egyptians are. They rely heavily on the effect of surprise. They are convinced that their only chance to achieve any substantial success depends on catching the Israeli Army napping. For more than a year they have carried out a large-scale plan of deception, prepared in close cooperation with us. Its object is to lull Israel into a false sense of security and spread among your military and civilian leaders the conviction that the Arabs are unprepared for war and that they won't dare to attack you for a long time to come."

Gonen interrupted him. "Was the departure of your experts from Egypt part of the plan?"

"Yes. Up to this moment the plan has been carried out to our full satisfaction."

"What's your interest in the project?"

"On a smaller scale my country wants to obtain a decisive influence in Egypt. But our main objective is to deal the West a crushing blow."

"How?"

Blagonravov reflected before answering. "As a matter of fact, the entire Egyptian-Syrian plan has been masterminded by us. It must start a sequence of events that we have carefully designed. We know that the West depends to a large extent on Middle East oil. We decided, therefore, to put pressure on the West by completely cutting off the supply of fuel to Europe and America. In order to do that we had to create a military threat to the oil-producing Arab countries and force them to stop supplying the West immediately."

"You don't need Egypt for that," Gonen retorted.

"Oh yes, we do," Blagonravov said heatedly. "Of course, we have an enormous arsenal of long-range ballistic missiles, and we can train them on any target in the

Middle East. But a direct Soviet threat would immediately trigger American retaliation. We might be dragged into an atomic world war. In no case could we consider such a possibility. For our plan to succeed it must be an indirect threat, sponsored by us but carried out by another country. We therefore built a pro-Soviet underground organization in Egypt. It is a powerful group, headed by the Chief of Staff himself, General Salem.

"The war against Israel will create a new reality in the Middle East and in the world. Immediately after the war ends—and we believe that it will end with a victory—Salem will seize power in Egypt. At that moment he will have the prestige of a national hero, and he will have no trouble whatsoever in overthrowing Anwar Sadat. Soon after the coup he will address an ultimatum to the oil-producing Arab states to cease all shipments to the West or else he will destroy their cities and oilfields. This ultimatum will be presented as a countermeasure to the help given to Israel by Western imperialists. Salem will then disclose that IRBM's have been set at various bases in his country and that they are trained on the main oil-producing nations. It will be clear that those missiles have been supplied by us but that they are now under Egyptian control."

"You think that will work?"

"It must. The Soviet Union will be involved, but not enough to justify an American nuclear strike. On the other hand, our involvement to protect the new Egyptian regime would prevent the West from any military intervention in Egypt. Under the Egyptian threat not a drop of oil would go to the West anymore. The West will have to capitulate and deal with us, which means to accept our political and military conditions for the resumption of oil shipments."

"What about the missiles? Are they operational?"

Blagonravov hesitated. "Yes," he sighed finally. "We have been smuggling them into Egypt for a long time. The Egyptian Government doesn't know that in our Air Force bases in Egypt we have deployed IRBM's. We succeeded in bringing the weapons to Egypt with the help of Salem and a small group of his friends. Two years ago, when you captured our guidance station in Marsa, you almost blew up our entire project."

Gonen dug his trembling fingers into his palms. He hoped that Blagonravov didn't notice how terrified he was. For the first time a Russian disclosed before him the details of that Machiavellian project he had stumbled upon two years ago. It was a flawless plan, and it had every chance of succeeding if it wasn't crushed at the start. It was clear that Israel faced the danger of extermination and the West a slow strangulation.

The General was watching him closely. Gonen pulled himself together. "Now, your missile system in Egypt," he said briskly. "How many, what kinds, where?"

Blagonravov's voice dropped to a barely audible murmur. His sentences were laconic and compact, like in an operational cable. "Project Aurora," he said. "Thirty-six missiles. Twenty SS-4, Sandal, built 1959. Sixteen SS-14, Scapegoat, built 1971. All of them mobile. Range twelve hundred miles. Atomic warheads. Arming only on operation's eve. Missiles mounted on trailers serving as launching pads, concealed in hangars. Five missiles at Kabrit. Twelve missiles at Aswan. Six missiles at Matruh. Thirteen missiles at Luxor. Control and guidance stations at Rãs Bãnas and Sidi Barrani."

"The names of the Salem group," Gonen demanded.

Blagonravov blurted out a long series of names: generals, diplomats, two ministers. Gonen was listening intently, striving to memorize details, names of people, points on the map.

Then he asked his last question, the most crucial one: "When is D day? When will it all start?"

"It will start in two days' time, Colonel Gonen," said an ironic voice from the door. "But unfortunately you won't live to tell anyone."

Gonen and Blagonravov stared in dismay. Immersed in their extraordinary conversation, they had not noticed the door opening. They wheeled around to face the doorway.

There, in the midst of several Russians, guns in their hands, stood General Yulin.

The little Director of the Eighth Department walked slowly into the cell. In his right hand he still clutched the crumpled form of a cable. He stared at Blagonravov with contempt. The handsome aristocrat looked away. "We just received the news about your betrayal, General Blagonravov." Yulin's tone was like a whip. "But we received it in time. Ten minutes ago we decoded this cable from Paris. You know what that means, don't you? You are arrested for high treason thirty years ago and now. You will be tranferred to Moscow, put on trial, and probably executed."

He beckoned two of his men, who took Blagonravov away. Stunned, Blagonravov made no objection, but went out obediently. Yulin waited until his steps had faded, then turned to Gonen. "And you, Colonel, you almost succeeded in fooling us, especially the second time. Will you accept the compliments of a professional? Who planned everything, old Jeremiah Peled?"

Gonen didn't answer. He was still in a state of shock. In only a few seconds he had sunk from the heights of a magnificent triumph to the depths of despair.

"Anyway, it was the plan of a genius," Yulin went on. "It was only when I received the cable about Blagonravov and found out why you had so readily broken down and talked that I understood what it was all about. What insolence, Colonel! Why, you used me as a messenger! By telling me the story about a report signed by Blagonravov, you got me to summon him here. I thought all along that I was using you, but the truth was that you were using me!"

Yulin paused and thoughtfully looked at Gonen. "How did you alert him?" he asked. "By his code word?"

Gonen nodded his assent.

"Was it Young Comsomol? Cossack of the Don?"

"Cossack of the Don," Gonen said.

Yulin paced a circle around Gonen, talking not so much to his prisoner as to himself, assembling the bits of the Israeli operation, putting the last pieces of the puzzle into place, and reconstructing the Old Man's project.

"What planning!" he muttered. "You work your way

into our hands. Then your people deliberately blow your cover and you give us your second cover story, about that 'leak in the Air Force.' This famous leak is used then to provide credibility for your second cover story, after we break the first. Or rather the first was intended to be broken! Very clever, Colonel. Your only assignment was to establish contact with Blagonravov. And so you did, while we were running on wild-goose chases."

He stopped walking around and peered into the lusterless eyes of his prisoner. "What a pity that you won't live to deliver my compliments to Mr. Jeremiah Peled! He was born in Russia, is that correct?" He chuckled. "Well, that accounts at least for his cunning."

His voice abruptly changed to a hateful hiss. "I'd love to kill you with my own hands. Do you hear me? Right now! But I can't. Unfortunately, we may need your help during the next few days. The Arab attack is scheduled for the day after tomorrow, in the afternoon. It's your Day of Atonement, isn't it? Maybe we shall make you atone for everything you did to us. You will be extremely helpful to our Arab friends, with all the military secrets you know. Just for once you'll talk and speak the truth. I'll take care of that!"

He shoved his prisoner roughly into the hands of his subordinates. "My apologies to you," he said caustically, "but we have to leave this place. It's getting too hot here."

Half an hour later several cars simultaneously left the villa and headed in different directions. In one of them General Blagonravov was taken to a private landing strip, where a light plane was waiting. He didn't resist, but got aboard the plane with his two guards. Yulin drove with two of his people to Nice Airport and boarded an Air France plane to Paris, with a connection to Moscow.

Gonen was walked across the beautiful park to the wooden pier, over the private bay that stretched in front of the residence. A motorboat took him to a Polish fishing trawler that was moored beyond the bay. His Russian bodyguards, waving their guns, pushed and kicked him all the way down through the filthy, foul-smelling passageways and locked him in a tiny compartment, half full of decaying fishing nets.

Meanwhile the remaining KGB agents—about a dozen of them—were rapidly loading the ship with crates of equipment and documents they had cleared from the villa. Two hours later everybody and everything were safely aboard.

Once alone, in the darkness of his new cell, Gonen collapsed. Tears of rage and despair filled his eyes, and he pounded his clenched fists on the wall until blood oozed from his bruised knuckles. All his will power, all his self-control were gone. He had just heard a death sentence pronounced on his country, and he couldn't do anything about it. In two days Israel would no longer exist.

At nightfall long convoys of trucks, half-tracks, tanks, jeeps, and other combat vehicles moved from Egyptian Army bases in the vicinity of Cairo to positions along the Suez Canal. The armored divisions of the Second Egyptian Army concentrated on the northern part of the canal. The Third Army units moved southward and were deployed between the Bitter Lakes and the city of Suez. Auxiliary units worked throughout the night to camouflage the huge masses of armor set at barely several hundred yards from the Israeli defense line, across the waterway. Engineering units hurriedly sorted the mobile parts of the Soviet-made pontoon bridges, needed for the crossing. Special companies of Navy engineers for the last time checked the multitudes of motorboats, dinghies, rafts, landing craft, and amphibious vehicles assembled at about fifty crossing areas along the 100-mile-long canal. Eighteen hundred cannons were zeroed in on the Israeli forts and positions. Several brigades of elite commando troops were en route to military air bases, where more than a hundred MI-3 helicopters were ready to fly them deep into Israeli-held Sinai at H hour. Messengers of the Supreme Command circulated among the advancing units, distributing to senior officers sealed envelopes bearing the stamp: OPERATION BADR—TOP SECRET. A first wave of forty thousand troops was ready to cross the canal when the order was given. On the Israeli side, in the forts along the Bar-Lev line, barely 425 soldiers, most of them reservists, were preparing for a dull and eventless Day of Atonement away from home. In the far north about eighty Israeli tanks were deployed along the cease-fire line on the Golan Heights. In front of them fifteen hundred Syrian tanks were ready to move forward in less than forty-eight hours.

Israel didn't suspect the deadly peril that hung over her during these pleasant, sunny days of early October. That very day, the 4th of October, thousands of soldiers went on leave, to spend Yom Kippur with their families. The front lines, the combat posts, the communication centers, were left almost empty, manned by skeleton crews. Confident, convinced of their overwhelming superiority, the Israeli leaders would not believe that the Arabs might risk a war. It would be equivalent to suicide for them, their experts said.

Jeremiah Peled came home late that night. He had spent most of the day in his office, trying to devise a way to save Gonen's life. He knew Gonen was living on borrowed time, because now that the Russians had discovered Blagonravov had been a traitor they knew why Gonen had worked his way into the KGB's hands. He had even considered an attack by a special unit on the villa at Cavalaire, but in the early afternoon he was informed by his men on the spot that all the Russians had left the place in a hurry. In the evening he drove to the airport to meet David Ron and Raphael Dori, the surviving members of the Minerva team. He questioned them at length and rode with Ron in the ambulance that took him to the hospital. He didn't leave him in peace until the wounded agent was taken to surgery.

The house was quiet and tranquil, but Peled's nerves were on edge. He knew that at that very moment Gonen might be tortured, dying, or even dead. He would never admit it to anyone, but he was deeply attached to the young man, who reminded him sometimes of his dead son. Or maybe it was just a sentimental urge, and he would have wanted his boy to be like Joe, had he lived. He sighed. He was a lonely man, feared, respected, and admired, with no real friends, living in the shadows, from where he would send people to kill and be killed.

With a great effort he pulled himself together. He went to his kitchen and made strong Turkish coffee, which he carried to his study. He locked himself in, to avoid being disturbed by the elderly maid who had been taking care of him since his wife died. He turned off all the lights except a powerful reading lamp on his large desk. Then he put the voluminous dossier of the Minerva operation in front of him. He started to read it carefully from the very beginning, page by page, line by line, taking notes on a pad. There were several documents in the file that he read two and even three times. He went over the Roehm list, the details about Minerva, the fragmentary descriptions of Soviet operations against the Minerva team in Europe, and the notes he had taken earlier in the night while questioning Ron and Dori.

It was three in the morning when he dialed a number and asked a question. The answer left him puzzled. For a long time he stared through the open window, while the night slowly began to fade and the first thin gray line in the east heralded the birth of a new day. And then, suddenly, his eyes lit up. He picked up the phone and gave several sharp orders. To the objections and the exclamations on the other end of the line he retorted impatiently, "Don't argue! Do as I say!"

At 6 A.M. he took off on the first plane to Europe. At a little past noon he landed at Helsinki.

20

October 5, 1973, noon

Sibelius Park in Helsinki was deserted. The fierce cold and the icy rain pouring from a low gray sky had driven away its regular visitors. The last to escape from the rain and cold were a blond-bearded giant, wearing a small white cap, tennis shoes, and blue training overalls, and an old lady in black, walking her snow-white polar dog. A depressing atmosphere of desolation hung over the abandoned park. The October north wind was moaning in the treetops, bending the young firs, tearing the desiccated yellow and reddish leaves of the birches and blowing them until they landed in packets on the wet grass. Black, sharp-edged granite rocks were protruding from the gently sloped green lawns. In the center of the park, over a rising mass of dark rock, was suspended a strange futuristic structure: a cluster of gray stainless steel pipes, unequal in length and diameter, some of them riddled with gaping holes, others scratched with deep, raw cuts that looked like bloodless wounds. This awe-inspiring structure was like a huge organ built to be played by a mythological giant or by the untamed elements of nature. Nothing, indeed, could better symbolize the genius of the Finnish composer Jean Sibelius, whose death mask, cast in steel and fastened to the rock, was severely contemplating this huge monument constructed in his memory.

From opposite directions two men emerged and marched toward the steel organ. One came from the nearby road, where he had left his black Volvo sedan. The other came from the small, misty cove that sheltered a row of wooden piers and tarpaulin-covered motorboats.

They climbed the steps carved in the rock on both sides

of the monument. Two small men, no longer young. They looked much alike. The same shrewd blue-gray eyes, delicate features, tightly pressed thin lips; the same watchful, sealed expression. Two people who were mortal enemies.

They stopped and faced each other under the steel organ. The heavy rain was drumming on the huge pipes, and the gusts of the autumn wind squeezed out of them an eerie, high-pitched vibration.

Yulin spoke first. "You were confident that I would come, weren't you?" he said in English.

"Yes," the Old Man said slowly, stretching the single syllable.

"Why?"

"Because you wanted to know if I knew," Peled replied in Russian. "I do. Minerva 6N. That is what they called you during the war, isn't it?"

Yulin didn't move, didn't utter a word. Only the knuckles of his small hands, which were clenching his gloves, turned white with the pressure.

"Last night I read all the details about Minerva," the Old Man said softly, almost conversationally. "His career when he was young. GPU, then NKVD. Then during the war he supplied inside information about Soviet leaders. That means he had to be somebody in the inner circle of the secret service, able to go in and out of the Kremlin at will. He also sent reports about the underground operations against the Germans in the Ukraine. He didn't ask for money, so he spied for political reasons. Therefore he must have been a man who loved his country but hated its regime. He could be a Ukrainian nationalist who wanted to use the Germans in order to obtain independence for his homeland ... And then, all of a sudden, I had a feeling of *déjà vu*. You see, we have a complete file on you, General. Do you want me to read it to you? To tell you how many years you were in the GPU and in the NKVD? To remind you that during the war you were attached to the Kremlin? That you were born in Kharkov, in the Ukraine? That you won your medals for those daring intelligence and sabotage operations you conducted so well with Red Ukrainian partisans behind the enemy lines? But I guess you had nothing to fear then—your German friends certainly took all the precautions needed to keep you alive."

He raised his eyes. The large drops of rain were pounding on the Sibelius organ, and thin filets of cold water were gradually soaking the two men wet to their bones.

"It's a pity," he added, "that the incomplete report by my surviving agents came only last night, after you had captured and killed their two colleagues." Yulin looked at him with expressionless eyes. Still he didn't move.

Peled went on. "However, what really aroused my suspicion was your zeal. You see, the Roehm affair, the search for the list, the hunting and killing of my agents, were not in your domain. We know the *modus operandi* of the KGB. These operations had to be carried out either by the Western Europe department, the Special Investigations Department, or the Mokroie Dela murder and kidnaping squads. Nevertheless, it was you who took the initiative. Everywhere we went—you were there. Too much zeal, Comrade Yulin."

Peled's eyes intently scanned the little General, attentive to the slightest change of expression in the wise, weather-beaten face of his enemy. "You made a mistake, Yulin. You killed my men." He sighed. "You see, I had sent a whole team to the Soviet bloc, to divert the attention of the KGB. They moved all about Russia, Poland, Bulgaria, East Berlin. They were followed, but nobody touched them. Your boss, Andropov, must have reached the conclusion that the Roehm list wasn't worth killing a foreign agent. So he let my men go free. But not you. Your agents killed my men mercilessly, on your orders. Karpin, your Chief of Operations, was in charge of those murders. You were ready to take all the risks, to kidnap and to kill. For the names. For the secret list of Heinrich Roehm. Then I understood: you were afraid, afraid that somebody else might find out about you."

For a few moments that seemed an eternity the two master spies stood motionless, staring at each other, their eyes fighting a fierce duel, a battle of will against will. The drumming rain, the howling wind, and the muffled thunder rolling far away, over the Gulf of Finland, were the only sounds accompanying this final confrontation of two desperate men.

And then one of them spoke. "What do you want?" Yulin's voice sounded old now, and very tired.

"I want my man back," Peled snapped. "Back with all the information he asked for, within twelve hours. You know what to do."

Then he turned and walked back to the pier, which had begun to disappear under white patches of fog. It was the afternoon of October 5.

Half an hour later General Yulin slowly drove his rented Volvo through the center of Helsinki. He had dismissed his bodyguards and secretaries without explanation. He went down Mannerheim Avenue, sitting woodenly behind the wheel, staring straight ahead as he passed the National Museum and the huge parliament building on his right. He parked the car carefully by the side entrance of a yellow brick building, the Main Post Office. He went in, past the black statue of the late Marshal Mannerheim riding his magnificent horse and looking quite satisfied with himself.

At the left of the entrance there was a small phone booth. Yulin had chosen it because it had ordinary concrete walls—and not transparent glass or plastic partitions, which revealed anything that was going on inside. He shut himself in the booth and with a swift movement wrapped his handkerchief around the mouthpiece of the phone. He dialed 003.

"Criminal police," an eager voice said in Finnish.

"Do you speak English?" Yulin asked in a muffled, low tone.

"A moment, please." In a few seconds a new voice said in English, "Yes, go on please."

Yulin spoke quickly. "I want to report a huge heroin-smuggling operation in the South of France. A ship, camouflaged as a Polish fishing trawler, has been loading a shipment of heroin on the French Riviera. The name of the ship is *Ian Chmielnizki,* and it is now cruising in

French territorial waters, very close to Cavalaire. The loading is done at night. The ship is scheduled to sail away at dawn. If you inform Interpol immediately, they will capture it with all the stuff on board."

"Who is speaking, please? Hello?" The police officer's voice exploded in the receiver.

The line went dead.

Yulin walked rapidly to his car. In less than a minute he joined the heavy traffic in downtown Helsinki and headed for the airport.

21

October 6, 1973,
2 A.M. - 4:35 A.M.

At 2 A.M. a search party of the French Police Maritime
boarded the trawler *Ian Chmielnizki* off the bay of
Cavalaire while she was frantically maneuvering to get
clear of French territorial waters. The surprise had been
almost total. Only when the two fast motorboats, all lights
and projectors ablaze, emerged from behind the southern
tip of the Saint-Tropez peninsula did the sailor on watch
give the alarm. In a matter of seconds Captain Kolajcyk,
a tall blond Pole from Gdynia, was on the bridge, bellowing orders into the loudspeakers. He tried a frenetic
escape: the *Ian Chmielnizki*'s extraordinarily powerful engines burst into a roar, the ship slipped her moorings and
in a few moments was on her way, leaving behind her a
wake of bubbling white froth. But she hadn't the slightest
chance. The sleek vedettes of the French coast guard
were designed and equipped to overtake any conventional
naval vessel. And *Ian Chmielnizki* was no exception. Soon
the two coast guard patrol boats were sailing on both
sides of the trawler and the race was over. A French senior officer, Police Colonel Jean Richet, identified himself
through a loudspeaker. He ordered the Polish ship to stop
and to cut her engines, which she obediently did. The
vedettes maneuvered expertly and stopped too, their hulls
almost touching that of the *Ian Chmielnizki*. Rope ladders
were thrown overboard, and two groups of French officials climbed to the ship's main deck. There were about
twenty men in the party: three plainclothes detectives of
the Narcotics Division of the Marseilles police, three Customs officers, and a squad of heavily armed gendarmes.
Captain Kolajcyk watched with interest as two frogmen in

black rubber suits deftly buckled the belts of their scuba equipment and plunged into the black water to inspect the keel of the ship.

He turned and politely greeted Colonel Richet, who reached the bridge and produced search warrants, duly signed and stamped. "We have reason to suspect," the colonel said dryly, "that an illegal shipment of heroin has been loaded on your trawler, Captain. I have orders to carry out a thorough search of the ship." Kolajcyk shrugged helplessly.

The party dispersed on the upper deck and started a systematic search, beginning with the captain's bridge and steadily proceeding downward. The sailors were confined to their quarters and asked through the loudspeakers not to move in the passageways and on the decks.

In the bowels of the ship Gonen's guards held a quick consultation. There was no chance that the search party might fail to examine the small cabin where their prisoner was kept. And they couldn't afford Gonen's discovery by the police. They had to improvise, and be swift about it. One of the guards unlocked the door of the cell. He threw a bundle of filthy sailor's clothes at Gonen's feet and pointed a Mauser at him. "Put that on, quickly!" he ordered. Gonen obeyed. "Turn back!" When he did, the Russian smashed the butt of the gun on the back of his skull. Gonen collapsed, unconscious, on a pad of rotten nets. The Russian knelt beside him and turned him over. He uncorked a bottle of cheap vodka and emptied its contents over Gonen's face and clothes. He threw the empty bottle by the unconscious man, then retreated from the cell, leaving the iron door ajar. It was the best he could do on the spur of the moment. Gonen would remain unconscious for at least a couple of hours. The French police would find a dirty, drunken sailor, sleeping off his liquor where he wouldn't be disturbed. His uneven breathing, the reeking odor of vodka from his clothes and face, the empty bottle rolling at his side should fool the most perceptive investigator. The French could search the cell as much as they wanted; they wouldn't discover anything but old fishing nets. All that mattered was that

Gonen didn't awake. And if he did, thought the Russian as he tiptoed into his cabin across the passageway, he would see to it that the prisoner didn't open his mouth.

After recovering from the initial shock the Polish captain calmed down. There was no heroin aboard, and the French police wouldn't find anything. In a few hours the ship would certainly be allowed to continue her voyage.

But he hadn't taken into account the Russian passengers who had boarded the trawler yesterday morning. In the heavy crates they had hauled aboard there indeed was no heroin, but there were piles of documents, some powerful transceivers of unusual design, and a quantity of weapons and instruments that had nothing to do with navigation or even sardine fishing. And when a suspicious gendarme ordered one of the silent strangers to open the crate that was in his cabin, the inevitable happened. The nervous KGB agent drew his Tokarev pistol. His companion plunged under the low sleeping bunk and produced a heavy Kalachnikov submachine gun. The stupefied policeman tried to escape, but he was mowed down by a short burst of the Kalachnikov even before he reached the doorway of the cabin. A minute later shooting spread all over the ship. The French policemen, alerted by the shots, rushed to the rescue of their friend. The Russians, who realized too late that there was no way back, hurried to their caches of weapons and opened fire on any Frenchman in sight. Their only hope now was to disable all the members of the search party and escape to the open sea. In a sudden metamorphosis the ship turned into a battlefield. In the passageways, on the decks, even on the captain's bridge, Russians and Frenchmen were fighting one another, while the Polish members of the crew ran for cover. The only initiative Captain Kolajcyk took to help his Russian masters was to cut off the electric power, which plunged the ship into total darkness and general confusion.

A close burst of machine gun fire woke Gonen. He rose painfully to a sitting position and rubbed his swollen neck. His head ached terribly. He had the feeling that something was cruelly hammering it from within in a steady rhythm. He felt weak and dizzy, and the stink of the vodka was nauseating. His eyes gradually adjusted to the darkness. On hands and knees he crept to the door. He didn't understand what was going on, but when he touched the steel door and it slowly opened he knew just one thing: he had to get out of there.

Farther down in the narrow passageway somebody was firing. He assumed that this was his Russian guard, taking part in the general shooting. He chose the opposite direction—away from the shooting, away from that blurred figure crouching barely fifteen yards from his cell and steadily firing at an unseen foe. He staggered through the passageway, his head heavy, his body swinging and hitting the walls. Over and over he fell, but he got back on his knees, and then his feet, and continued moving like a somnambulist. He knew salvation was to climb the rusty iron ladders. Laboriously he worked his way through the hatches separating decks and passageways. Now and again the ladders led him to dead ends or to locked hatches he couldn't unscrew, and he had to retrace his way. Now and again he was caught in the middle of a cross fire and had to flatten himself against a wall or dive into a cabin to avoid a hail of bullets. But doggedly, painfully, he crawled and climbed upward, determined to get out of the ship.

He never could tell how long that hellish journey took. But when he pushed the last hatch and the sea air hit his face and he saw the stars far above, he knew he would soon be free. He was on the poop deck, somewhere at the back of the ship. He crawled to the guard rail on his right and saw the police boat clinging to the ship, a little ahead. To the north he could make out a thin row of white lights—the shore. He stumbled on an unseen obstacle and almost fell. Quick steps resounded ahead of him. He didn't stop to think. He turned around and in a final burst of strength ran to the poop. Behind him he heard shouts in French. Someone emptied a gun at him. Panting, he heavily passed one leg, then the other, over the guard rail and jumped into the dark, cold sea.

At 4 A.M. the heavy thumping on the outer door woke
Gaston Benoît, an elderly Provençal who was the owner
of the only café in the small fishing village of Bellecagne.
It took him a long time and a good deal of courage to get
up from his bed, throw an old woolen robe over his pajamas, walk toward the door. *"J'arrive, j'arrive,"* he muttered angrily. His plump wife, Ernestine, stopped him
with frightened screams. "The rifle, Gaston! Take the
rifle!" The Riviera was swarming with gangsters and rob-
bers. Recently there had been several holdups in nearby
Cavalaire and Saint-Tropez.

"Keep quiet," Gaston ordered angrily. Nevertheless, he
took the old hunting rifle that hung on the wall. Ernestine
joined him, and clung to him, trembling, while he fumbled
with the lock.

They were both taken aback by the unusual sight. A
man was standing in the doorway, leaning heavily on the
wall. He looked utterly exhausted. His face was covered
with bruises, and his wet blond hair clung to his skull. His
hands were swollen, his eyes bloodshot, and he was
shivering uncontrollably. His clothes were soaked, and a
puddle of water had formed at his bare feet.

His voice was almost a whisper and his words hardly
distinguishable. "I must use your phone, Monsieur
Benoît," he said in French. "I was told by your neighbors
that you had the only telephone in Bellecagne. I have to
call Paris. It is a matter of life and death."

Benoît eyed the stranger suspiciously. "I don't know,
this seems to be a matter for the police," he said uncertainly. His frightened wife nodded agreement.

"You can hand me over to the police if you want, but
first, please, let me use your phone," the stranger im-
plored. "See, I'll pay you for it." He stretched out his left
hand. "Look! I'll give you my watch, just to pay for the
call. It's a pilot's watch, and it's quite expensive."

Benoît felt a rush of pity at the sight of the shaking
hand. He didn't hesitate any longer. The man was in such
bad shape that he couldn't hurt anyone. *"Bon,"* he said.
"I'll let you phone. Go and walk around the corner to the

café. I'll come through the back door and let you in. The telephone is there."

He turned to his wife. "Ernestine, fix him some coffee. This young man is sick."

A few minutes later Gaston and Ernestine Benoît stood beside the old wooden counter of their small café, staring with dismay at the disheveled young stranger, who was trying to shout into the mouthpiece of their phone. The cords in his neck bulged with the effort, and his words were in a strange, rather barbaric-sounding language.

The amazed Gaston looked at his wife and shrugged. *"C'est de l'Hébreu pour moi,"* he whispered, meaning that he didn't understand a word their visitor was saying.

But it really was Hebrew, and Gonen's phone call saved Israel.

The War

October 6, 5 A.M. - October 26, 1973

Dawn hadn't appeared yet when Peled brought the astounding news to the Prime Minister. A few minutes later a wave of telephone calls swept Israel, rousing ministers, generals, reserve officers, diplomats. The Defense Minister, the Chief of Staff, the commanders of the Air Force, the armored corps, and the infantry dashed to the War Operations Room at headquarters. An extraordinary Cabinet meeting was convened.

When the sun rose in a cloudless blue sky, Israel was far from offering its traditional peaceful image of a nation devoted to prayer and atonement on this Yom Kippur of 1973. On October 6, Israel was a nation struggling desperately to survive, to check the forthcoming blow. Military cars were racing through the streets, picking up reservists at their homes, interrupting their prayers in the synagogues and carrying them to their units, still wrapped in their white and blue prayer shawls. At the Air Force bases perspiring soldiers were frantically arming and refueling the combat squadrons of Phantoms, Mirages, Super Mystères, and Skyhawks. Convoys of tanks, half-tracks, automotive heavy guns, trucks laden with ammunition moved from bases in the center of the country to the Golan and to Sinai.

Israel hadn't enough time to mobilize all its reserve soldiers. At 1:50 P.M., in a smashing first strike, hordes of Egyptian and Syrian soldiers attacked. In the north, more than a thousand tanks swept through the Golan Heights, crushing Israeli resistance. In the south masses of soldiers and tanks crossed the Suez Canal and advanced eastward.

But total surprise, which could have been fatal to Is-

rael, was prevented. When the Syrians and the Egyptians
moved, the Israeli Army was ready. The Air Force was in
the sky; fresh units were streaming to the front lines.
Hundreds of thousands of reserve soldiers were hurriedly
equipped and dispatched to the battlefields. After the set-
backs of the first few days the Israelis stopped the Arab
offensive. Five days later they had repelled the Syrian in-
vansion, thrust deep into Syrian territory, and halted at
cannon range from Damascus. In the south the paratroops of General Sharon crossed the Suez Canal and
opened the way for the armored divisions, which advanced deep into Egyptian territory. The Third Egyptian
Army was encircled on the east bank of the canal. Israeli
units reached the Suez—Cairo highway, and only sixty
miles lay between them and Cairo. The Presidents of Syria and Egypt contacted the big powers and asked for a
cease-fire. On October 23 the war was over.

During the October war American-Israeli cooperation
reached its peak. A huge airlift of giant Galaxy airplanes
of the U. S. Air Force supplied Israel with much needed
arms and ammunition. But the real, closely coordinated
American-Israeli operation was carried out in carefully
guarded secrecy. On the fifth day of the war, under the
cover of a general air strike on Egyptian air bases, a
special task force of Israeli Phantom jets swooped on the
airfields of Kabrit, Matruh, Aswan, and Luxor. With pin-
point accuracy the Israeli pilots destroyed the hangars
where the "Sandal" and the "Scapegoat" powerful missiles had been stored. At the same time Mirage fighter-
bombers dived on Sidi Barrani and Rās Bānas and blew
up the guidance and control stations built by the Russians. At sunset all that remained of the Aurora project
were smoldering, twisted piles of steel, wire, and rubber.
That same night, following a prearranged timetable, the
unofficial American representative in Egypt paid a call at
Kubbeh Palace. He brought a detailed, handwritten report
and a set of aerial photographs to President Sadat. The
documents revealed to the Egyptian leader the treacherous Soviet plan to get hold of his country and to use it in
a drive to overpower the West. Sadat reacted promptly.

On the pretext of a state of emergency he dispatched some of his most devoted officers to the destroyed Soviet bases. The angry protests of fearful Russian officers didn't stop the Egyptians from inspecting the hangars, the command posts, and the guidance stations, some of which were still burning. The evidence was there.

The next day, while the fighting was at its height, General Salem was secretly dismissed from the office of Chief of Staff and put under house arrest. General Gamasy, a pro-American officer, took his place. The members of Salem's entourage and his political accomplices who had taken part in the conspiracy were also quietly arrested.

They didn't take over Egypt. And the Russians didn't take over the oil sources of the Middle East. During the following months Soviet-Egyptian relations grew worse. Gradually President Sadat moved closer to the West. The Russian experts and advisers were politely, but firmly, asked to leave Egypt. Nine months after the Yom Kippur War the President of the United States came on an official visit to the Middle East, and an enthusiastic crowd cheered him warmly in the streets of Cairo.

The Aurora project, which could have made the Soviet Union master of the planet earth, came to its end amid the smoking, blackened debris of Kabrit, Luxor, and Aswan. And the man who was behind the project, he who had hoped that Aurora would bestow fame and honor upon him, didn't outlive it long. Found guilty of high treason, General Lavrenti Alexeievich Blagonravov was executed by a firing squad in the backyard of Lubyanka prison.

On October 10, the day that the Israeli Air Force carried out the death sentence of project Aurora, the KGB sent its men to execute a different kind of death sentence, which had been pronounced ten days earlier. Three men arrived in Washington from Montreal. They came on different flights and carried Canadian and French passports. The first one disembarked in the morning. He was in his thirties, with brown hair and black eyes, dressed in a conservatively cut dark suit. He might have been a West European businessman, but there was something in the hard look of his eyes, in the bearing of his thickset shoulders, that didn't fit that image. A little past noon, a second foreigner arrived, a small man in his forties, stocky, thin-lipped, and gruff-looking. The third man was blond and tall, and had a pleasant face. There was something catlike in his quick, supple walk. He nonchalantly crossed the large arrival hall, hailed a taxi, and disappeared.

The three men were members of the operational team of the Eighth Department of the KGB, and had been sent to the American capital to carry out an operation on the personal orders of General Yulin. Actually their assignment was top priority and was to have been executed several days earlier. But the three men had been delayed in Paris in the operation against the Minerva Israeli team. Only after the manhunt in France was over could they devote themselves to their new assignment in Washington. Had they checked again with General Yulin, their orders might have been canceled, for after the Helsinki meeting conditions had changed, and nothing justified another senseless killing. But nobody checked, nobody asked questions, and the deadly machine of the KGB carried on.

The initial stages of the operation were flawlessly executed. The KGB killers didn't register in any hotel. The meager luggage they had was left in lockers at the airport. Each went his own way—one to a stationery store, one to a drugstore, the third to a small coffee shop. Upon pronouncing a password, each man was given a revolver. The blond received the keys of a Chevy Vega, parked close to the coffee shop. It had been stolen the night before, but its plates had been changed.

The three men spent most of the day in various cinemas in town, dozing in their seats. They met finally at 6 P.M. in the bustling lobby of the Statler Hilton. They spent barely a quarter of an hour together, to study a pencil-drawn sketch that had been left in the glove compartment of the Chevy. They did not need to examine any photos on their way to Washington; they had already memorized the features of the blond girl they were after.

They did not have to rehearse their plan, either; they were trained professionals.

A little past seven they reached the secluded house in the quiet residential suburb of Chevy Chase. The blond man parked the getaway car on the other side of the street, across the entrance to the garage. On a gaily painted mailbox was printed the name of the house's owner: Lieutenant Colonel Robert Bacall, U.S.A.F. Nobody was in the house. Smoothly the three men moved into positions in the bushes planted along the path that led from the garage to the house itself.

The hours slowly passed by. The KGB people had thought of almost everything. But they could not have foreseen that because of the war in the Middle East, Jenny Bacall would be late coming home. Since the war started, she had volunteered to help the personnel of the Israeli Embassy in sorting the heaps of letters, parcels, and donations streaming into the embassy on Twenty-second Street. Late at night an exhausted Robert Bacall would leave the situation room in the Pentagon, where he followed every move in the Mideast war, and would pick up Jenny at the embassy. So it happened that on that night when Jenny came home she was not alone. Sometime after midnight Colonel Bacall's old Dodge Dart stopped in the drive. When two figures alighted from it in the dark, the waiting agents were momentarily confused. They had no instructions to kill Robert Bacall. It took them only a few seconds to reach the inevitable conclusion—but those seconds turned out to be crucial. Jenny and her husband were already halfway along the path when two figures appeared ahead of them and opened fire. The third Russian, who was left behind, didn't move, fearing to enter the field of fire.

Everything happened with lightning speed: Jenny was hit by several bullets and collapsed. Robert Bacall was only superficially wounded by the first shots. Instinctively he hurled himself on his attackers. His unexpected reaction threw the Russians off balance. They emptied their guns at the figure moving toward them, then jumped in the bushes and ran to the waiting car. Their third com-

panion was already behind the wheel. The Chevy darted
forward and disappeared around the first corner. Barely
two hours later the KGB killers had left the country, following a prearranged escape plan.

When a police prowl car, sirens screaming, reached the
scene of the shooting, two bodies were lying on the
ground. Robert Bacall, bullet-ridden, died on his way to
the hospital. Jenny, badly wounded in the chest and abdomen, was rushed to surgery. Peter Wilkie reached the
hospital at 3 A.M. The young surgeon who came to him
shrugged helplessly. "We may as well start praying," he
said, looking away.

Only on the last day of the war could a badly shaken
Jeremiah Peled break the news to Joe Gonen. Joe had arrived in Israel on the 8th of October, two days after the
war started. Without even taking time to change he had
rushed to Air Force Headquarters and plunged into the
War Room, to emerge on the 23rd of October. It was
then that the Old Man told him the truth about Jenny.
"She's badly wounded, Joe, and her chances of survival
are very small," Peled said softly. Joe listened to him in
silence, his face ashen. The Old Man went on to tell him
the truth about the role Jenny Bacall had played in the
operation. But he never told him—for he didn't know—
that all Jenny did had been done because of a promise to
see Joe again.

Suddenly, in the midst of Peled's words, Joe turned and
ran toward his car and headed directly for Lod Airport.
He managed to get on one of the last Galaxies that had
been used in the airlift and was now returning to America. Twenty-four hours after the war was over, Joe Gonen
arrived in Washington. An hour later he was heatedly
quarreling with the plainclothesman guarding Jenny's
room at Bethesda Naval Hospital. The guards refused to
let him enter. Finally one of the security officers agreed to
telephone his superiors in the CIA. But even before Peter
Wilkie called back, Joe was approached by a young doctor. "So you are Joe Gonen," he said. "I am Doctor Kel-
ler. Mrs. Bacall's been calling your name over and over

again." He looked at him gravely. "She is in a critical condition, most of the time in a coma. I am very worried by her total lack of will to survive. You must see her."

The room was dimly lit. Joe sat in the chair close to her bedside and bent over the immobile figure. She was wrapped in bandages, and her breathing was irregular. He sat motionless, gazing at the woman he had come to love so deeply, her life sustained only by the slow drip of plasma that entered her body through a thin plastic tube.

What seemed like hours later the huge green eyes suddenly opened and looked at him. She didn't seem to recognize Joe, but he bent close to her and whispered into her ear.

"Jenny, it's me," he murmured.

She didn't move.

"Jenny," he said again, "the last time I saw you I asked you a question. Remember?"

The figure in front of him remained motionless. He repeated the question over and over, clenching his fists. All of a sudden he thought he saw a new intensity in the look of the big misty eyes.

"I asked you to come with me and marry me," he went on. "Can you answer me? Please, darling, try to make an effort. I beg you, please. Will you, Jenny?"

Slowly her eyes closed and opened again. The parched lips finally moved. Her murmur was low, almost inaudible.

"Yes," she whispered.

Then he knew she would live.

When Joe Gonen landed in Tel-Aviv, the Old Man was waiting for him by a side exit at the airport. Jeremiah Peled put his hand on Joe's shoulder in an affectionate gesture that left Joe stunned. For a second he even had the impression that he saw tears in the Old Man's eyes. But he hurriedly dismissed the thought.

Jeremiah Peled drove Joe home, where several close friends had gathered for a modest party in his honor. It was a quiet, informal gathering, and Joe relaxed for the first time since his mission had started. Slowly he realized that the nightmare was over. His country had been saved.

Jenny was alive. The dramatic stages of the operation
came to life in his memory. He dragged Jeremiah to a
corner and asked him candidly if he had informed the
Russians—or the Americans—of the true identity of
Minerva 6N.

The Old Man smiled. "No," he said, his shrewd eyes
twinkling. "Gentlemen don't tell on each other."

Or maybe he had another reason.

The Laromme
Nelson's village
Eilat 1975

About the Author

Michael Barak is a pseudonym for a well-known Israeli author who served as press secretary to General Moshe Dayan during the Six Day War and later, as a paratrooper, crossed the Suez Canal into Egypt during the Yom Kippur War. *The Secret List of Heinrich Roehm* is totally authentic in detail, down to the popular Portuguese expressions used in a São Paulo bar, the color of the carpets in the KGB chief's office, and the machinations of the spies themselves.

Other SIGNET Bestsellers You'll Want to Read

- [ ] **THE PLACE OF STONES** by Constance Heaven.
(#W7046—$1.50)

- [ ] **PLAYING AROUND** by Linda Wolfe. (#J7024—$1.95)

- [ ] **DRAGONS AT THE GATE** by Robert Duncan.
(#J6984—$1.95)

- [ ] **WHERE HAVE YOU GONE JOE DI MAGGIO?** by Maury Allen. (#W6986—$1.50)

- [ ] **KATE: The Life of Katharine Hepburn** by Charles Higham. (#J6944—$1.95)

- [ ] **SANDITON** by Jane Austen and Another Lady.
(#J6945—$1.95)

- [ ] **CLANDARA** by Evelyn Anthony. (#W6893—$1.50)

- [ ] **ALLEGRA** by Clare Darcy. (#W6860—$1.50)

- [ ] **THE HUSBAND** by Catherine Cookson.
(#W6990—$1.50)

- [ ] **AGE OF CONSENT** by Ramona Stewart.
(#W6987—$1.50)

- [ ] **THE FREEHOLDER** by Joe David Brown.
(#W6952—$1.50)

- [ ] **LOVING LETTY** by Paul Darcy Boles. (#E6951—$1.75)

- [ ] **COMING TO LIFE** by Norma Klein. (#W6864—$1.50)

- [ ] **FEAR OF FLYING** by Erica Jong. (#J6139—$1.95)

- [ ] **MISSION TO MALASPIGA** by Evelyn Anthony.
(#E6706—$1.75)

THE NEW AMERICAN LIBRARY, INC.,
P.O. Box 999, Bergenfield, New Jersey 07621

Please send me the SIGNET BOOKS I have checked above. I am enclosing $_____(check or money order—no currency or C.O.D.'s). Please include the list price plus 35¢ a copy to cover handling and mailing costs. (Prices and numbers are subject to change without notice.)

Name_____

Address_____

City_____State_____Zip Code_____
Allow at least 4 weeks for delivery